To Sophie (Lucy)

Hope you enjoy

A Limey in the Court of Uncle Sam

by

Ken Wise

authorHOUSE®

AuthorHouse™ UK Ltd.
500 Avebury Boulevard
Central Milton Keynes, MK9 2BE
www.authorhouse.co.uk
Phone: 08001974150

This book is a work of fiction. People, places, events, and situations are the product of the author's imagination. Any resemblance to actual persons, living or dead, or historical events, is purely coincidental.

©2009 Ken Wise. All rights reserved.

No part of this book may be reproduced, stored in a retrieval system, or transmitted by any means without the written permission of the author.

First published by AuthorHouse 3/5/2009

ISBN: 978-1-4389-4378-7 (sc)

Printed in the United States of America
Bloomington, Indiana

This book is printed on acid-free paper.

Table of Contents

The Early Years	1
Growing Up Is Hard To Do	24
Hey, Good Lookin'…	44
Window Shopping…	49
Baby We're Really In Love …	54
Lovesick Blues…	59
Honky Tonk Blues…	62
I Can't Help It…	71
Take These Chains From My Heart…	76
My Bucket's Got A Hole In It…	82
Nobody's Lonesome For Me …	86
Weary Blues From Waitin'…	90
Settin' The Woods On Fire…	98
I'm So Lonesome I Could Cry…	108
Your Cheatin' Heart…	122
Mind Your Own Business	125
Crazy Heart…	140
Move It On Over	150
I'm A Long Gone Daddy…	156

Why Should We Try Anymore…	162
Rootie Tootie…	180
I'm Satisfied With You…	191
The Blues Come Around…	200
Why Don't You Love Me Like You Used To Do…	208
Honkin Tonkin'…	215
I Saw The Light…	228

The Early Years

Most people cannot remember too much of their childhood and I guess I am no exception. The bombing of our Kentish home in 1939 was, fortunately for me, a blur; that and the subsequent move to Reading have resulted in just a few flashbacks, some of which were a source of embarrassment and others a milestone in my growing years.

My earliest embarrassing moment was when my infant school teacher failed to notice that I had put my hand up in order that I might be granted the privilege of using the toilet. I never made it and I could not understand the pool of water that had suddenly appeared beneath my canvas chair. Someone should have informed the teacher that a four-year-old, waking up after a two-hour enforced sleep, might possibly need to use the toilet.

No one seemed to notice until one of my 'friends' informed my mother (who had come to collect me) that 'Ken has wet himself.' As he shouted it at the top of his voice, it seemed to me that the whole street now knew – bless him! My face must have been a shade of beetroot!

That happened in 1941 and Britain was in full battle with the Nazi foe. Bombing London was by then a normal event but bombing Reading was still relatively scarce. It did happen but fortunately Albany Road where we lived came through unscathed. I do remember looking up at the night sky, ablaze with searchlights and ack-ack gunnery fire and hearing the drone of German planes en route to God knows where. To a six-year-old it all seemed exciting and a little unreal, just a picture of something that was happening miles away.

I can remember the almost nightly visits to the Anderson air-raid shelter that my father had dug out himself and made into a 'home from home'. My mother recalled banging my head on the side of the entrance on one occasion and that, she used to direly inform me, was one of the reasons I was 'not quite right'. Thanks, Mum…

When you get a little older you are expected to grow up with not only larger feet but a degree of increased intelligence. I believe I was about six years of age and lucky enough to own a three wheeled tricycle. It was a sturdy bike with nice firm handlebars and two large wheels at the back with space for one of your mates to stand on. It had one brake that operated the front wheel. It also had a great bell. I had two best friends, Mike and Jim (we were all about the same age). We used to like playing on things such as handmade carts and some of these even had their own steering apparatus. Although not totally safe, they were generally OK for negotiating along the pavements. Reading consists mainly of hills and a rather steep hill rose sternly above our own Albany Road.

We used to love going down the hill in our cart – turning off the hill just in time to stop us shooting out into the road running across at the end.

One day our poor cart had an accident and we found to our dismay that it would not be available for our day of fun. No dad was available to repair it and for several minutes our faces were crestfallen; what a bummer.

'I know,' said Mike, 'let's use your bike.'

Now, as I had already been diagnosed as a sandwich short of a picnic, I couldn't think of any reason why we shouldn't go up this giant of a hill and ride on the bike down to the bottom, just as normal. Climbing to the top of the hill was hard enough but, the big question was, who would be left out as there were three of us and the bike would normally only hold two.

'Don't worry,' I said, 'one of you can ride on the front handlebars if you like.'

'Yes, OK!' Mike exclaimed. Within seconds, with Mike on the front and Jim on the back, we started down the hill.

'Mike,' I said, 'I can't see anything; you're in the way!'

Silence; I guess Mike was pondering where exactly he should move to. And the silence continued from the three of us as the bike gathered speed. I knew one thing: I would have to be careful when applying the one and only front brake or we would all tip over, not an option that I wanted to experience. I then had what I thought was a really good idea; I rang my little bell – like mad! I knew in the back of my little brain that it would not actually stop the bike hurtling down the hill. That left me with only one option and, hoping the other two were doing the same, I closed my eyes – still ringing my little bell. It was certainly a good thing that in 1941 there were not many cars, or anything else, on the intersection of Albany Road. We went straight across, speeding onward on our sturdy steed, all three of us holding on like grim death, on and on until, with a sudden bump, we stopped. Opening my eyes gingerly, I found that an even larger machine had stopped our onslaught – a car. Luckily it was parked and as it had a small bumper there was no apparent damage either to my bike or the car.

'That was good,' exclaimed Jim.

'Yeah, wasn't it,' Mike and I offered without any real conviction. I looked at Jim's beaming face, realising happily that I was not the only one with something missing from my picnic basket.

One thing that Jim had, that Mike and I really enjoyed, was his parents' large pear and apple orchard. To us, it was enormous. Running parallel to our famous hill, it ran down a similar slope. We used to play hide and seek in the orchard with Jim trying to find us. Can you possibly imagine a better place to hide? Can you imagine a worse place for parents to allow three healthy boys to play in? Compared to mad dashes down hills and potential traffic accidents it was obviously safer but what real value do you put on your apples and pears? Perhaps Mr Beard, Jim's dad, used the many half eaten cores for compost. We never did wait around to ask. I can honestly say that not once in my childhood did I have to break into any orchard to do any 'scrumping' for apples and pears. Perhaps I missed out.

I can recall the day the war ended. Walking into the house after playing some street football the announcement came. My mother and the rest of the mothers all piled out into the streets shouting and screaming, 'It's all over!'

I remember saying, 'That's good!' but my mother replied that I did not know the half of it! I should have realised that perhaps my mother even then had some severe doubts as to the level of my intelligence

With the cessation of hostilities there was only one logical thing to do: have a street party. All the mums and dads miraculously came up with all kinds of goodies: rolls, jellies, fancy cakes, custard, ice cream and plenty of ginger beer.

I remember being completely gobsmacked. Where did all this lovely food and so many people come from?

We had about one hundred houses in our street and I guess we must have had four hundred children sitting down. It was the biggest 'birthday' party I had ever seen. No one was turned away! Multiply that by a thousand streets in Reading plus streets all over Britain! I guess the message of the day was 'thank God' and never again. Many a child went home just a little bit worse for wear with an overful tummy. The sense of relief in that road and all over Britain was immense; a kind of hush came over all the houses when darkness fell. While the children slept contentedly, the parents slept peacefully in their beds for the first time in many a year.

My father was more lenient with regard to my mental state and I remember him being very instructive and informative when showing me how to do things, enabling me to learn more about life than just kicking a small ball with my friends in the street. He was an extremely gifted man who, at that time, commanded a good job setting out stainless steel projects. He earned a good wage of around twenty-four pounds per month – an enormous sum in those days. Not that we saw much of it, although he did treat my brother, two sisters and me equally when it came to having things like new bikes. If you could not pay cash for it, my father went without. Oh, how I wish now that I had followed many of his earlier examples.

After the war ended I remember the deep, close family atmosphere that my parents created when raising my brother, sisters and me. We ate at the table at the same time when possible, which was most days, and even when my elder brother started dating and eventually got married he and his wife came and visited nearly every Sunday. I remember Dad buying a new contraption called a television.

I also remember the numerous power cuts that happened on a regular basis, normally when I was trying to watch an afternoon movie. In addition to watching the TV we used to play darts; this was very competitive and nearly always ended with a win for the boys or complete exhaustion. It was really nice on Sundays, when we had the Sunday roast and Yorkshire pudding. The meat, although still scarce, was even nicer when Mother made her own special Yorkshire puddings.

We had an old grandfather clock; it gave me many wondrous hours peering into its dark interior looking for secret passages. I had gleaned this idea after watching one of the many children's shows. I did, however, quickly become bored with shows such as 'Muffin the Mule' and 'Watch with Mother'.

I guess it was about this time that I was introduced to my first experience with death. My mother was part of a large family and had five sisters, one of whom was called Cissi; she had a niece called Lillian. One day my mother and father received a very disturbing letter informing them that Lillian had passed away. It was quite sudden and at of thirty-three years of age it was obviously very distressing for all the remaining members of the family as, of course, it is with any close family.

I was suddenly consumed with grief; I could not understand how someone so relatively young could possibly die. You were not supposed to die until you reached old age, at least seventy years of age; had not one of my grandparents lived until he was ninety-two? I remembered that because my father had told me that people of that age always die and go to heaven. My mother also came up with the fact that Lillian's favourite song was Lilly-Marlene, an old wartime song. How this particular tune had become Lillian's favourite tune was never explained but there it was, a very young girl passing away suddenly without any apparent warning. Perhaps there had been many prior signs but in Britain, the 1950s communications were not as streamlined as they are today. Either way, I had many disturbed nights wondering to myself just how such a tragedy could possible happen. It had a profound effect on me despite the fact I had never even met the poor Lillian. My mother and father attended her funeral; fortunately I was spared that ordeal and I was happy to stay at home playing football in the street. It is amazing that, while certain people are experiencing such sorrow, other people are able to carry on with normal life. Such is life.

Coal fires were the only form of affordable heating but what better taste can you experience than eating crumpets which had been toasted over dying embers? The coal was normally delivered via the 'coal hole', which was located in the walkway or path up to the main front door. It emptied directly into the cellar which stored the coal. I soon realised who was to be appointed 'coal monitor'!

My father (being a very prudent kind of fellow) would make most things rather than buy them. He made a very large chicken pen and after a very short time the chickens, Rhode Island Reds I think, were producing many fresh eggs every day. This all went very well until, Dad decided, why stop at chickens? So he purchased six lovely fluffy ducklings. Up the garden path they waddled, one after the other, quacking as only ducks can and soon the neighbours from both sides were coming around to view the amusing new arrivals.

After my father had made a temporary pen for them we all went in for lunch. Whilst eating we were disturbed by a loud commotion coming from the garden. I rushed out and to my horror I could only count five ducks! Of course, everyone else came out and checked my maths straight away. Yes, only five ducklings; someone, or something, had stolen one! The remaining ducklings were strangely quiet considering that one of their siblings had gone missing. We looked around the long garden and, as I looked over the garden wall, I saw a very disturbing sight.

A cat was eating the missing duckling. He looked up, seemingly unconcerned, almost as if we were at fault for disturbing his dinner. He had bitten the head off and was working his way around the rest of his feast. He was a stray cat with no markings and looked as though he had mange in his coat. My father looked at it, did not comment, and just left it eating its prey. He went to the dustbin, emptied the contents onto the floor and filled it up with water. We all watched in silence.

'He's tasted blood so he will not stop at one,' my father explained. He produced a sack and, with a firm hand, grabbed the unfortunate cat by the scruff of its neck, put it straight into the sack, then plunged the sack and contents down into the murky and watery depths of the dustbin. This was a father we had not seen before; we knew him as a fair man and a good father, but we were now seeing an almost callous side to him. After a brief struggle and a few wails the cat went silent and my father released his hold. He pulled up the wet dripping sack with its now motionless contents; we all looked on, almost speechless with mixed emotions. That was a bit drastic, Dad, or perhaps we should have been thinking about our poor duck – headless and half eaten. Still, I guess

Dad with his summary justice was just another learning curve for us young disciples of life.

Guy Fawkes Day, November 5th was always a special day for all the young residents of Albany Road. The daily collection of fireworks added to the anticipation of the event. We would normally band together with the next-door neighbours and, with a few invited friends, have an extremely large bonfire, fireworks and plenty of noise. I particularly liked the Catherine wheel, if I could ever get it to spin around properly. For those not familiar with this particular firework it only works correctly if you bang a nail precisely into its centre. When lit, the firework rotates making a loud fizzing noise and of course creates a spectacular effect for several minutes – sometimes!

One year, towards the end of a very successful bonfire night (one that I would come to remember well), we had let off all our fireworks and our 'Guy' had been dispatched in the usual manner (by burning it on the bonfire). I was prodding the fire to get a nice final glow from it - a vain attempt to keep alive the magic of the night. I turned around to see Colin, my very young friend from next door, coming toward me. Colin, bless him, had a present for me, my hammer; I had used it for putting up the Catherine wheel. I guess Colin suddenly decided that the best way to return the hammer quickly would be to throw it to me – but he did this without warning me first! Bang, the hammer caught me just above my left eyebrow and down I went, seeing stars that were in addition to those already twinkling in the sky. Lying prostrate on the cold garden pavement, I soon realised that the warm liquid seeping into the corner of my mouth was blood, my blood! Why did Colin do that? Was he after my new Dan Dare comic that had just come out that day? He only had to ask! Well, maybe not.

Blood everywhere, anxious parents running to my rescue and poor Colin, looking helpless and just a bit worried, thinking that maybe he had killed me! What was Colin trying to do, finish off what my mother had tried to do years ago in the Anderson air-raid shelter?

'He will need a stitch in that,' my father said, almost uncaringly. Stitch, what did he mean stitch? I did not fancy the sound of that. My mother had some sharp needles but surely that was going to hurt. An ambulance was called and I was put in it; with bells clanging I was soon speeding, with my mother and father, to Battle Hospital which fortunately was close by. I had heard that 'a stitch in time saves nine' but this was really ridiculous!

The wounded soldier duly returned home from hospital. If nothing else this had to be worth some TLC from my mother; perhaps no jobs for a while, special treats and nice gifts? What a silly billy I must have been. 'Get on with it,' Dad said, 'you'll get worse than that in your life.' Nice one, Dad, but you were not the one on the receiving end of the hammer!

There were several enlightening events in my early years. One of these was my education in the art of lovemaking. All of us younger boys had been grappling with rumours passed down to us by much older, experienced boys. They were of course, to us, even more knowledgeable than our fathers (we could ask them more in-depth questions without the eyebrow raising). We had a local hero called Blackie who was really old, at least fourteen! We were told that he had been with a girl, in fact not any old girl, a prostitute!

We all gathered at the meeting place where we knew Blackie would be holding court. He emerged from the shop that his family ran.

'What was it like, Blackie?' was the earnest question of the day. To our young minds, he was undoubtedly the prelude to one of the characters in 'West Side Story' or 'On the Waterfront'. Marlon Brando springs to mind. Blackie's husky overtones conveyed the information that we young males needed to know. Information that we expected would transform our lives into something amazing.

'She took me in the back room.'

(I hoped it was not his dad's shop or I could never go in there again). I need not have worried as apparently the 'event' happened in downtown Reading.

Blackie continued, 'She unzipped my trousers and took out my thing.'

'Yes! Yes!' was the murmured chorus that came from the surrounding youngsters.

At last, the truth from a real live person who would not gloss over the naughty, interesting bits, like they did on the TV and in the papers.

'She took out the letter and placed it over my thing'.

All eyes were open wide by now and glued to Blackie's face – awesome, just awesome.

After a brief pause, when our hero made sure that he had all of our attention, he continued, 'And then we did it!'

'What did it feel like, Blackie?' said one young voice, who like the rest of us could hardly contain himself!

Again the necessary pause: 'It was like sandpaper being run up and down my dick.'

There, we had it, the vital piece of information that all of us young men of the future could take with us to our first heavenly encounters with the female race. Blackie had spoken, and with such conviction that no one at that historic gathering would have ever dared question those mind-boggling facts. Moving away we all drifted back to our homes, deep in thought, recalling, step by step, the amazing event that our friend Blackie had shared with us. I can only imagine that there was a sudden increase in 'wet dreams' for many of the boys residing in Albany Road at that time.

Christmas time at the West home was idyllic, with the lead up to Christmas normally starting around the first week of December. I remember the usual preparations, which normally started with the making of paper chains out of strips of coloured paper stuck together with paper glue. There were none of the fancy decorations that are freely available nowadays: if you wanted to join in the fun it meant you had to contribute something yourself, which of course we kids were only too pleased to do. The only decorations we did purchase were bells made of crepe paper that had small metal clips to hold them in shape. I remember part of the build-up to Christmas was when Mum took us kids up to the Reading town centre to do our Christmas shopping. I remember going around Woolworth's and buying some Brylcream hair cream for my father and brother. What gunk we used to put on our hair in those days! Hence the description that labelled many of the rising stars: 'Brylcream Boy'.

I remember standing opposite one of the highly decorated stores with its giant Christmas tree looming above us. I just could not believe there were still ten days before the 'big event'. Ten days, that was an eternity, surely! I guess nothing has really changed even these days for the millions of children waiting for the 'big day'.

Oh, how I wish now that we could provide every living child in the world today with a special present, but sadly this can never be.

The Christmas tree was always a real one which Dad purchased around the twelfth of December. We seemed to strictly observe the twelve days before and after Christmas. Of course nowadays it is not unusual to see Christmas decorations available as early as October.

As things became available more, turkey and pork were a must as far as Christmas fare was concerned. Like her mother before her, my mother used to make her own pastries; the sausage rolls and mince pies were fantastic. The other addition to the Christmas feast was, of course, the Christmas pudding, which was made many weeks before Christmas with dried fruit and spices. We all had to stir it and make a wish.

I guess one of my dad's wishes did come true when he eventually won the football pools, but unfortunately not 'the big one'. He had eight draws, when half the teams playing drew. Still, he won ninety-nine pounds – a tidy sum in those days. He bought my sister a new bike but, despite my pleas for a new 'proper' football, he returned with a six-shooter gun for me. Bloomin' heck, Dad, how do you expect me to be the next Stanley Mathews if I cannot practise!

Christmas lights were available, but who can forget the endless problems of getting and keeping the string of lights working all the time over the Christmas period. It seemed to be part of a lottery that we endured and accepted without too much fuss. I guess we will never forget the standard movie that was shown then and still today: Miracle on 34th Street. Could this have been possibly one of the first imports from the United States? Either way, it was a welcomed import. Every city should have a 'Maceys'.

Another ritual in our house was that after the 'visit' by Father Christmas, all the other presents were not given out until after the Christmas tea. This ensured that if we kids did not eat up our Christmas dinner and tea, there was a good chance of no more presents afterwards. I guess we would call it practical blackmail these days but, by golly, it always worked. It also guaranteed that you had plenty of time to play with the toys given to you by Santa and perhaps a little peace and quiet for Mum and Dad.

As the days grew to a close one of the duties that was passed down to us kids was the turning on of the gaslight, normally suspended from the centre of the ceiling similar to today's electric light. A lighted match of course was required, with extra care not to damage the fragile gas mantle which was made of chemically treated gauze. This gave out a nice soft light which of course was not as bright as the electric lights of today.

It was soon decided that thanks to my parents' prudence we could now afford to move to a larger house. My father and mother found one at the other end of Reading in a street called School Terrace. Did that mean it had a school close by? Yes, in fact opposite. I remember not being amused as surely the teachers would always know where I was and could bang on the door – day or night!!

The start of my junior school years was fine once I had forgiven my mother and father for taking me away from best friends, Mike and Jim. I remember being taken into the headmaster's office, then taken down to the classroom to which I had been assigned, plonked down in a seat and left! Where did my mother go?

Who was going to protect me from all these scary kids? Didn't she know I was a natural target, the new kid on the block? Mothers can be cruel sometimes and from the perspective of a seven-year-old, I was being treated cruelly.

Where were the good guys that were meant to protect us poor kids! I moaned at her when I went home for lunch and I moaned again when I went home for tea. I did not like the school, the teachers and, was she listening? I didn't like the other kids! I would stand in the schoolyard, opposite our house, staring up to my room at the top of the house, wishing I was there and not stuck in this 'bloody school'. Of course I would never forgive my mother, or father, for moving me to this place!

That's where I was standing the next day when Dobby, one of my classmates, stopped suddenly. 'Want to play?'

'Err yes, suppose so!'

Away we went, running all over the schoolyard, chasing some darn Red Indian that had suddenly appeared! Perhaps this was not such a bad place after all. Good one, Mum and Dad!

Moving to the other end of town and a new school brought its own sort of problems: having to make new friends and of course meet the new teachers. The dreaded Jacko comes to mind: the head teacher whose stern look was seemingly enough to send fear into the sturdiest of hearts. Then there was our amiable history teacher Tommy, who was Welsh. He would repeatedly grab one ear, then the other, and then ask the unfortunate child if there was anything between 'ere and 'ere?

The expected answer was 'Yes, sir' to which he would then reply, 'Well use it then!' Again, Mother's prophecy of me being a sandwich short of a picnic would seem to be correct, because the first and only time I was asked the dreaded question, I replied, 'No, sir.' For a while, having buggered up his punchline, I found Tommy's eagle eye always seem to fall on me when requesting an answer to a difficult question. Mind you, most of the questions seemed difficult to me.

Now, playing football was something I could manage. Scoring a few goals at the right time soon enabled me to get back into Tommy's good books as he also happened to be the school's sports teacher.

Jacko, the maths and science teacher, was a different matter. You didn't become his friend until thirty minutes before you left the school for good; then he would shake your hand and wish you well.

Before that, his way of communicating with you was a piece of chalk that would unexpectedly bounce on your desk top should you show any signs of not paying him the attention he richly deserved. I cannot remember any mother or father rushing to the school shouting 'child abuse' or anything like that.

Firstly, Jacko was 6 feet 4 inches tall and secondly, I reckon the mums and dads of the day knew he was a damn good teacher. If you could clone Jacko today, I suspect we would not have so many of the problems we have in our schools. I often mentally thank Jacko for teaching me at least one thing - that by paying closer attention you might just learn something to your advantage.

One good thing about moving to School Terrace was that we were also closer to a large cinema, about fifteen minutes walk away. Saturday morning visits were a must with the cowboy films and the subsequent galloping up and down the aisles. This was something I never got involved in but I did enjoy the Roy Rogers and Hopalong-Cassidy films except when they started singing, - ugh!

I remember one dinnertime when my dad was playing a rather silly game of sprinkling pepper over my dinner. Of course he didn't actually do it, concealing the fact that he had his finger over the hole where the pepper came out. I, of course, kept up my usual daft behaviour by returning the favour but without placing my finger over the hole. A clip around the ear followed, and I hurriedly left the room with protests from my mother, stating it was Dad's own fault for doing it in the first place; he should have known what Ken was like! Another slight against my intelligence!

I went up to my cold room at the top of the house and did my usual sulk! No amount of pleas from my brother and sister to come down had any effect on me. Even Dad coming up and telling me 'not to be so bloody silly and to come down' had no effect. This was perhaps the earliest example of Ken West being a 'stubborn son of a gun'.

My dad was a man of all trades and, contrary to the saying, he was a master of most. He soon set about sowing seeds and plants in the new garden and he required a basic fertiliser for the growing rhubarb plants. This was readily found – in the street taking the form of 'horse poo' better known as 'horse manure'. Guess who was conscripted to collect this treasure? Little ol' me! As soon as a horse and cart passed our house and as the giant of a beast dropped his load, I was sent out with my bucket and shovel to collect the steaming heap of poo! I had to be on the ball in case any other would-be gardener wanted this treasure. If nothing occurred then I was expected to follow the horse to at least the end of the street.

You would be surprised just how many tradesmen used to peddle their wares down our street. It was like something out of Lionel Bart's musical 'Oliver', 'who would buy my red, red roses,' except they were not roses. There was the milkman (who delivered daily), the knife-sharpener, the rag and bone man, the fish man in his well stocked little van, the coalman and, for a while, the soft drinks man, selling 'Tizer' and 'Corona' before he got himself a nice new van. I never had a clue what the rag and bone man used to call out: 'bone o', or something like that! I remember the boy who asked me what I was doing collecting the poo and, when I answered it was for my father's rhubarb, he remarked that his mum always put custard on theirs!

I remember the pigswill man coming into the school with his bin on wheels to collect the leftover food from the school meals. The bin emitted a very unpleasant aroma, but I never heard of any of the pigs complaining. I guess nowadays they have to be fed with nuts or something like that!

We kids always ran everywhere to comply with our mother's wish: 'Oh, Ken, run down to the paper shop and get your dad's paper.' On a Friday, which was the 'Eagle' comic day featuring Dan Dare, earth's handsome space captain, fighting the evil Mekon, the super-intelligent ruler of the Treens, from the planet Venus, I never needed any bidding.

I guess we never had the chance to become obese. In fact I remember my mother taking me to the doctor to see if anything could be done to put weight on me. Comments such as looking like a Belsen victim were not meant to be unkind to the memory of those poor people who perished in the Nazi labour camps but after seeing pictures of those terrible scenes in the newspapers, the mothers were always conscious that their offspring should put on weight and look fit and well. They never realised that, without the constant television as we have today, all the children enjoyed being out of the house and playing frantic games which only kids of the day could dream up. Something had to keep off the effects of the spotted dick steamed puddings that the mothers used to make at least once a week. Hmm, don't tempt me! The normal result of those visits to the doctor was a prescription for 'cod liver oil and malt'. I liked it, but it did leave you with a jaw ache after trying to eat the huge spoonful that mother thrust eagerly into my mouth.

One thing that did not have to be delivered was the fish and chips. This shop was conveniently located at the end of the street, so I didn't have far to run for 'cod and chips four times and sixpence worth of scratchings, (the very small bits of batter that used to fall off the fish)'. The fish and chips were always wrapped in newspaper which seemed to add to the flavour. Taking old newspapers to the fish and chip shop always ended up with the kids being given some of the already mentioned scratchings. It made a smashing treat for us kids who were always hungry.

'Wash days' for the mums were not a pleasant task and normally involved a scrubbing board on which they had to rub furiously in order to get the rings of dirt out of the men's shirt collars. In those days changing shirts was not a daily thing and when detachable collars were not used, the washing of such items was tiring, time-consuming work for the 1950s mum.

The other task, normally carried out by the mums, was 'bath night'. This was at least once a week! Good God, we were a clean lot! Anyway, our 'bathroom' was normally to be found hanging on the rear outside wall of the scullery (kitchen). The four-foot long galvanised bath was brought in for 'bath nights'. Many kettles and pans of water, from the built-in wood-burning range which provided the hot water, were emptied into the bath. Some of the stoves would be looked on and classed as antique nowadays but, as things improved in 1950s England, gas stoves became more the norm. It was quite normal to 'share' a bath which normally meant the youngest, me, being the last. Through the week, Mum would give us what she called a strip wash, up on the dining table and God help you if you twitched or 'played up', as she used to say…You got a smacked bottom!

Another mod con was linoleum or lino! This was a must as most of the British did not have the money for such luxuries as carpet or, in some cases, even rugs. We did have lino in all the bedrooms and of course, no modern 1950s house would be complete without the potty under the bed - yet another task for Mum!

Long trousers were normally forced on us boys around twelve to fourteen years of age; mine arrived on my twelfth birthday - as a 'birthday present'. Swell, eh. I did not like them! When told to go down to the shop, I started to take them off and my mum's hand came down, smack! Right across my bum! This happened in front of my mates, who had gathered to witness the final 'grooming' of their friend. They were not impressed; if this was going to happen when it came to their turn they all reckoned they would stay in short pants!

Life at Newtown Secondary School proved rather good after that, with a few exceptions. I did have the privilege of receiving the cane once. As I walked into the classroom after break someone started shrieking at the top of their voice. Mrs Jones, the teacher, came in, looked around, could not tell who the culprit was, so sent the three of us who happened to be in the room at the time to Mr Reeves the headmaster. We waited outside his room like lemons.

The headmaster arrived. 'What are you doing there?'

'Sent here for making a noise, - sir!'

'Okay, inside,' barked Mr Reeves.

We entered the headmaster's office and I was immediately struck by how dark and dingy the whole room appeared. The headmaster went to his desk and extracted an evil-looking cane from the drawer. I wondered briefly if he had a selection of canes for different occasions. I guess I should not have worried too long about this as he proceeded to bend it between his two hands as if to test the strength and flexibility.

I remembered seeing similar illustrations of headmasters bending their canes in the Billy Bunter stories, of which I was an avid reader. I suddenly realised that headmaster Reeves was about to act out his part and guess which poor individuals were going to participate in this real-life episode? Me and two others! One by one we were told to hold out our hands. Whack, whack, whack and out we came. I was only just getting around to saying, 'It wasn't me, sir!' Talk about being a bit slow; that bang on the head years ago had certainly stopping something working properly – my tongue.

With stinging palms we all returned to our now fully occupied classrooms and Mrs Jones directed us to our seats. Did I see just a glint of sympathy in her eyes? After all it had been she who had sent us to the headmaster's office in the first place. Looks from our fellow classmates were a mixture of glee and most likely relief that it had not been any of them that had been caught misbehaving! Me, I was innocent! Wasn't I?

At times like this with justice being dealt out with such firmness, I was beginning to wonder. However, perhaps some of Mr Reeve's instant justice could help with some of our present problems in our schools.

We did have another rather upsetting experience with a cat, this time with our pet cat, Tabby. She had the habit of sitting on top of one of the brick columns that fronted our small front garden. One day we had a knock on the door. One of my friends informed us we had better come and see our cat as two greyhounds had her. How could this be? We had a gate that was almost certainly closed at all times. My mother and I ran to the end of the road and there, lying in front of the local butcher's shop, was our Tabby, with a very anxious greyhound owner bending over her.

'What happened?' my mother asked.

Ray, a neighbour who the family knew well, was very upset. He had been walking by with his two greyhounds (without a lead) and they had spotted Tabby sitting perched on the column. Evidently, if she had stayed there she would have been quite safe, or even if she had jumped back into the garden, but no, she panicked and had run up the street with the hounds in close pursuit. She had no chance against such adversaries. They caught her within minutes and, with one dog at each end, they started pulling her literally into two bits. Amazingly Tabby was still alive and mewed pitifully at me as I attempted to stroke her head to give her some comfort. It was almost like she was trying to say, 'Look what they have done to me.'

The vet was called and mercifully put Tabby to sleep. My dad, in his usual manner, dismissed the unfortunate incident as a part of life's natural happenings and he and Roy remained friends. I was less forgiving and as far as I was concerned, he was certainly not my favourite man of the moment. Bloody dogs!

Becoming a 'senior' at school was a milestone as it meant we were getting to be the big guys and could boss the smaller kids around. Talk about tribal tendencies! The school was set out with a full curriculum that included sport, cookery, metalwork, woodwork and, of course, the dreaded maths, English and science.

One day, in the sheet metal class, Mr Rabbit, our metal and woodwork teacher, was demonstrating the precision cutting of metal. He had a large cutter with a handle about four feet long and needed a lot of space for him to manoeuvre it. Everyone was crowded round and interested in how he did this. Of course there was always one in the bunch who daydreamed and walked about, looking at everything but what Rabbit was doing and - bonk! Straight on the head! I saw stars – straight down on the floor – it must have been seconds, but looking up at a concerned but laughing Rabbit, who was asking how many fingers could I see. I felt an absolute idiot.

I finally began to notice there was something different about some of my classmates; they smelled different. I am talking about the girls not the boys, but I guess some of them did as well, not that I noticed. Sonia Jamieson was certainly different and, when I had to work with her in the science lab, I started to feel a rather strange reaction to her nearness. Not that we were that close of course but, having to hold the microscope for her to look into and vice versa, I noticed she didn't have any of the spots that all of us boys had! In fact she was rather nice, in a funny sort of way… Perhaps she even felt some attraction towards me because both of us started to delay our going-home time and staying behind (with Jacko's permission), strictly in the interest of science of course, to further investigate the bugs and clean up the slides.

Oh, how the teachers' staffroom must have tittered with laughter at the two of us, experiencing something other than learning at the end of a microscope, particularly as we did not really know what was actually happening to us. I guess the sap was rising at last in two young persons' lives. This platonic fling lasted two weeks until my best friend Dobby suddenly asked what we were doing after Jacko's science class; I told him and he started staying behind …and stole my girl! Oh love, I feel thy sting!

I was in Jacko's class for my last year of school and on one particular day I was counting the hours until we could go to football, the highlight of our week; well, for the boys anyway. We had all taken numerous tests and today was results day. Jacko had come up with the idea we would be seated in order of our test results. The smart ones at the back and so forth which meant, of course, that the duffers would be at the front so they could receive extra attention; a good idea, I suppose. The results were handed out with the marks shown on the top. We had done four tests so the mark was the total of all four. To make things worse everyone received someone else's test paper results. As Jacko called out the marks from the top starting with '200', the maximum possible score, everyone moved around to their new seat. Can you imagine the chaos as all the kids moved to their new places and, as usual, not quietly? The scores continued to be called out; 148, 145, 140…. and soon the halfway mark was reached with everyone waiting for their marks and, even more importantly, their final year's position in the classroom.

I suddenly felt great fear; they were now filling up the last row and still my name and marks had not been called. Oh no, not the duffer's place, not the last place in the class, not below Hilary Jones, the recognised dunce of the class! The suspense was killing me; still the places filled up and, at last, the very final place. I closed my eyes and awaited my fate.

My name was not called.

'Please, sir, I don't appear to have a place!'

Jacko looked at me in his bemused way. 'Who has Ken's paper?'

One of my classmates put their hand up. 'I did call it out, sir!'

I had to go to the front of the class while everyone looked at their results again and then started moving to make room for little ol' me. I was seventh! Thank God! I was saved, seventh out of thirty-eight was not bad but surely it was the wrong time to have copped a deaf 'n.

Actually, Hilary Jones was quite a dish, and I guess I could have done a lot worse than sit next to her. I could start carrying her books to and from school. The problem was I only lived across the darn road. What would Mother say?

One of our fellow classmates lived in an orphanage and, unfortunately, the orphanage chose to put their charges in large heavy boots. The boots would clink due to the 'Blakeys', steel studs that were fitted on the toes and heels to make them last longer. My father did the same to my shoes but, with the heavy boots, our classmate seemed to have a problem walking, and playing football in the playground with a small ball must have been really difficult. I felt sorry for 'Clippie' as his heartless classmates called him. I used to ask him to play on my team even though it gave us a disadvantage with his slow and sometimes lethal challenges; however, it did make the opposition move out of the way faster. We all liked to think that by asking him to join us we made his life at school a little bit more bearable.

As many of us lived in the same area, we used to go for bike rides to the lovely places around Reading at the weekends. Places such as Woodley with its miles of evergreens and bluebells which seemed to go on for ever. With the present demand for housing seemingly taking precedence over nature, I often wonder what is actually left of those exquisite woodlands now.

We were out one day on our bicycles and coming to the main road. Most of us stopped as required, but a few of the front riders, seeing that nothing was coming, went straight across. Not one of us had seen PC Evans; hand up, he gestured for us all to stop, which we duly did.

'What stop sign, Officer?' Out came the book and fifteen names went in to it. The case came up one month later and we all were fined 10/- (ten shillings), quite a sum in those days.

No argument with the law. The policeman's word was the law. Perhaps nowadays more policemen like PC Evans would be welcome on some of the crime-ridden housing estates.

We had a couple of girls in class who, with rather deep voices and being tall of stature, would act more like boys. One such girl was Pat Ford; she had her 'gang' trailing after her wherever she went. We all gave her a wide berth but really she never did any harm as far as I knew. However, one day Sally, one of her lieutenants, who I did quite fancy, came up to me and asked to speak to me privately. Oh well now, I guess I could fit Sally in for a few minutes, as she had asked me so nicely…I imagined that things had come to a head and she was obviously going to declare her undying love for me!

'Yes, Sally, what can I do for you?' I said, smiling nonchalantly.

'Pat wants to know if you will go out with her.'

I do believe the smug smile froze on my face as the implication of what Sally was asking me sank in.

'I'm, er, what did you say?' I replied, knowing full well that I had not misheard. I was like a condemned man asking for time to say his prayers. Sally repeated the request and I glanced across at the waiting Pat who, although not unattractive, just filled me with absolute fear (and I was not the only guy that had such a fear).

'I'm sorry, I can't,' I heard myself answer in what could only have been classed as a whisper. Not quite sure what she heard, Sally returned to the Godmother and conveyed my feeble answer. Fortunately I received no other requests and no horse's head was ever placed in my locker!

Now if Sonia had revitalized her interest in me I would have been honoured, but Pat, God bless her, just scared the life out of me!

We were all sitting in our newly allocated seats when the headmaster came in and informed us of a devastating event: 'King George VI has died.'

No one spoke; it was if the news had struck dumb everyone in the class and perhaps even everyone in the school. A hush descended on the whole class, such was the devotion that existed in the country at that time. We all knew that both the King and Queen had refused to leave London while the blitz was happening and that had made every citizen, young and old, even more devoted to the King. The funeral was a great occasion and to us mere children it seemed to go on forever, as indeed they do even to this day. The next big occasion was the Coronation of Queen Elizabeth, the young princess who had rushed back from Africa when the untimely death occurred. I remember it well. My Uncle Bob, my father's brother, came down from Brentford together with his family; this included his daughter Barbara and, being a delightful blonde, she soon became the centre of my world.

An instant attraction occurred between us and we started drifting outside to the backyard whenever we thought we would not be missed. Even then we had great respect for the occasion and perhaps even more respect for both my dad and his brother. They did not seem to mind; I guess they had been young once themselves and realised that the pomp and ceremony of the occasion was a little tiring on us younger mortals. Years later, when Barbara visited on a more sorrowful occasion, the passing away of my father, she admitted that the attraction had been there for her as well. Just as well it did not go any further as I do not think a good case of incest would have gone down well in those days.

When we had first arrived at Newtown School, we were placed in 'houses': Kennet, Thames or Loddon (names of local rivers); I was in Loddon. Pupils were awarded house points when they did something outstanding. As you can imagine, this created quite a rivalry between the different houses, lasting all year and climaxing with a presentation to the house with the most points. I remember going camping to the Isle of Wight and playing cricket. We had knocked Thames out of the competition and were playing Kennet for the points. I was captain of the team, had batted first and scored most of the runs. Kennet were in and now needed six runs to beat us. I took the ball as the captain and, being a fast bowler for the school team, I decided to stop Kennet in their tracks.

Everyone was watching from the sidelines, including Sonia Jameson and her friends. I hurtled down to the crease and soon five balls had been delivered at a cost of only two runs. (Both byes as I had bowled so fast the silly wicketkeeper could not stop them). I made an extra effort and again the ball skipped safely by - we had won by three runs, my 'house' Loddon had won extra points and Ken West was saviour of the day!

We trooped off the field and I looked around for Sonia. Where was the girl, for God's sake? Surely she had seen my fantastic efforts? I had to wait until after mealtime for the answer. As the boys were sitting talking around the campfire, I overheard John Trenary, a 'friend' of mine, calmly announcing that he had been in the girls' tent and, asking what lipstick Sonia had on, he had leaned across and tested it! This must have happened while I was slogging my guts out on that cricket field! For God's sake, had neither of them any feelings? I was devastated and what made it worse was that it had only been a game to John; there was me pining all this time, whereas he had only been window-shopping! I never had the opportunity to ask Sonia about it; well, a gentleman does not ask a lady such things, does he?

While we lived at School Terrace, we had a lodger for a while, a chap called Russell Parks who was going through university and wanted a place to stay.

'Yes,' said my ever-obliging mother

'He can have Ken's room'.

That was understandably the first strike against poor Russell as I really liked my nice and cosy room. I was moved to the spare room opposite, which was large, spacious and bloody cold!

Everything Russell did was fine – with my mother and father. He was a Labour supporter as was my dad. He had nice manners which my mother adored and he knew when to butter up my brother and sisters (not that he was at all my sister Coral's type).

Anyway, Russell was there to stay and he did, for about a year, before moving onto university and, no doubt, better things. One thing he did leave with me, which was something really special, was a short wave radio. By now I had forgiven Russell for nicking my room and bed and would often go up to his room with a cup of tea, sent up by my mother, when he was studying. He used to have this strange-looking radio on and would often tune into the different foreign stations of countries I had not even heard of.

Leaving me the radio was perhaps Russell's way of making amends to me for the upheaval; upon moving back into my room I was content to continue with the wave listening interludes.

One of my firm favourites was Radio AFN: the American Armed Forces Network. Staff Sergeant Chuck Berry was the American DJ. He was from the southern states of America and had a very distinctive southern drawl. He used to play all the favourites of the day: Nat King Cole, Frank Sinatra, Pat Boone and his sign-off message was one I can still remember to this day: 'This is Staff Sergeant Chuck Berry signing off, asking you to drop in any time, any day; we will be tickled to death to have yur.' It must surely have been a sign of things to come!

My father and mother like many mums and dads of the day liked to go to the pub now and again, which normally meant every weekend.

'The Jack of Both Sides' was my dad's 'local' and he soon became involved in putting on shows and 'acting the goat' as we used to say in those days. In fact he was quite good at it. Being a rather quiet chap it was surprising to see him up on the stage singing songs such as 'Don't laugh at me cos I'm a fool', an old Norman Wisdom number. He also liked to do 'Cigarettes and Whisky', not that he preached the wild, wild women stuff. My mother saw to that!

In the early days of the pub visits we were left outside on a wooden bench with the customary lemonade and a packet of Smith's crisps. I never ever used the twisted blue salt packet which had been placed in the bag but at least it was fun looking for it. Even when the weather was a little on the cold side, us kids used to put up with our lot. We often had to stand in the doorways of the pubs in an attempt to get some warmth from the heat generated by the bulging crowd of people inside. They seemed to be oblivious to the chilled bunch of kids gathered around the entrances to the busy public houses. When you wanted more drinks or crisps you just sauntered into the bar where Mum and Dad were and tugged on Dad's coat pocket as if to remind him that we were still in some way his responsibility. He would normally gladly reach into his pocket, pull out a shilling and place it in my outstretched hand. It was a small price to pay in order that he could rejoin his many friends in sorting out the day's problems. As an afterthought he would gently remind us that we should not be in there. It was a ritual that was repeated many times during the weekend visits to the Jack of Both Sides public house. Talk about having it both ways, we all seemed to win on those occasions!

It is said that things 'run in the genes' and I look back with fondness to those years with my father doing his stuff on the pub stage. Perhaps without realising it he was setting the scene for me. It was no coincidence that in later years I became a club manager and ended up on the stage compering shows with acts like The Platters, Gerry and the Pacemakers and Vince Hill. I hasten to add that I reckon my father had me beat when it came down to the singing. Anyway, that is another story…

Growing Up Is Hard To Do

The next few years saw me grow from an aimless boy to a rather aimless teenager and, when asked what I wanted to do when I left school, I was pointedly informed that joining Reading Football Club as a player was not an option in any way. Had they not seen me score those four goals against Battle School? Just goes to show how little head teachers know!

Upon leaving school I managed to get a position with the Sutton Seed Company in Reading. I worked with people like 'arry Brown, an ex-matelot, who soon completed my education concerning the opposite sex. It seemed the only thing Harry had on his mind was sex and more sex…A fellow co-worker called Alan had the misfortune to mention he was courting and for weeks Harry would constantly asked him if he had 'dipped his wick'. Poor Alan, he would just go an instant shade of red and when, finally, he had to admit he had 'dipped his wick', Harry, seemingly satisfied, turned his attention to me.

I immediately said I had and, remembering Blackie's step by step account, gave a rendition that was sufficient to satisfy poor old Harry.

We all knew whenever Harry had 'dipped his wick' as he always came into work with a spring in his step. Unfortunately for him that did not seem to happen too often!

A friend of mine, Barney (another misfit of his time), and I used to go down to the local dance halls, hang around all night for the last dance and then try our luck with the girls, but we often found our luck was well out!!! How did we know you had to spend money on them!! Girls had to be wooed, whatever that was…

Across from the dance hall was a respectable dance school. My friends and I joined in order to get our hands on some of the pretty girls that seemed to frequent it. This was harder than we anticipated as the dance instructors, a husband and wife, would keep us all separated while they gave us instruction. However, we found that, after six or seven lessons, we had learnt to dance correctly. I even took and passed the Bronze and Silver dancing tests. To this day I find dancing quite a nice way of relaxing, if I can ever find the time.

Learning to dance had the compensation of finally getting to dance with the girls. It was a bit of a pickup place as you could make dates if you were lucky enough to score. One embarrassing moment came in turn to all of us boys. Julia, the married dance instructor, used to make us guys dance with her without holding her hands. This is actually how you learn to dance and how the men are supposed to learn to lead, by the hips. Can you imagine the red faces when we were told to push our hips into hers to enable her to know which way we wanted her to turn! We were only fifteen years old, for goodness sake! It must have made a comical sight when we all took turns in pushing Julia around the dance floor with our hands held high.

Another favourite was the ladies' choice: when a lady can actually choose whom she prefers to dance with. This is twofold for the ladies as they can save their feet if they know the guy is not a good dancer and, if they fancy you, well…!

I remember a delectable girl called Maureen, whom I had long fancied, actually asking me to dance. Ladies' choices are nearly always slow dances and you might be able to use an opportunity such as this to ask the lady out! Maureen must have been in a loving mood that night; she clung to me, wrapping herself close to me as only a lady can. I had never experienced such closeness, it was fantastic and an emotion I could only dream of or sigh for when going to the movies. Hold on a minute, what was that? Up to that point I had always believed I was a slow starter, my urges only went as far as looking and sighing at bums and boobies. There was suddenly another link between Maureen and I and I did not know how to deal with it! Maureen seemed to enjoy it; in fact she seemed to move even closer if that was at all possible. Had she got the response she desired or maybe much more than she bargained for!

The dance finished and, with a blushing face, I thanked Maureen. She in turn thanked me and looked at me expectantly; did I have anything to ask her said her expression. I stood there for a moment with three legs and just moved away with what can only be described as a gait or kind of awkward stroll. It looked like I must have inadvertently copied it from a John Wayne movie. Ask her out? I could not even look her in the face. Another chance missed by a movement of nature that only comes to those who wait. The problem was how did you control those natural movements?

I often wondered where everything was leading me; I was in a dead-end job and had no idea where I was headed. I did not have to wait for long to find out. I was to head a very long way…to The United States of America…

About the time that Barney and I were trying our luck with the local girls in the Reading dance halls, my sister Coral met Staff Sergeant Nelson (Hank) Snow of the American Air Force and soon, very much in love, they became engaged. This was to change her life and inadvertently the lives of the rest of the West family. Nelson (being from West Virginia) was very fond of country and western music, especially Hank Williams. This is why he was nicknamed 'Hank' by his buddies. He would often bring many of Hank's records to the house.

I became a firm admirer of Hank Williams's music and started collecting all of his records, so much so that I got to know all of the words by heart. In fact, even more than Frankie Laine, a big name in those days, 'Hey Good Lookin', and 'Take these chains from my heart' were soon, along with many others, to become big listening in the West household.

I do remember the Yanks taking us all out to dinner in appreciation of Mum and Dad's hospitality. Nelson and five of his buddies informed us they wanted to treat us all to a steak meal. Now steak was not a common commodity for most of the families in England and, even with Dad's reasonable wage, we rarely had steak. So off we set in three cars and sped down the A4 to a restaurant situated just outside Maidenhead in Berkshire.

It was a nice sunny day and we all started enjoying the day out, soaking up the sunshine. Within a short time we reached the restaurant and ordered our meal. Drinks were plentiful and soon both Dad and

Mum were really enjoying themselves. Dad, being a natural gentleman, certainly knew how to charm our hosts, and they in turn gave us back some good old American hospitality.

I was sitting back, just observing the proceedings, when I started to notice that the guys seemed to go missing in turn. I never thought much about it at the time and put it down to them answering a call of nature. It was only later that my sister Coral informed Mum and Dad that the restaurant was a 'whore house' and the guys were making use of the desserts that were available at the time!' Nelson excluded, of course. If my mother had known that at the time I guess she would have choked on her chips!

During correspondence between Hank's mother and father in America, it was suggested that my father and mother purchase a forty-acre farm that belonged to Hank's parents. Now, forty acres seemed a lot of land to a townie like my father, but soon our family and Hank's were making arrangements for the possible purchase of said farm. Dreams of becoming the next Clampit farming family became rife in the Wests' family home.

The subsequent wedding between my sister and Hank seemed to finalise things. Soon all the West family were applying to the American Embassy in London for the necessary visas for entry to the United States. After many months, and visits to London, they duly arrived. Then there came a problem: what to do with Ken?

'Me! What's wrong with me?'

'You are coming up to draft age,' my father informed me. It was the normal procedure in the 1950s that you had to register early in order that the government could send you the 'greeting' at the appropriate time. Up to that time, joining the army or anything else was the least of my intentions. For goodness sake, didn't they realise that I was still learning how to dance and how to show those lovely girls some of the talents I had in rich abundance. The outcome of all this was that it was decided to send me on ahead – on my own.

My father booked my berth on the ocean liner TSS New York. It sounded quite grand. I was really looking forward to it and, after some rather apprehensive goodbyes, I arrived at Southampton and sought out the assigned ship. I did not see it at first as it was sheltering under the bow of a rather large ship of the day, the Queen Mary, 83,000 plus tons. The TSS New York: 19,000 tons.

The ship left Southampton and proceeded to plod its weary way across the Atlantic. After first calling at the port of Cork, in Southern Ireland, it then headed to, what seemed to be to little ol' me, the other side of world. Perhaps it was! Oh my God. I will quickly gloss over the nine-day voyage as I really do not want to recall any of the incredibly terrifying time spent on that rust bucket. I spent most of it lying on my bunk. I can still remember the six-inch gap that was all that was left, between my head and the ceiling, every time we hit a wave. My roommate was a card sharp, or so he seemed to me. He would always have a deck of cards on his person. He was obviously using his talents somewhere on the ship as he would often come back to the cabin in the early hours. I did not see any heavies chasing after him the whole time on board, so I guess he was just a normal maverick and not the devious type. He spent time with me showing me new tricks but never for money. To this day I have never played cards for money so I guess my time spent with my maverick friend was well worth the effort.

We finally hit dry land, calling at Halifax Nova Scotia, and then proceeded to eventually dock at Long Island, New York. The entry point did not greatly inspire me as it appeared to be only a slight improvement on what may have been experienced by the Ellis Island immigrants all those years ago. I do jest a bit but, at sixteen years of age, I guess I was expecting the red carpet treatment after all that swotting up on the delights of my new adopted country. I do recall that many years ago a chap called Dick Whittington had similar ideas about the streets of London being paved with gold! If I remember rightly they made a pantomime out of his experiences. Well, at least the hero in the story did eventually get the girl! That was a good sign…

I did learn something though: if your tip to the cabin steward was not deemed to be sufficient, you end up lugging your heavy suitcase back up to the top deck yourself. I can only assume that the ten dollars I gave him was not deemed adequate. Bloody Yank! Passing under the Statue of Liberty was, however, a fantastic experience and one which will stay with me for the rest of my life.

My father and mother had arranged with Hank that one of his friends would meet me at Grand Central Station, feed me and let me stay over in their Manhattan apartment for a few hours. They would then put me on the next long distance Greyhound bus which would travel all night, with few stops, all the way down to West Virginia. This would drop me off around 10.30 a.m. when the hillbilly clan would meet me.

The couple, Jim and Susan, met me at the assigned meeting place. Americans make it easy; they called it 'The Meeting Place'.

'Just a minute,' I remarked. 'I haven't got my bike!' I will never forget the look of amazement that spread over Jim's face.

'You have a bike?'

'Yes, my dad said I should bring it; it was brand new for my last birthday'.

'Oh fine,' Jim remarked, seemingly unfazed by this new revelation 'Where is it?'

It had been taken off the ship, and efficiently delivered to the 'bulky luggage' department. The Americans have a name for everything.

I remember walking down the middle of Grand Central Station huge forecourt with my Raleigh four-speed bicycle. The stares that came our way were immense – people just do not use bikes in New York City, not if you value your life you don't. How Jim and his wife managed to get it in or on his American car is a dim and distant memory but they did. It was suggested however that perhaps, large as the luggage storage was on the bus, we had better leave it at the apartment and perhaps they could send it down by train. Not wanting to upset things, I agreed to leave my lovely four-speed bicycle with two complete strangers. So be it, but I must have been mad! My new friends lived in Manhattan and showed me the sights of New York. It was awesome and they gave me the royal tour, stopping at all the noted landmarks that everyone has to visit.

I managed to get down some food and have a sleep before getting on the bus. Thanking my hosts, I got on and spent the next few hours looking at amazing sights while leaving New York and then New Jersey. I'd only been used to Smith's charabanc coaches when going to Weymouth for our holidays. I'd thought they were luxurious. The Greyhound buses were smooth, air-conditioned and quiet, very quiet. I soon became drowsy and drifted off to sleep in serene comfort. The bus trip down was to be incredible.

I was awakened suddenly by the bus stopping and the driver shouting that there was a thirty-minute stopover.

I stepped off the bus into another world – it was 2 a.m. in the morning and there was a very busy diner, open for business! Surely this could not be right? In the UK everything used to close at eleven in the evening. I had promised myself a giant American cheeseburger and a coke, which I duly ordered, but what was that small kind of box sat on the counter? What is more, there were many of them placed everywhere along the food counter. Where the heck did the sound come from? Not to worry; putting in a dime and selecting the latest Pat Boone record from this jukebox was a real treat and I did just manage to hear it before we had to get back on board the bus.

I thought I had just died and gone to heaven when, as if by magic, a Hank Williams song came over the PA, it was called 'Ramblin' Man'. The driver must have had a sense of humour or perhaps he knew I was on the bus going to my new home. We will never know…

Waking up early was not hard, as the morning sun streaked suddenly across the window of the driver and we were given coffee if we asked. American Greyhound buses had two drivers on board and they used to interchange as they sped across the American states. Galax, Virginia, where I was heading, was only one small stop. It was said that a Greyhound bus could outrun a Cadillac, if you were silly enough to challenge it, such was their power under the hood. Travelling in the USA was new, exciting and it was happening to me. I certainly was a 'Ramblin' Man' and if this was how things were going to be in the USA, then perhaps I could just about put up with it.

I should not have worried about my bike as Brady, Hank's father, arrived to collect me in a large pickup truck. Either way, the bike was back in New York and there it was destined to stay. I soon found out that, down on the Blue Ridge Mountains of Virginia, no one biked anywhere. They drove in nice large cars. Even kids that were my age managed to get driving licences. My bike was finally sold for thirty dollars and I never had the heart to ask about the money.

I met all the friends of Hank's younger sister Ann Marie. Although we had corresponded it was soon clear that there was never going to be any love interest between us. One of her girlfriends however, called Leslie, was gorgeous and I fancied her the moment I saw her. So, when I was invited to go with Ann Marie and her friends to Galax, the nearest town, I readily agreed. Leslie was driving and I was just imagining that she was paying me 'extra' attention when she suddenly stopped the car and got out! Ann Marie took over and Leslie went off with her 'secret' boyfriend. My dreams were shattered. Did she not realise that I had travelled all this way to be her new English lover!

Oh well! Ironically, Dean Martin was crooning 'Sweet dreams are made of this' on the car radio.

The time at the farm flew by with me helping out doing odd jobs and herding the cows from one field to another. At one of my first mealtimes I was amazed at the taste of the food, especially the beef. Being on a farm, we of course ate the beef which had been reared there. I had never tasted such tasty food. I used to love the American TV shows such as 'The Dick Van Dyke Show' and 'The Amos and Andy Show'. I also enjoyed 'The Rowan and Martin Show' where they promised if you blew in their ear they would 'follow you anywhere'. Just priceless comedy!

I loved this kind of comedy and soon became addicted to it. I guess a lot of my own humour these days can be traced back to the situation comedy shows that I used to watch back in those Blue Ridge Mountains of Virginia. Soon the American draft was mentioned. Now too old for the local high school and too young to get serious work, it was suggested that I joined the Air Force and I readily agreed.

I was taken down to the local Air Force recruiting centre, given countless tests, a medical and, hey presto, I was in the American Air Force. What was more, I did not have to go back to the farm. I was loaded onto a truck, then a train and again moved across the States of America, finally arriving at Lackland Air Base, in Texas, for my basic training. God, here we go again, new place, new friends and in a different country. What on earth was I getting myself into now?

I vaguely remember buying a new suit just after starting work at Sutton Seed Company in Reading. The colour was the closest thing to the American Air Force blue, which I now found myself in. Deep down it appears our subconscious may just play a part in our future!

The first thing you notice in Texas is it is hot, very hot. A haircut leaving you completely bald meant that you did not have to worry about your hair when roused at 4 a.m in the morning and informed that you are to SSS in fifteen minutes. The last two S's were Shower and Shave; I will leave the first letter to your imagination. Fifteen minutes was the designated time for having breakfast, then 'on parade' just in time to meet the morning sun (which at six clock in the morning was nearly as hot as we used to get (or hoped for) in August in England).

Dousing your head with soothing cold water is NOT recommended – someone should have warned me. Having done this I lasted about five minutes and then hit the ground without any warning, my first and only taste of Texan sunstroke! This did mean however, that I managed to sit out the remainder of the drill that day in some comfort. I was not going to complain about that.

Life in basic training was hard, with drills and more drills, then finally an overnight camp-out under so called 'enemy fire'. It was a chance to play soldiers but did I not join to be an airman? Airmen don't soldier, do they? The drill instructors were a mean lot or this was the impression they tried to implant in you. They would often pick on one poor individual who had caught their eye,

'Come here, airman. Are you some kind of nut? You are nothing but a dip shit!' Or even worse, 'Your ass is grass and I am the lawnmower.' It was surprising how quickly you got used to such abuse. So this was how they modelled you into the modern fighting man, but had I not joined the air force to be the poor man's fast gun? The new English Top Gun. I mean, the airman I had met in my little ol' town of Reading, the handsome Nelson with his gleaming white teeth, his Yankee accent, clad in his air force blue, that is what I joined for, not this constant abuse! Our only recourse was, when drilling and marching miles and miles across the endless countryside (which was seemingly always available to Uncle Sam), the woeful lament of 'TI, TI, don't be blue, Frankenstein was ugly too.' How pathetic was that?

The Air Force also had its little ways of keeping you on your toes. Just when you had settled in for a reasonable six hours' sleep, the hut door would open and in would come two or three instructors, bent only on one thing: to strike sudden fear at this sudden intervention and to get you out of the sparse but cosy hut. Believe me, it did work!

I will never forget the almost daily miles of strict order marching which we were forced to endure.

It was quite eerie, when returning from an extremely early morning squadron march, to hear only the loud explosion of boots pounding the dusty roads which led back to the base quarters. It seemed endless when looking ahead to see fellow airmen disappearing around bends which appeared only to be followed by yet another bend. The only break in the noise of the boots was the instructor's occasional sharp demand to pick up the cadence. Perhaps he wanted his breakfast as well. We could only hope.

Another little gem the sergeants used to pull was to come unannounced into the barracks. They always consisted of sergeants that were not of your squadron but they were always senior in rank, such as Top Sergeants (six stripes). Every day an airman basic, the lowest of the low, which of course was all of us at that time, was assigned the task of CQ, short for Charge of Quarters for the day.

This lasted until six in the evening when another airman would take over. One evening I was on the late shift which meant I would be there until at least two in the morning. My duties were to keep everyone safe and prevent such things as fires occurring, etc.

On this particular evening around eight o'clock, two sergeants entered the hut barking orders. One was a Senior Top Sergeant and the other a Staff Sergeant.

Without any word to me sitting at my small desk where every Charge of Quarters sat, they shouted to the few airmen in the hut to do their bidding. They proceeded to instruct the four men in the hut to take the footlockers of every man billeted in the building out into the compound. I watched intently as, one by one, the forty or so footlockers ended up on the outside road. I naturally assumed they would be transported to where the sergeants had in mind.

The two sergeants nodded to me and left the hut only to return ten minutes later to ask if it was normal for me to let them or anybody else in and allow the removal of forty fellow airmen's footlockers from the hut.

I was perplexed; please let the ground open up and allow me to disappear into it. I was sent out to assist the men in bringing the lockers back to their original owners. I was pleased that most of my fellow airmen were out enjoying themselves; I certainly would not have enjoyed the ribbing that would surely have followed the next day. Not to mention the mandatory report that would also follow; the limey fell for it. Dull bugger!

About this time I had my first 'run in' with an Air Force '90 day wonder!' These were the officers that were made up to second lieutenant after just 90 days of training, hence the nickname. I was rather short-sighted when in basic training and, not wishing to wear my glasses (due mainly to vanity), I did not recognise the bars on the approaching lieutenant.

'Airman, don't you salute an officer when you see one?' came the smart rebuke.

'Oh, sorry, sir.' Up went the arm and the salute was made. He was not satisfied with that salutation and informed me that the thumb should be in line with the rest of the hand.

'Sorry, sir, unfortunately I am double-jointed in that hand and I can only move my thumb in place.'

I remember the '90 days' face; the years of good college education had not prepared him for this meeting with a 'funny' speaking Limey, who was of course daft enough to believe that anyone of average intelligence would believe such piffle. He watched as I placed my thumb in the correct position, sighed, and then dismissed me! If my mother had seen me that day, she would also have shaken her head in wonderment. .

She would also not have not been too impressed if she had heard about the night (again in basic training) when I was given the task of keeping the fires going in all the twelve huts which the airmen occupied whilst training. Simple task, yes maybe, but one is expected to stay awake, so as not to only wake up upon hearing the commotion of two hundred agitated airmen also waking to find no hot water. Airman West was certainly the only one in hot water that day, which is more than could be said for the rest of the airmen who went short of their daily shower!

I guess that losing the hot water was not the only problem I experienced while in boot camp. An incredible thing happened. Perhaps due to the heavy pounding my feet were taking I started to develop in-growing toenails. Not something I had had any problem with before.

'Better go to the medics and get it fixed' was my flight sergeant's advice; I was no good to him hobbling around on one foot.

'Ugh yes, nasty,' said the giant black medic looking at my swollen large toe.

'Don't worry, we will fix that,' he said, picking up the largest needle I had ever seen in my life.

He could not be serious about putting that bloody thing in my poor toe? If one has ever had, even for a fleeting moment, a notion to allow a giant needle to be put into the top end of one's toe for any reason, I would honestly recommend them to think very hard about allowing this to happen.

'This sorts the men from the boys,' my 'friendly' medic remarked. Friendly – this man was not friendly; he was downright sadistic in every way. Tears rolled down my cheek as they offered me a tissue and, while not a sound came from my mouth, they knew I had been hurt, really hurt. Needs must was the sympathetic look I received from the two men.

The needle did its work and I watched with some trepidation as they proceeded to cut half of my toenail away. I was amazed by the amount of blood from such a small appendage. With the toe bandaged up and having been given some sticks to hobble with, I soon realised that every problem has a silver lining. No drilling for at least four weeks and no parachute jumping that just happened to be scheduled for that particular week.

Oh, how sad. I was really looking forward to that!

This was, however, not to be my only experience with Uncle Sam's medical establishment. Soon after my experience with the 'giant needle', I had a smaller encounter! Up to this point of my life I had, fortunately, been reasonably free from exposure to any hospital visits, outpatient or inpatient. This was, unfortunately, about to change. While in Texas, even with its plentiful sunshine, for some reason a lot of new recruits, myself included, went down with a throat infection. The Americans called it 'strep throat', which is a type of severe tonsillitis and at that time there was only one kind of treatment, penicillin, which of course was at that time delivered only one way - by the dreaded needle!

I was lying on my hospital bunk at some insanely early hour (why do they wake sick people up so early in all hospitals?) and waiting for the doc. Along he came, looked down my throat, muttered a quick retort that I could not quite catch and left. Within minutes at the end of the ward a couple of medics (who just happened to be black, but not my friendly duo) started working their way along the line of beds.

Bang! Down came a hand on the patient's bare bottom, followed by a fast injection of the penicillin. I swear the man was on piecework and he must have had some Indian heritage (or perhaps some harpooning experience) because he seemed to aim the needle at the poor recipient's bottom from a distance. I would think he could have been listed in the Guinness Book of Records such was his desire to do a good, fast job or perhaps he just wanted to get to the commissary for his lunchtime cheeseburger! We all thought this was a bit overplayed until, unfortunately, we did indeed lose a fellow airman one night due to this serious infection.

The toe operation did not stop me going to Technical Training School, which was the main reason that we were all there after all. I was assigned a classification of 72050 which meant I would be a pen-pusher not the 'Top Gun' fighter pilot that I initially had wanted to be. Oh well, the Air Force's needs came first. I guess they had enough pilots at that time. If Uncle Sam needed a good, hard-working administrative office boy – look no further.

Touch-typing was one of the tasks we had to master and for some reason I found my fingers ill-equipped for the old fashioned typewriter they gave me. All the other guys and girls in the class obviously had better typewriters because theirs did not make the mistakes mine did. Bloody thing! I found I was in a unique position; I was one of the top three in the administrative tests that we were given but I could not type well enough to pass the final test. I just froze up and could not get the speed. Being phased back two weeks created an embarrassing moment again as my classmates celebrated their 'passing out' and were given their orders to go on to their next station.

I was sent back to start again with the class two weeks behind my present one and duly informed that if I could not get the required speed I would be relocated to the supply section. Relocated! The American way of saying duffer!

In those days, rightly or wrongly, most 'supply specialists' as they were called were from a poor working-class background with a poor education. I needed some help and fast.

To this day I do think that fate has a part to play in all our futures; while I did try to get the speed and accuracy required to pass the final test I did not feel confident in any way. '34' was the lowest mark you needed to achieve for a pass; that meant that, at the correct speed, you were allowed only four mistakes. The day of the test arrived and I walked in with a slightly heavy heart and sat at my desk. The bell rang and straightaway the air was filled with the clash of eager participants hitting their keys in unison, all except me. I seemed to freeze as usual and then I began my paragraph. The only way to do speed-typing is to touch-type, which means you do not look at your keys and just watch the words come up in their sequence. The strangest thing happened; I seemed to relax and I became more resigned to my fate. The papers were handed in and then handed back; my mark was 34. I had made it by the skin of my teeth. Someone up there did like me!

Now for my new assignment: Columbus, Capital of the State of Ohio, in the Midwest. Again I was moving into the unknown.

Before shipping out to our new postings, we were granted a weekend pass and the chance for some light relief after the hard work of passing the exams. We eagerly caught the local bus to the town of San Antonio. We all knew the legend of The Alamo with Davy Crocket and Jim Bowie and his knives. After arriving in the centre of the town we soon sorted out the nearest cantina and ordered our first round of drinks, all ten of us. I can just imagine the local population groaning with despair at yet another invasion of the fly boys from the local training base. Then, I guess there were many that liked and enjoyed the trade generated by the airmen's visits. I would imagine this must be true all over the world when it comes to the military personnel getting some time off. The memorabilia on sale, the Davy Crocket Hats, the Jim Bowie knives, all made the visit that much more attractive to this Limey, who could not get enough of this glimpse of the past. I had read about these things in Tommy's history class and now, here I was, almost reliving the past, actually in this historic town. I could just imagine Clint Eastwood with his sombrero and poncho walking down the main street, lighting a cheroot, and saying 'Go on, punk, make my day!'

I was a little concerned about purchasing one of the Jim Bowie knives and settled for just a smaller token of the visit. We all managed to drink a good quantity of the local beer and, after a further visit to a lively cantina where we were treated to an excellent display of flamenco dancing; we made our way back to the air base. A nice change from all the schooling we had endured (in my case, two weeks more than anyone else). Either way I was just pleased to graduate with the AFSC (Air Force Speciality Code) I had been awarded.

I had enjoyed my brief visit to one of America's most legendary places and, for the first time since my arrival in the United States, I felt part of the great nation that had become my home. I again gave silent thanks to my parents for having the fortitude to make that decision to embark on a new life. I remember with affection that old adage: 'When I was fifteen I thought my father a fool, now I am twenty-five, I am amazed just how much he had learnt in the last ten years!' Good one, Mum and Dad!

My father, mother and sister had arrived in the US shortly before I left Texas and before I took up my new position in Ohio. After a brief stay in Virginia, they had decided against purchasing the farm. They eventually moved to Delaware where my father obtained a good position in a company dealing with precious metals. Now all the West family were at least in one country, with exception of my brother Derek who had remained in the United Kingdom.

Arriving at my new posting near Columbus, I soon found that my fellow colleagues were very pleasant to work with. I did have some problems with the language however; well, not me actually. The incoming callers on the telephone had to listen very carefully when they heard this very keen and very English-speaking Limey rushing through his standard greeting. You can imagine it: 'Squadron 742 administrative support. Can I help you, airman second class West speaking, sir!' The normal response was 'What the hell did you say, airman?' Had they heard right, what planet had I arrived from! Oh well, guess I had better slow down just a bit!

I actually found my new posting quite nice; now that all the problems of testing and judging were well behind me I settled down to work in the squadron orderly room and even started to improve my speed and accuracy in typing. I also found time to enter one of the base's little incentives, a jingle contest. I happened to be up at headquarters and, seeing an entry form for a jingle, I sat down and wrote one.

My top sergeant was Robert Bizzack, a giant of a man and a really nice guy, always trying to pull a trick on everyone. He came in one morning saying that the bloody Limey, me, had won the base jingle contest and I should go and get my prize at HQ as the base commander was waiting.

'Oh yes, sarge, great.' I returned to my desk and started typing.

A now very agitated Sgt Bizzack came into my office. 'What the heck are you doing there. The base commander is waiting for you!' Bloody heck, I double-timed it to the base HQ and received my prize of fifty dollars. Nice one. I managed to have a picture taken as well. Bit of a swank that day! No big deal really though, could have been one hundred dollars; now that would have really recognised my genius.

I soon made many friends with my fellow airmen, one in particular: Will, whose family came from a strong Polish background. He was asked to attend the wedding of one of his many cousins and he invited me to go along. So we set out to drive up to Windsor, Michigan. The state of Michigan is very famous for its numerous lakes and it happens to be one of the nearest states to the Canadian border. In fact, Will used to joke about seeing the British flag flying across the border.

I will always remember the drive from Ohio to Michigan; tall trees lining both sides of the road which cut straight through towards the Canadian border where Will's family lived. In England we had a problem building a straight motorway despite the Romans showing us the way all those years ago.

We arrived at Will's house and soon it was arranged for me to see the sights. We first had to meet some of his many cousins and, as he had many, it did take some time to catch up with everyone. We ended up on the bank of a fantastic lake; it was crowded with many young people sitting around drinking beer and eating snacks from the numerous snack bars. The sun was shining and we both started to relax in the warmth of the sun and the extremely congenial welcome that was extended to us. I started talking with a nice young lady who was keen to know about England and how I liked living in the USA. We were getting on great and I was hoping to see more of Greta, my newly found Polish lady, when one of her friends called out for her to go on one of the boats which were on the lake. Greta turned around and asked me to join them but, being a non-swimmer, I declined. One thing I have always regretted is not learning to swim. Another missed moment.

That evening Will and I went to join the wedding party which, surprisingly, was still going on. It was the third day of the celebration, the Polish people certainly know how to celebrate, and I found the atmosphere electric, almost riotous as the dancers joined in vigorously to the beat of the Polish band. The music was very infectious and similar to the hillbilly music that I had encountered on the Blue Ridge Mountains of Virginia. The five hundred or more people were all sitting on benches in front of tables which were covered with white tablecloths that could only just be seen through literally hundreds of glasses and bottles of beer that were strewn on them.

I was quite enjoying the atmosphere when Will decided he had more cousins to visit and we left the busy wedding party, with me slightly regretting us having to leave. This was made worse when we passed the smiling face of Greta who smiled sweetly at me; smiling back I wondered for a second what would have happened if I had caught that boat trip with this pretty young lady. With my luck, I guess it would have tipped over!

Before we left Michigan we did manage to drive over the border into Canada and visit the other side. Will was not amused when I informed him that the grass was certainly greener on the other side with the British flag flying. I guess you never really leave your roots behind entirely. Either way, Will and I had a great time, and I thanked him for allowing me to see just a little more of this great country that I had now made my home.

As my chores took me up to the head office on a daily basis, I soon became very friendly with many of the personnel. 'Hey Limey' was the normal call from fellow workers, even from some of the officers. One in particular, Staff Sergeant Joe Werenski, seemed to take to me. Joe had been married to an English girl for some years and coming from West Virginia seemed to bring us closer together.

'Hey,' Joe remarked one day, 'fancy going out on the town?' Joe was married but, as his wife had returned to England on holiday, we could hit the hot spots. I had an English friend, Ed, on base so we readily agreed to go, not that we intended to drink too much. Twelve noon found us piling into Joe's car, speeding out of the base and, within one hundred yards, stopping at the first bar. Oh great, didn't realise Joe had such a thirst.

'Ever had a 7/7?' Joe asked.

'What's that?' I asked.

'Rye whiskey and 7 Up,' Joe replied.

'Bartender - three large ones!'

And that was it, my introduction to 7-high, as it's known. Seagram's VO or, as it is sometimes called, Canadian Club rye whiskey. If ever a devil was born without a set of horns it was you, Canadian Club, it was you.

Now you would think that two sane, healthy English guys would have some sense of their own capabilities and, perhaps even more importantly, an appreciation of the drinking capabilities of a man who had lived on the Blue Ridge Mountains of Virginia where, everyone knows (or should know) – they make their own whiskey! Perhaps moonshine is a better term.

Six o'clock in the evening came and found us arriving at Joe's home. We'd only taken six hours to travel eighteen miles – rather a long time? It appeared that Joe seemed to know every bar and the name of every bartender on the route from the base. Should we have been a little concerned? Not on your nellie; we felt great, a little drunk, but great. Some chow followed and then back into the car to continue our journey and do what we had planned to do seven hours earlier - hit the hot spots of the town of Columbus.

It was 2 a.m. in the morning. I was in the back seat of the car, my friend Ed was slumped in the front seat, but where was Joe?

'Where is the driver of this vehicle?' asked the policeman who had poked his head through the open window on the driver's side. I was blind, completely blind; the man had no face at all. I could only see the badge on his hat and the badge on his shirt. He sounded like he might be a policeman but why would he want Joe?

Ed waved in the air vaguely; he did not have a clue where Joe was either.

'Tell him to move this vehicle when he returns,' retorted the cop. We could only imagine that Joe was answering a call of nature. However, when Joe did return, we learnt that he was visiting an old friend; his wife was out of town and he was taking the opportunity to catch up on old times. At 2.30 am in the morning! Yep, good one, Joe!

Yes, Joe was a friendly guy like I said and perhaps his nose was getting a little longer than before.

'If you feel sick, put your head out the car,' hollered Joe to us both. Moving the car was not a good idea because, within minutes, Ed was opening the car window and yes, it went straight out onto the street as we sped back to Joe's place. Never had so much been drunk, by so few, in such a short time. Since that day I am glad to say I have been immune to the problems of this rye whiskey, although give me Scotch whisky and I would be anybody's. Any excuse, eh?

Joe was up bright and early and anxious to return to being the normal loving husband. He was ready to collect his wife from the airport. His wife was travelling by air force transport, so he could drop us back at the base and resume his marriage without any fear of anyone dropping him in it! Not that we would; Joe was an all-round American guy and we loved him, figuratively speaking of course.

Joe worked on the assignments to bases all over the world. When he rang me up and asked me did I fancy going to Okinawa, thinking this must be close to Hawaii, I said, 'Yes please.'

Now that I know exactly where Okinawa is, it's a good job that the base was denied the pleasure of my company. I did not go as I did not have a security clearance. Just as well; it might have been better in the long run though; I might have found me a Geisha girl! That would have been nice.

Within a few weeks Joe was back on the phone. I like to think he was trying to help me, not get rid of me.

'Want to go home? No problem with security clearance, they have given you a Top Secret Clearance.'

They had given me a TOP SECRET clearance?

Now that does show just how lax the American Secret Service was then; who in their right mind would give me any type of security clearance, let alone Top Secret? If anyone ever told me a secret I would normally tell the first person I met; they didn't call me blabbermouth Ken for nothing! I wasn't even granted a library pass without my dad co-signing. It was quite obvious now that my importance had been recognised by the American government and they now wanted me in a certain place at a certain time.

I could only conclude that this administration job was just a cover; they more than likely wanted me as a spy! To go where no one else had gone before; but, hold on a minute, could this be dangerous? Oh well, those who dare win!

With bated breath I huskily answered, 'I'm in.'

Joe asked again, 'Are you sure?'

'Yes,' I croaked, 'count me in.'

No doubt I would be receiving my orders later. Obviously I would be asked to eat them after reading them, or maybe they would just disintegrate and dissolve after being read – cool!

No wonder I had been taken out by Joe and put through the drinking test; it had all been training to prepare me in case some Russian female spy tried it on with me and, my mind raced, here was a Limey going into the depths of a 'Top Security' situation, going back to my old country in the pay of Uncle Sam. Perhaps I could be a 'double-agent', MI - Double Pay! Deep down, in my subconscious, I could hear Peter Sellers (of Goon Show fame), 'You silly twisted boy!'

Hey, Good Lookin'...

Hank Williams and his Drifting Cowboys:
Say, Hey good lookin', what you got cookin'?
How's about cookin' somethin' up with me?

The American Air Force transport plane banked sharply and turned its position in readiness for its approach to Croft Air Base in middle England. The early rays of sunshine lit up the interior of the plane, stirring most of the ninety-two air force personnel who had attempted to sleep during the epic thirteen hour trip, from Columbus, Ohio, to the United Kingdom.

Airman Ken West glanced out the small window closest to him and noticed with some pleasure the patchwork of fields that glimmered through the early morning mist, laid out as usual above the English countryside below.

It was 12 June 1957 and now I, Airman West of the United States Air Force, was coming home, albeit much earlier than I had anticipated when leaving the shores of England four years ago. Now I was back - a Limey in the court of Uncle Sam. Croft Air Base was a holding point for the numerous personnel due to be dispersed to the many USAF bases scattered around the United Kingdom.

The landing was surprisingly smooth and after a small bump, the aircraft was soon taxiing to a pre-designated parking bay where the airmen were ordered off the plane in the usual military manner – double-quick time! Initial processing was surprisingly fast as the final paperwork would be completed on the following Monday. This being Friday, the airmen were granted a weekend pass to explore the nearby villages and towns and to meet the local population.

I was allocated a comfortable room with a bed that looked particularly inviting after the long flight but sleep would have to wait. My mate Don, who I had made friends with in San Antonio boot camp, called me with an enthusiastic 'Come on, let's hit the town'…Such were the hardships of being in Uncle Sam's Air Force. Meeting up with fellow airmen, they soon gave us both a piece of good advice…be permanent! You are not passing through! The local girls will not look at you twice…Made sense, so as soon as Don and I met up with Maria and Jane, two local girls, the short response to their first question of residence was just short of the truth: 'Sure, just been posted here.'

Being in the American Air Force 'blues' helped me get over the fact that my accent was still very English in normal speech, with only the occasional American phrases that I had collected over the last four years. Perhaps it made me a little more interesting.

Walking around the area was great and I soon realised that while England would never have the excitement that America offered, it was still very nice with its lovely green fields and, as usual, its frequent rain showers. We enjoyed ourselves and, apart from some heavy petting, nothing much happened on the romance side and we parted until the next day.

Falling into bed was a welcome relief after such an exhausting forty-eight hours. After a good sleep we ate some chow and then headed back to town to meet the girls. The meeting was tempered with the news that the girls, who happened to live close to each other, had arranged a meeting with their mothers! It is one thing feeding a line to two young ladies but to answer more searching questions from two worldly mothers was not what we guys really wanted to face at this stage. 'Love them and leave them' was always a guy's dream plan. It was quite obvious that the two girls had taken our previous assurances of being 'permanently based' not without some scepticism.

We were soon to realise that too many false promises had been made by previous visiting airmen and we would not get any further with the two girls without more time passing, time which of course the two of us never had. Cutting short the liaison seemed to be the best move and after a respectable time, we made our excuses, retreated from the scene and returned to the base.

Undeterred by this setback we got ready for the move south. This is also when the two of us got ready to say goodbye to each other as we had been assigned to different bases: Don to Upper Heyford and myself to Oxford.

Arriving at Brize Norton near Oxford I was duly processed in. Within hours of my arrival I was soon settled into my new quarters which, in terms of military accommodation, were quite luxurious. I then received my new assignment: the office of CAMS (Consolidated Aircraft Maintenance). The B-52 Squadron, guardians of the free world – a squadron on 24 hour alert – seven days a week.

England in 1957 had a certain quaintness about it, which one could only recognise after returning from the environment of gloss and excitement that I had experienced in the US. Another plus for my move to England was that I was entitled to overseas pay: extra money paid for being overseas from the USA! This was most welcome and soon became part of my income, and expenditure, but, like most US airman, I was often broke many days before pay day.

For transport, to travel to cities like Oxford, we got to rely on the excellent English buses which came to the base several times a day. When staying on base there was plenty to attract the airmen: the commissary with its cheap drinks and food and the Airmen's Club that held dances which attracted many of the local girls from Oxford. The airmen's favourite nickname for this event was 'Hog Call'. This did nothing to deter the twice-weekly attendance by the Witney and Oxford girls. Perhaps they never knew.

Getting used to life on the base came easy and I loved the excitement of planes coming in and out. The giant B-52s had replaced the ageing B-47s. The B-52s were so large that their wings were actually designed to swing up and down in order to prevent them breaking off. David Valentine arrived on base shortly after my arrival and, due to our similar duties, we soon became firm friends. Dave had many strings to his bow, one of which was that he was a first-class mechanic. He often assisted many of the mechanics, who worked and kept the B-52s in the air, with their own cars, such was his talent.

My brother Derek was still living in Reading, the town in which I was brought up. One weekend, I invited Dave to come with me to visit Derek and his wife. We caught the bus from the base, and soon we were walking through the Oxford town centre towards the train station. Deep in conversation, we became aware of a sudden drop in the level of noise at the point where we were walking. As this was the main road through the town we were a little surprised, until we looked up and saw with some trepidation that we were about to walk through a group of approximately twenty Teddy boys who were looking menacingly in our direction. We were dressed in our Air Force blues as our civilian clothes were following by sea. My only previous dealings with Teddy boys had been when I lived in Reading in my teenage years. I was more of a Mod, certainly not a Teddy boy by any stretch of the imagination. I did not feel this was the time for any explanations. They divided into two lines forcing us to walk straight through…all that was missing were the strains of High Noon.

Both of us braced ourselves for the worst, but nothing came! We were about ten feet past the Teddy Boys when suddenly there was a very loud retort: 'Bloody Yanks.' I remember breathing a sigh of relief; if they only knew!

One of my first tasks was to buy a car. There were always plenty of cars for sale, with personnel coming from and others returning to the States. For two hundred dollars I managed to pick up a nice Dodge car which had many extras such as electric petrol caps and dashboard lights which changed colour when driven at certain speeds. Many times, when stopping to fill up, I had to ask the petrol attendant to stand back as he puffed and pulled to open the petrol cap. Pushing a button in the car allowed the cap to pop open.

'Hey, do that again,' was the normal response whenever this occurred. There was one problem; I never had a driving licence! The base issued a provisional one based upon American law which the British accepted for five years. I had no trouble driving on English roads and, as I had not actually driven in the USA, I had no bad habits. The gods must have been smiling on me, because the Provost Marshal of the base informed me that if I brought back to him a letter of competence from an English driving school, he, the Provost Marshal, would issue me a full American driving licence for UK use. I quickly obliged and was issued with a new licence; I was then able to drive to Oxford instead of taking the bus. The legality of this action was never challenged such were the laid-back conditions which everyone experienced in 1950s England.

I do remember my brother coming to visit me. When he arrived, he expected to be asked to stop for a visitor's pass but the air police on the gate just waved him through. He did have the presence of mind to stop in the car park and walk back to get a pass. There were some embarrassed faces that day as the security on the base was supposed to be second to none. Still, it was nice to show my elder brother exactly what I was up to. He left later that day quite impressed with his 'daft' younger brother who evidently had found his place defending the 'free' world and perhaps might just have regained a little of his 'loss' of intellect!

Or had he?

WINDOW SHOPPING...

Hank Williams
You're window shopping, just window shopping,
You're only lookin' around!

MEETING LOCAL GIRLS BECAME A rather pleasant pastime and it could easily be defined as the main pastime of most airmen on the Brize Norton Base. One of my many tasks was to process marriage applications that came over my desk which, in turn, had to be sent to HQ for final processing. The number of applications steadily grew over the months. I often wondered if I would ever process my own.

On July 4th, Americans love to celebrate their Independence Day. A trip to London was suggested to mark the occasion. Having a car, I was selected to drive; nice to be popular! Armed with assorted bottles of booze, five GIs piled in the car and we proceeded happily in the direction of London, via the A4. We stopped off at numerous randomly selected pubs on the way for additional refreshment.

Arriving at Hyde Park at midday, an amazing sight greeted us with piles of empty beer cans forming pyramids over thirty feet high. I remember counting around thirty piles of these pyramids due to the tremendous support for the July 4th celebrations. As it was only twelve o'clock, I can only guess what the final tally would have been. Independence Day started early that day. Many girls had joined the throng of GIs and, coupled with the ongoing beat of Elvis & Co, a good time was had by all. Gosh, were there that many GIs in England?

On the way back to the base, rather later than anticipated, one of our group, a small, usually quiet baby-faced guy called Bates finally woke up to the fact he was enjoying himself. That it was 2 a.m. in the morning and we were driving along Maidenhead High Street seemed not to matter to him. However, when he started throwing out the now empty spirit bottles, one after the other, I decided it would be more than prudent to put my foot down and leave the lovely town of Maidenhead before relationships between the local police and the American Air Force reached a all-time low. American Air Force policemen did not take kindly to being called out to collect any of their wayward servicemen; it was just as well that the merry men's departure went unnoticed…

Up to this time my new life in my country was going rather well; with plenty of female companionship, an easy workload and overseas pay, life was rather good. However, this was about to change and not necessarily for the better.

It started at one of the 'Hog Call' evenings. Everyone seemed to be having a good time when a few coloured guys walked across and asked some of the girls to dance. Most of the girls readily agreed as, in 1950s England, racial overtones were not something anyone was too concerned about. The atmosphere suddenly changed when a large group of white GIs, from the southern states of America, decided it was not proper or acceptable for black men to dance with white girls.

Another High Noon situation quickly developed. It was almost eerie; in the subdued club lighting you could just make out the white faces of the men from the south, twisted with apparent hatred and dislike and, on the other side of the dance floor, the black Americans, their eyes glaring with defiance. Most of the black Americans had been born in the north of America and knew their rights. Things had moved on from the old 'nigger' days. The stand-off seemed to last for an eternity, it was just as if time was standing still. The bar and its staff went quiet; the music seemed to fade even though we could all hear it playing.

If a pin had dropped no one would had looked for it and the dance area held everyone's attention. This did not seem to matter to the white boys from the South and soon chairs were flying and tables were being overturned; years of hatred, born into both sides, erupted and the two sides clashed, each searching for a moment's supremacy.

Dave and I, always looking for a good fight but one we could observe from a safe distance, decided that now was a good time to get a beer and a cheeseburger from the commissary. As we left the club, the Air Force

Police started arriving in their droves. 'Never knew we had so many police,' remarked Dave dryly.

After that, things settled down and no more problems of that kind emerged during the whole time I spent at the base. Other problems came in different ways and some of those were much harder to deal with than the occasional fight.

A couple of my friends and I were spending a pleasant evening at the club, dancing with a few of the usual girls that frequented the dances. I noticed two rather attractive girls standing near the bar and decided to try my luck and asked the nearest girl to dance. She obliged and, while dancing, I became aware that I had picked one of the most attractive girls that I had seen in the club in a long time. In fact, it was her first visit. Her name was Pauline and to say she resembled Bridget Bardot would be an understatement.

I spent the rest of the evening with Pauline and I was rather disappointed when the dance ended and I escorted her to the specially arranged bus that the base supplied for the girls.

Waving good bye through the coach window Pauline smiled broadly, and then silently mouthed the words 'I love you' which came, astonishingly, as a complete surprise to me, standing by the side of the coach. Had I seen and heard correctly? Walking back to the barracks I told Dave what had transpired but finally had to agree with him that I must have been mistaken; it had been dark and Pauline seemed too intelligent a girl to express her feeling so soon after meeting, especially to a dozy guy like me. Thanks, Dave, you certainly know how to keep a buddy's ego up.

Either way, I had a rather disturbed night's sleep. I was unaccustomed to such declarations of apparent love, especially from a very attractive member of the opposite sex.

Part of my job was to process all arrivals and departures from the squadron. One particular day a Staff Sergeant arrived, a huge black man who had large staring yellow eyes: Staff Sergeant White (six stripes).

'Sit down, Sergeant, I'll be with you in a minute,' I said affably.

'How long is this going to take? I've had a long day,' came the sharp reply.

'Not long,' I answered.

'Just as well,' Sergeant White replied with a grim and, what I took to be, a little hostile face.

I could not quite understand the sergeant's apparent offhandedness as I certainly had no problems with colour of any sort, that is, if this was a colour situation. I remember being downtown in Texas with a black friend and going into a restaurant. My friend began to get very worried about getting served. I was most indignant at the time and when the waiter came up with that 'look', I ordered for both of us with a very distinctive 'English' voice, more like Prince Charles than anything else. We got served. I could not understand this latest episode in my life at all.

I processed the sergeant and then directed him to visit different offices to finalise his arrival on the base: base finance, housing and so on. Walking around the base did not seem to improve his demeanour in any way and he arrived back at my office in an even worse mood. After he had left I remarked to the assistance CO that the sergeant had 'seemed pleasant'.

'He must have got out the wrong side of the bed,' said Captain Henderson who had witnessed what had been happening from his office. I did not know at this time that Staff Sergeant White was going to be a big influence on my stay in the United Kingdom and not a particularly a good one!

I proceeded to make trips down to Oxford to see Pauline on a regular basis and as our mutual attraction seemed to grow it became an almost daily occurrence.

'Got it bad,' said Dave, who was used to having me on base with him, debating all the numerous daily events and rumours that came with a large base.

'Yes, I suppose I have,' I agreed.

It was almost unreal to be back in England and to be going out with an English girl. I met her parents and several times I enjoyed their hospitality and the meals cooked by her mother. I started experiencing feelings which I had not felt since my schooldays with Sonia. I experienced a special feeling of desire and well-being whenever I was with Pauline. She became my centre of attention and the way she looked at me made me feel special. I knew that I was falling in love with this young lady and it seemed that she also had feelings for me. The touch of her hand electrified me and, when we kissed, I felt the hairs on the back of my neck stand up, just like they tell it at the movies!

Often people would comment that Pauline looked like Bridget Bardot. I was just happy that she was with me. The more I saw her, the deeper I was falling in love with this girl who had accepted my invitation to dance. Pauline and I took many photographs which we sent to my parents and my father and mother duly welcomed her to the family. It started to look, in the time-honoured way, like the number two son had met his future partner. Surely nothing could end this deep affection that we both had for each other! I was on cloud nine and, with my job going rather well in the Air Force, I guess life was sweet – really sweet; Airman West was walking on cloud nine!

BABY WE'RE REALLY IN LOVE ...

Hank Williams
If you're lovin' me, like I'm lovin' you
Baby, we're really in love

OXFORD MUST BE ONE OF the most pleasant places to court a girl and, in the mid-l950s, it seemed even more idyllic, with walks down by the river watching the students with their punts being poled along as in the olden days. One day, going down to Oxford on the bus was almost hypnotic as I reminisced on all the recent events that had taken place since my arrival back in the UK. Yes, things were going very nicely.

'Let's sit down,' remarked Pauline as we strolled along the riverbank. I glanced at her face and clearly she was not at all her usual self.

Oh God, I thought, looks like she is fed up with me,

'Mum said, as we have been going out for three weeks, I should tell you something.'

'What's that?' I asked.

'I'm married,' replied Pauline.

For once in my life, I was speechless.

'What are you doing here with me?' I whispered in disbelief at what I was hearing.

'It was a mistake; I thought I was doing the right thing and it's been more than eighteen months since we split up,' Pauline answered.

For the next few minutes, which seemed forever, neither of us spoke and the silence was deafening. I knew Pauline was just nineteen years of age and girls did not normally get married that young in the 1950s without a reason.

'No! I was not pregnant!' Pauline added as if she had read my mind. 'Mum said I should give you time to think about it and let me know. I don't want to stop seeing you but I would understand if you wanted us to finish.'

I asked several questions: 'Who is he?' 'Do you see him now?' 'Have you any feelings for him now?'

Numerous questions and, one by one, Pauline answered. Her husband was a local boy and she had met him many years ago.

I looked at Pauline and I knew, without any doubt, here was a girl I wanted to be with and I wanted her to be part of my life; the point was, at what cost? We walked, held hands and talked but we did not mention the marriage again; it was just as if we both wanted to block out anything that might affect us being together now. The future would take care of itself; Cupid's arrow had not fallen out and, if anything, it had become even more embedded in our hearts!

Life carried on in its usual manner; many trips to Oxford to see Pauline and life on the base became routine. With the exception, of course, of a few base alerts which Uncle Sam sprang on us to keep us on our toes. I remember one particular alert which came one afternoon and we all sprang into action. A man was seen running towards one of the giant B-52s parked on the runway. The alert was soon stepped down when they caught the intruder; a Limey workman who had been running after his lunchbag which was blowing towards the plane. Men have been shot for less but then this was mid 1950s and war, fortunately, seemed a long way off.

Dave and I often commented on the quality of the technical expertise which some of the mechanics appeared to possess. Dave remarked that, if some of the guys repaired the aircraft like they attempted to repair their own cars, it's a wonder we did not have more crashes. Fortunately we never did or rather, none that were brought to our attention.

It was, however, like living in two worlds. Firstly, we had the American side which seemed rather luxurious with food and drink a'plenty; then the English side which was always short of such things even in the mid 1950s. The one thing the Americans could not copy was the English fish and chip shops and a lot of us would make frequent use of them in the nearby village of Witney (home of the Witney Blankets and now, of course, the home of a senior political figure in the Conservative party).

Having made the decision to court Pauline, I held onto a slender hope that things would sort themselves out in the future. The one thing we all knew was that, in those days, divorce was not an immediate option. This was due to the law that required a waiting period of at least two years before you could even file for divorce.

Our relationship intensified and grew to the stage of me staying overnight at Pauline's house. Not in the same bedroom, even though I would admit to some hanky-panky which was inevitable due to the level of passion that we were experiencing at the time.

I did feel honour-bound to try to remember that I was in someone else's house. I liked Pauline's father and mother; they had made me feel extremely welcome. However, self-control was not easy due to the intense passion that I, for one, had never experienced before.

I remember the first time I stayed over, in the spare room of course. I awoke to a knock on the bedroom door and Pauline in her lemon pyjamas entered with a cup of tea. I was thrilled when she suddenly drew the covers back and got into the bed and just for a moment our two bodies seemed to entwine as one; I felt heavenly urges and some earthly ones at the same time! It was not to last long as the sound of Pauline's mum's shrill voice broke our mutual embrace before things could get out of hand.

I drank my tea and anguished that the English had not adopted cold showers as their daily washing routine as we had on the base!

I soon realised that this was probably the most intense love affair that I had ever experienced in my life. Pauline was a lovely young lady; she had poise and a nice manner and I could only wonder why the earlier marriage had not worked out and who was to blame. It takes two to work at institutions like marriage and marrying too early can be one of the main reasons that such break-ups happen.

I was late; I had just finished work and after a quick change of clothes I wanted to get to Oxford and Pauline. Staff Sergeant Augustus White looked into the dormitory and out of twenty airmen present there, his eyes fell on me.

'Airman West, come here, I want you to relieve the Postal Clerk while he has his dinner.'

I groaned silently to myself. 'Not now, Sergeant.'

Then I had an inspiration. 'I can't do that, Sergeant, I'm not an American citizen and not being one, I'm not allowed to handle any post, or even enter the Post Room.' This was correct as one thing I knew well were the administrative laws which I had to deal with every day.

I saw Sergeant White's yellow eyes glare and I remembered our first meeting when I processed him into the squadron. 'Cantankerous' was not the word. For a moment he seemed stuck for words but he would not be bettered by a mere Airman Second Class.

'Don't matter! Just guard the post office!' he growled.

It was crazy – I was to guard something I could not enter! It also meant that no one could enter and retrieve their mail as they had to be given it personally by the Post Office Clerk. I did as I was told. While the clerk went for some chow, I stood outside the post office. He came back after an hour and I then journeyed to Oxford some two hours late. What would be said the next day? I could not see Sergeant White leaving it alone.

Actually nothing was said about the incident so I knew that Sergeant White must have been informed that, technically, I had been right. I was soon to find out to my detriment that this was by no means over!

Staff Sergeant Augustus White was a key person on the promotions board. Even with the highest administrative score on the base, it soon became obvious that I was never going to make Airman First Class. It seemed that Sergeant White made sure of that, despite several heated exchanges that ensued between him and some of the other board members who had wanted to promote me.

Captain Henderson could not apologise enough. It was clearly a case of the Supply section against the Administrative section and they had three votes more. To this day, I never learned what Staff Sergeant White had against me – perhaps just being English was enough.

About this time Dave was selling his car, a convertible Hillman Minx, which was much more economical with fuel. Having already sold my car, due to its large consumption of petrol, I was keen to purchase the Hillman but we found it had a small hole in the felted roof. Dave assured me that we could fix it, so we set about repairing this small problem. Why I needed a convertible was questionable because the weather at that time was wet and cold but I was full of optimism, or was it beer left over from the night's drinking at the base bar? Either way, a deal's a deal, and with a large roll of self-adhesive felt we spent several hours cutting and sealing the whole of the roof. That should do it, and the joins looked good – really!

We reckoned that it was a job well done and, for several months, I experienced no leaks. However, on the first sunny day, things changed. While we still had no actual leaks from the original small hole, the rest of the roof started peeling off in strips; driving around I found my roof seemingly waving at everyone as I passed. Felt quite daft really!

I do remember driving to Oxford one freezing cold night and going down a narrow small hill. Seeing a car approaching, I applied my brakes to slow down and wham! The car hit some black ice and started sliding all over the road.

It was just like the dodgem rides we used to have at the fairgrounds; it was with more luck than skill that I managed to control the skid and ended up going down the hill backwards. You should have seen the look of surprise from the occupants of the car coming up the hill who had not apparently seen any of the previous skidding.

Why was this guy driving down the hill backwards? Was he drunk or more likely one of the local inhabitants of the air base, which would make sense! I was quite glad of the anonymity the darkness afforded me.

Lovesick Blues...

Hank Williams
I got a feeling called the blues, oh lawd since my baby said goodbye...

ALL GOOD THINGS DO COME to an end, and one of my favourite sayings is 'nothing stays the same'. When the end cometh you can normally see some signs but perhaps you can always choose to ignore them. I do believe that what happened was due to Pauline and I being together too much.

I came to visit one weekend and, having worked late, I had not even managed to shave and change. Pauline met me at the door.

'Let's go dancing!' she said.

I remarked that I had not even had time to shave and change.

'Oh, you look fine,' came her retort. We arrived at the dance, which was at the Oxford Carfax Centre and went upstairs to the dance floor area. Within moments, I did not feel right. I knew something was wrong. I got some drinks and sat down.

'What's wrong?' I asked.

'I don't really know,' Pauline replied, gazing over her shoulder.

I then realised the object of her attention was a group of guys over on the other side of the dance floor. One guy in particular resembled a picture I had seen of her husband.

'I think I would like us to take a break for a while'...Pauline was talking but I could barely hear her words.

My first response was typical of me,

'Okay, if that's what you want.' I could hardly believe it was me saying these words; such was the maze I could feel myself falling into.

The dance hall was busy but I felt alone, hearing words that I did not want to hear and saying words that I knew were not really how I felt. I also felt ill-prepared; I felt scruffy, I needed a shave and I was not at ease. If I had seen this coming maybe I might have reacted in a different manner but fate had played its card and at this moment it looked like my card was the Joker.

With the both of us having apparently agreed, Pauline left the table and joined some of her girlfriends at the other end of the dance floor. They all looked my way and I could only imagine what was being said. One of the girls Marlene, who was with Pauline when I first met her, got up and started to head my way but Pauline pulled her back. I sat there, knowing that, whatever was to occur, I did not want to be there when it happened.

I walked out of the dance hall, down the steps and out into the cold night. I automatically headed for the bus station and caught the next bus back to the base.

The trip back was a blur; why was this happening to me? If there was ever a time for some C&C, now was that time. I can't remember leaving the Airmen's Club. However luck was with me and Dave managed to see me back to my quarters. I just hoped that the nightmare I was experiencing would be different the next morning.

Waking up early did nothing to phase out the events of the previous evening and, not receiving any phone calls from Pauline then or that week, I resigned myself to a single life again. If it had been anyone else but her husband it might have been different, but it wasn't. It seemed so final. In the 1950s you could not compete against a husband and wife. Didn't people marry forever? With a heavy heart I went on with my various duties around the base.

Oh Pauline, 'Why don't you love me like you used to do?' Hank Williams's sorrowful song said it all.

Greg Harman was a fellow airman who owned a fabulous collection of LP records and he used to play them continuously almost every evening and well into the night. No one seemed to mind as he used to wind up his nightly rendition with Jackie Gleason's 'Music for Lovers' which included songs such as 'My Funny Valentine' and 'Misty'. This type of music seemed to be warmly welcomed by the tired airmen returning from a long day's work and it serenaded everyone off to sleep.

Now, however, the playing of this type of music had a different effect on me; it did nothing to boost my self-confidence and esteem. Lying on my bunk in the wee small hours of the morning I would often wrestle with my thoughts of Pauline; her certain smile, her caress, they were not there with me and I missed them. I wanted them back! If music be the food of love Pauline, you eat while I fiddle! This had been my first serious love affair and I had been hit by Cupid's arrow, warmly welcomed though it had been. However, nothing in my previous experience of 'love' had remotely prepared me for this; I had been, 'bedded, measured and been found wanting' and I didn't like it – not one bit!

Honky Tonk Blues...

Hank Williams
Well I left my home down on the rural route
I told my pa I'm going stepping out
And get the Honky Tonk Blues, the honky tonk blues
Oh Lord, I've got them, I got the honky tonk blues.

One of my duties was to keep the Squadron Recall Plan up to date. This meant keeping track of any personnel returning to the US, moving to another base and, of course, new personnel. Everyone had to be incorporated into the Squadron Recall Plan.

I decided to produce a new one: an 'all singing, all dancing' recall plan. It was a pyramid system, colour-coded so that everyone could see at a glance the individual part they would play in the event of an alert. It was really impressive; every officer that came into the office was shown it. Airman West was the bee's knees.

All it needed was to be tested and it was, two weeks later. We had an alert at 2 a.m. in the morning. All the B-52s were made ready for action for flying off towards Russia, normally to be recalled just before they reached the halfway point. But where was Airman West?

I had taken up with a nice young lady called Doreen, just to assist in my recovery of the very emotional break-up with whatshername. 'Plenty more fish in the sea' was my motto of the day.

Doreen's house never had a telephone so, being on the ball, I had arranged for a slight change in the recall plan. This meant that if I was not on base (which by now was most nights) best friend Dave would, when contacted, call a taxi company in Oxford who would come to

Doreen's house. I would pay him and then get in my own car and return promptly to the base. Nice and easy!

I was in bed but not what you call sleeping and was just about to ravish my new partner Doreen when we heard a knock on the front door of the house. I looked at my watch. It showed 5 a.m. and then I looked out of the window. Taxi – had a message for me – Base Alert. Great – everything was working well. With some reluctance I got dressed, let myself out of the house and was soon motoring out of Oxford and back up the A40 to the base. I had used this road many times and made good time. Speeding was not a problem at that time in the morning.

I looked around – hmm quiet, I really must have a headstart on the rest of personnel living in Oxford, Farringdon and even Witney. I knew them all; had I not put them in a certain order to get them to the base on time, ready for action? I was waved in by the Air Police with my security pass clearly visible on the car window.

'Hi, Captain,' I remarked, coming into the heart of the control centre which seemed unusually quiet for once.

'Where have you been?' asked Captain Henderson.

'In town, but I came as soon as I received the call.'

'According to your plan you were supposed to be here before me!' came the response.

'Yes, Captain, but I didn't get the call until 5 a.m. when the taxi came to the house!'

'Airman West, the alert started at 2 a.m.!'

'Oops!'

That bloody taxi driver had apparently come to me after doing all his other calls on his way home. To think I gave the bugger a good tip too! I was lucky I was still allowed off base but only on the basis that I came back every night by eleven o'clock and signed in with the Charge of Quarters. This was supposed to last for two weeks. I continued to do this for the two weeks but after three nights I used to return, sign in and then go back into town. I was very fortunate that we never experienced another base alert or I may have had to process my own court martial. Perhaps recent emotions of the heart had affected my state of mind more than I realised. Maybe I was becoming a little unhinged?

Doreen also lived in Oxford but a little further out of town from Pauline. She and her mother Janet shared a house with a portly gentleman called Jim. I guess you could call Janet Jim's 'live-in housekeeper' or, maybe, 'bed-keeper'!

We used to have many parties at the house with plenty of food and drink. I would bring down some of the booze from the base, which was most welcome. At one of these parties I suddenly found that all there was to drink was the brown beer which at that time English people loved to drink. In the time that I had spent in the US, I had become addicted to the lager-type beer which Americans loved.

I looked around and found the only familiar drink was a bottle of malt whisky – how bad was that! Not the Canadian Club that I was used to but then 'beggars can't be choosers!' The outcome of this was, however, that I soon became rather drunk; neat whisky is not my forte. The end result was that it was decided that I should stay overnight. Now, this was the first time I was to stay over and 'keeping up appearances' was always important in those days. Doreen showed me into a room with a large bed. I sank into the exquisite feather mattress and was just about to drift into oblivion when I suddenly became aware of someone else getting into the bed. I knew it was not Doreen as I could hear her talking to Jim! I was at that time also very grateful to learn it was obviously not Jim! I then heard Doreen's voice.

'Mum, where are you?' I heard a loud gasp!

'Oh hell.' It was Janet, Doreen's mum! She leapt out of the bed and fled from the room. I was quite pleased at this because, nice as she was personally, she was certainly not my type or age! Peals of laughter came from Janet, and recriminations from Doreen.

Next morning smiles all round and Janet informed me, 'The next time you stay over Ken, you had better stay in Doreen's room and be on your best behaviour!'

'Yes Janet.' Nice one! – good idea, lady! Christmas had come early that year.

Doreen and I dated for several months more before we fell out over something really trivial; perhaps I was comparing my present lady to a past one!

At the airmen's club we had many dances laid on by the Air Force and we all enjoyed the numerous English bands that played at the club. I remember the Ted Taylor Four, an English band that certainly had that something special and soon had the customers up dancing. I quickly forgot the stricter English dancing that I had been brought up to perform. I really got into the American jive dancing and, to this day, whether my partner likes it or not, the American jive is my favourite. It does look a bit daft though if everyone else is doing the waltz!

Dave and I would often go to Reading, my old hometown and usually visited the cinema. On one particular occasion we inadvertently sat in front of several girls. The usual talk started with us 'Americans' trying all the best chat-up lines we knew. After the film we ended up in a bar and I noticed that Dave was deep in conversation with one of the girls. Now Dave was no Casanova and, if anything, was rather shy with the opposite sex. It was then my turn to kid him about Gloria as she was called. I started dating her friend Jenny and trips to Reading became commonplace.

Jenny was a superb creature, very similar in looks and style to the actress Hannah Gordon, a lady that I had admired for some time. Dave and I used to stay at a small hotel in Reading which was located just around the corner from the Majestic Ballroom (which by now we used to visit very frequently).

We travelled by train from Oxford to Reading and, on one particular occasion while we were in Oxford, we decided to purchase some wine from one of the local wine stores. As usual, we were not flush with money as pay day was not until the following week. We looked at the many bottles on display and selected a bottle of VP Wine each. This was attractive both on design and price. We boarded the train and started to have a drink. It was very nice and within a short time we had finished both bottles.

I have already related my time in Columbus, Ohio, so I was obviously no stranger to strong drink such as Canadian Rye Whiskey. This wine, however, had an amazing effect on us both! We disposed of the two empty bottles out of the carriage window just before approaching a station called Didcot, which was approximately halfway to Reading. Fortunately we never hit anyone or anything but by now our actions must be in question. We alighted at Reading Station and headed towards the hotel where we were staying, with people looking rather bemused as we approached them. It was only 11.30 in the morning and our feet were having difficulty walking in a straight line. It was not long before we both realised that the cheap refreshing wine was affecting us much more than we had expected and that we would not make it the short distance to the hotel without some help - strong coffee.

We stopped, drank many cups of coffee and arrived at the hotel. Then we went straight to bed and stayed there all weekend. Returning to the base early did nothing to assist our basic well-being. We spent the rest of the week in our beds nearly every minute we were not working. The six shillings and six pence wine was much too much for us little ol' Yankees to handle.

To this day, the smell of VP wine can make me nauseous and I will not go anywhere near that particular brand of drink. What a wasted weekend, not to mention the following week. The following week indeed spent rebuilding our relationships with the two girls; we had had no way of contacting them and it was definitely a no-show. Luckily, we were forgiven and took the girls out dancing - which was quite nice.

Jenny and I then decided go out on a more permanent basis and we spent most of the rainy days that weekend doing what many couples do when the heavens open to release their refreshing downpour on the good old English countryside. Perhaps that is why it is so green. Either way, all I can say is that I enjoyed that weekend very much and it would not be gentlemanly to disclose too much.

Jenny and I went out for several weeks. However, it was soon obvious that maybe we wanted this relationship to progress at different speeds and levels. I believe in the end that Jenny wanted a more orderly relationship, maybe with a ring involved, but I guess I just wanted a good time and everything that went with it.

One day I suddenly received a 'dear John' letter from Jenny which set out how she viewed our relationship and what she wanted from it. I was sorry to receive the letter but she asked to see me when I went to Reading next. We could meet and then Jenny and I could perhaps talk about both our feelings and what we both really wanted out of the relationship. Another few weeks went by and suddenly Dave came into my office and asked me in a very business-like manner if I would process his marriage papers!

'You're a dark horse,' I exclaimed. 'Are you in trouble? Do you want help? Do you need to get out of the UK? I'm sure I can arrange for you to return home!'

'Don't be stupid,' Dave remarked sternly. 'Gloria and I love each other and want to get married and no, we are not being forced into it.'

Well, blow me down and hog-tie me, my best friend was going to beat me to the church!

I was very pleased for Dave as he was a great guy and he had found a really nice girl in Gloria. They got married shortly afterwards, with me as the best man. It was a really nice event. About one year later they had a little girl who they called Kim-Ann, a name which I really liked and in years to come I actually named one of my daughters after her. However, that is another story.

Mail call was always a big event and it was nice to receive post, especially from my family back in the US. My father wrote quite often and sent me poems now and again. He asked me to get him copies of old poems like 'Albert and the Lion' which I managed to find by writing away to newspapers, etc. Computers were not an option then but when I managed to get hold of a copy my father was really pleased. It was nice to be able to please him for once.

I remember Dad did not speak much about the last war, not many people of his age did. I think they wanted just to forget it – too many bad memories

He did however mention that he had, during the war, worked at the Woolwich Arsenal in London. The Woolwich Arsenal made all types of weapons and the Germans were always trying to take it out. One day the air-raid warning sounded. My father went to get into one of the many air raid shelters and, seeing it was quite full, hesitated.

'Come on, Art, always room for one more,' one of his work colleagues said.

'No! You're quite full,' said Dad, and moved onto the next shelter. Within minutes a bomb fell with a direct hit and wiped out the shelter he was about to get into.

There were no survivors! It was, perhaps, just not my father's time.

One day I was happy to receive a good selection of mail: from Mum and Dad, my sister Coral, and another one whose handwriting I vaguely seemed to recognise.

Opening it, it was quite a lengthy letter from Pauline and she informed me that things had again not worked out with her husband. She said she sent me her love but she guessed I would not want it. A day or so later, I received a telephone call from her, much more direct and saying she would like to see me again.

What did I think?

Old thoughts plundered my head, old wounds opened up as if a knife had been plunged into my chest. This could not be happening! I was over her, I was Jack the Lad, man about town, always loving and leaving them…

Suddenly, I heard myself saying: 'Yes I'd like that.' Oh God, will this man never learn?

Pauline's mum thought it would be better to meet and see how we both felt, maybe get out of Oxford for the weekend. Go and visit my brother, perhaps? This was agreed and we arranged to meet at the Oxford train station at twelve midday.

I was there early, looking at my watch, seemingly, every few minutes. Twelve noon and I looked down the hill leading up to the station. Would she show after all?

Suddenly there she was, walking towards me in a black coat with a white fur lined collar that highlighted her pretty auburn hair. I believe the saying is 'looking like a million dollars'. I gasped, reached out and took her hand and we walked into the train station, I was walking on air and, with a spring in my step, we boarded the train.

We did not talk much on the train to Reading; the individual compartments filled up with people and then emptied as and when people got to their destinations. We just held hands and, on arrival at Reading Station, we got out of the train and caught the bus up to my brother's house which was in Tilehurst, a suburb of Reading. He welcomed us warmly; after tea we sat talking, but when my brother and his wife left us to arrange some further refreshment, Pauline leaned across and kissed me.

Poor sap, I did not stand a chance!

My brother Derek thought that Pauline was amazing, her looks and everything. He was much older than me and always the 'older brother' but at times he acted as if he was almost in awe of Pauline's presence. He had married his childhood sweetheart and I really believe to this day that he may have just envied my 'free and loving' lifestyle. His own marriage unfortunately ended in a divorce some years later. Perhaps his desire for another life started on one of my visits.

The old life seemed to begin again with regular visits to Pauline's house, a holiday in Weymouth with her parents and snatched romantic interludes at convenient times.

The holiday in Weymouth was really nice. Pauline's mother and father had booked a six-berth caravan for the whole family. My arrival back on the scene did cause a few problems but they soon sorted out the sleeping arrangements. 1950s attitudes to sleeping around did not normally allow 'carrying on' without a ring being on the finger but, of course, the wedding ring was not mutually ours.

There were six of us in the caravan: Mum and Dad Davis, Pauline, her brother David (who was around twelve) and Marion (who was seven). The sleeping arrangements worked out okay with Mum and Dad having the main room, Pauline and Marion sleeping in the next sleeping area and David and I having the two single beds at the other end of the caravan. Love-ins were not acceptable so Pauline and I used to excuse ourselves from the beach and return early to hopefully make use of the empty caravan. This was not a daily thing as we did like to keep up appearances for the sake of the younger children.

On one of the rare occasions that we did make the effort to slip back to the caravan, we were suddenly aware of someone trying to get back into the caravan. It was David who could not understand how and why the door was locked. Had he not seen us walking off in the direction of the caravan? He also could not understand how the small window in the main bedroom suddenly shut when he went around to try it! It does not take much for something like this to dampen someone's ardour. Blooming kid!

We would often just sit in my car and kiss and cuddle, such was the relief of just being back together. The longer the kisses were, the better we seemed to enjoy them. It was inevitable that a more passionate relationship would be resumed. Pauline's mother was always keeping an eye on her daughter's 'time of the month', but we only had one scare and I do remember a feeling of severe disappointment when the all-clear came. Perhaps things would have ended quite differently if the result had been affirmative. Even in the late 1950s it was still frowned on to have a child out of wedlock. The love songs that arrived in the late 50s and early 60s had many meanings for young lovers at that time. Pat Boone's 'Love Letters in the Sand' and Tommy Edwards's 'All in the Game' had many connotations for the would-be lovers of the time. Normally however they were just extremely pleasant tunes to sing and listen to. Music for young lovers!

I guess Pauline and I were just happy being together to worry or to listen carefully to the words that went with all the tunes. That is always left to when you find yourself reflecting on past events. As long as you were happy at that time what was all the fuss about?

My own family in the USA was growing older and my youngest sister, Rosslyn, was getting to the boyfriend stage which, of course, kept my mother and father on their toes. Coral, my other sister, was happily married to Nelson and they moved around the states as Nelson's job required.

I often wondered where or when would the Wests actually be reunited as a family and would the family be increased in numbers? A lot of water had passed under the bridge since we all used to sit around the coal fire, toasting crumpets and playing cards. We were all now busy doing our own things; perhaps it was far from our minds that sometimes if you stay too close to the fire you can burn your fingers and maybe the cards may not always fall favourably for you.

I Can't Help It...

Hank Williams
Today I passed you on the street
And my heart fell at your feet
I can't help it if I am still in love with you.

Looking back, the air base used to arrange a lot of activities for its personnel and give them many opportunities to enjoy them. I heard that the BBC 6-5 Special television show was going to stage a live broadcast at Burford, one of our American bases, and Burford was only a short distance from Brize Norton. I obtained four free tickets and Dave and I with the two girls, Pauline and Gloria, went on the coach provided to the show. It seemed that we had to get there early, in order to be seated, so that the show could start on time as it was live.

We arrived there and I showed the tickets to the producer's assistant. 'Oh yes, dancers,' he said pointing to a spot near the large stage. Dancers! We looked at each other and it was only then I noticed 'Dancers' in the top left-hand corner of the ticket. No wonder they were free. Oh well, I could not change things now.

Dickie Valentine, Lita Rosa and Dennis Lotus were appearing and would be starting shortly. Starting shortly? It was only three o'clock; so much for live shows, ha. We should have known better; they rehearsed all the chat, the so-called ad-libs and, of course, the songs which we all enjoyed immensely. The problem was that we had to do the dancing again as well. I do not know about the rest but I was knackered by the time we had a ten-minute break for a cup of tea; then we were off again, live!

The show was about halfway through and Pauline and I were dancing to a rather nice slow, smoochy, number deep, or so we thought, in the middle of the dance floor. Even then television was all seeing and we learned afterwards that the camera picked us out for nearly two minutes, a long time in television. As I said before, a close-up of Pauline was most likely good television and the fact that millions of people had seen it did not concern us at the time. I guess this was mainly due to the fact that we were not aware of this sudden exposure.

Pauline's mum and dad, knowing that we were going, tuned into a show they would not normally watch just in case they could spot their daughter in the crowd. They were quite taken aback when, suddenly, there we were, framed for everyone to see, performing practically pornographic images on 1950s TV. I do jest, but it must have been a bit of a shock to see us both, kissing on the TV screen. Fortunately they took it in good humour and said we looked very much a couple. Anyway, being TV stars did not last forever and, getting back to the routine things like running an office (along with the Captain) was always anything but quiet.

Unfortunately, not everything goes to plan and I do remember, with some sorrow, a young Flight Supervisor who had his name in the base weekly newspaper. He was described as the youngest Flight Supervisor in the USAF. This was a responsible job and we were all very pleased for him. Being based at Brize Norton, this was of additional interest to us and was viewed, quite understandably, with some pride by all the Base personnel. One week later, however, he mistakenly walked just too close to a B-52 warming up and was pulled directly into the huge jet engine. I understand they did not have much left to retrieve and send back to his parents in the States. This tragedy affected every person on the base. Deaths did not occur often at Brize Norton; it was normally considered that the base chaplain had a really cushy job. No one envied him his job that day as, the bereavement not being local, he had to accompany the remains of the body back to the States.

One of my most pleasant and amusing memories was when a fellow airman decided that, as his name was Bedford, he must have some relations in the nearby town called Bedford. No amount of scorn poured on this way of thinking could persuade him otherwise. Would we all like to go with him to discover his roots? We had many black guys looking for their roots, but the fact that this was a white guy making such a song and dance of this search was simply too good to miss. It would also be a good day out – any excuse would do!

It was to be a men-only trip so the five of us set out to find the Holy Grail. Now we all knew that any direct link would be most unlikely. After a few hours walking around the town probing and talking with the locals we were, as expected, no further to finding anything concrete for young Bedford. The guys were debating what to do next, so I excused myself to use the toilet at a nearby pub, which we had not yet been in. Whilst in the pub I talked with the landlord and some of the locals. I told them of our quest and I gave some background details about Bedford. They all promised to help, prompted by the offer of a few free drinks. I suggested to the guys that we might take time out and have some refreshment, possibly an English Ploughman's Lunch (cheese and pickle with crusty bread). We then entered the pub and, after eating, we of course started asking the locals about any possible local tie-up with Bedford. The landlord turned around and asked his group of locals who were sitting around a nearby table. 'Anyone heard about a family called Bedford, lads?'

The group of drinkers looked at each other, one by one shaking their heads. Suddenly a voice came from an old man, sitting in a corner, who had appeared to have been engrossed in his newspaper. 'Ere, you looking for old 'arry Bedford?'

'Yes, yes,' young Bedford answered.

'Well, 'eez been gone many a year, I can't quite remember 'xactly what 'appened,' said the old man, looking straight at his glass.

'Have a drink,' Bedford gushed.

'Cheers!' Six empty pints were straightaway offered for refilling. These were quickly filled to the brim.

'One for my mate, the landlord,' retorted the man in the spotlight, now apparently enjoying himself and rising to his part. 'I do remember he had a sister who, with her grandma, went to Australia or America or somewhere like that'.

Poor Bedford, he was now hooked, coming so close to finding the 'Holy Grail'.

'Could it have been America?' he asked breathlessly.

'You know, I do believe it was,' said the old man, who we now knew as Fred. He surely must have been in amateur dramatics in his youth. 'I do believe she ended up marrying a general or someone.'

Bedford was almost speechless.

'A general? Fantastic! Please go on.' Fred's glass was offered again, along with the other five who had all mysteriously finished at the same time.

'Oh, don't forget the landlord.' By now the guys were in stitches and, even without the wink from me, had soon realised that this was a set-up.

I was completely transfixed and just could not believe how well the joke seemed to be going.

Surely Bedford would soon twig? It could not go on, not one of us could hold out much longer.

Bedford actually put an end to it himself. 'Can you remember the general's name?'

Fred thought carefully, was about to offer his half-empty pint but thought better of it. 'I do believe it was Custer.'

It seemed that everyone in the bar erupted with laughter.

Bedford was speechless; was it true? Then the penny dropped. He looked at my face, the faces of his 'friends' and, of course, the locals, who were curled up with laughter.

'Bastards,' he said. 'Bastards.'

However, being good sports, the locals then took Bedford into their fold and he eventually left the pub much later that night, a bit drunk, but feeling rather good. He had not found his lost kin but, by golly, he had made some darn good friends. I was to learn later that he made many trips back to that public house in 'Bedford' and enjoyed immensely the hospitality they heaped upon him. I would like to think that fifteen minutes of being the butt of the practical joke had worked in his favour; perhaps the joke had backfired a little on us. We certainly did not have anything like the rapport he was to build up with his newfound friends.

When I was not 'hot-rodding' it back to Oxford, I began to spend more time on the base as the trip to Oxford did take quite some time. Also the continuous cost of bus fares and petrol (when I did drive) soon became a drain on my finances. So trips to the local bars became more the norm.

We had a nice old-fashioned public house located in Carterton, a nearby village, close to the base. Years later I returned to the pub but found to my horror that they had turned it into a theme pub, the Robin

Hood Retreat or something like that. If I remember rightly, to the best of my knowledge, Robin Hood never came that far south.

Anyway, many a nice evening was spent having a lager in 'The Golden Fleece' which I believe it was then called. The English public house definitely has a charm all of its own.

Pauline and I continued with our romance and it was decided that she should take a turn and come up on the special bus from Oxford for the weekend dance. It was on one of these visits that we had an immense argument and Pauline got back on the bus with a curt goodbye. We had, by then, been going out together again for over ten months.

I went to my car and sat there for several minutes, wondering if I should follow the bus back to Oxford and make amends. I sat there almost transfixed but making no effort to start the engine. I remember a tear coming down my cheek but I did not know exactly why I felt so down. I got out of the car and went back to my barracks. No, I was not in the wrong and it was not up to me to make the first move to put things right. She will come around, I know she will.

Pride comes before a fall but whose pride were we talking about?

I went to work the next day and waited hopefully for her call. I just knew she would see sense! I did not receive any call that day or the next. I thought she was just being difficult. I would not give in; had she not asked me to come back to her? The days became a week and then two weeks. Was this the end?

I decided to wait it out. Pauline, however, never phoned or came back to the base and I never ventured down to her house again.

It was almost as if something or someone had said, 'Stop! You're not going down that road, you must go another way.' I guess also that my stubbornness prevented me from making that call. Even then I was on the road to becoming the fatalist that I am now; I believed that 'what will be, will be' but why did it hurt so much?

This was the most intense relationship that I had ever experienced in my life up to then; I cannot remember ever having had such strong feelings for anyone. I was still in love with Pauline, so why did I not try to resolve what appeared to be a lovers' tiff? Perhaps, just perhaps, during the argument I had seen something in Pauline's eyes that was not previously there or, maybe, I was just being my usual downright stubborn son of a gun.

Take These Chains From My Heart…

Hank Williams
Take these chains from my heart and set me free
You've grown cold and no longer care for me.

THE NEXT FEW WEEKS WERE not a happy time, with me fighting every instinct I had to pick up the phone and call Pauline. Every time the phone rang I half hoped it would be her just calling to make friends again. The songs being played daily on the radio did nothing to ease my unhappiness: songs like 'Pretend you're happy when you're blue' by Nat King Cole' and, of course the heart-searching 'April Love' by Pat Boone; just what you wanted to hear…I don't think! I steeled myself and said something I had heard my father say many times. 'Sod it.' Ladies, Ken West refuses to play your silly game any longer. 'Sod off.'

The days came and went, seemingly slowly to start with, but then sped up, until one day I found myself down in one of my old haunts in Reading, 'The Majestic Ballroom'. It was rather a nice place with a mirror ball hanging from the ceiling, which rotated for the slow dances. I had come down with a few of my friends. Dave was not with us as he had taken his marriage vows very much to heart and was happily being a married man. Perhaps I envied him, because what happened next was completely out of character for me.

Getting a beer at the bar, I looked around and noticed a bunch of girls parading down the centre of the dance floor, as they do. I could not help but notice one of the girls. She was stunning with a gorgeous figure and dark black hair that glinted under the twinkling lights of the dance floor. Wow! A bit out of my league? She had that look about her; a bit snobbish maybe?

I turned back to the bar and suddenly there she was, next to me, ordering a drink.

'Would you like to buy me one?' I ventured. I got the real look, a dressing-down with her smouldering dark eyes. I expected the worst; it wasn't a good chat-up line anyway.

She said, 'No, but you can buy this one!'

I had made contact. Bingo! I was, hopefully, 'in like Flynn'. Her name was Shirley and we sat and talked and then had the last dance.

'How are you getting home?' I asked.

'By train. I live in Slough,' she replied.

Slough was the next largest town to Reading. I then offered to walk her to the train station which was nearby. I wanted to know more about this new lady who had come into my life. Her dark eyes were almost hypnotic and gave me the impression that she was more than likely to have a gypsy background.

I took her to the train station and within minutes I had purchased a ticket for myself.

'You're mad,' Shirley remarked. 'You'll never make it back to Oxford; it's nearly eleven thirty now.'

So it was, but I pushed any sound reasoning to the back of my mind. I wanted to have just a little more time with this endearing girl. I had to learn more about this 'gypsy lady'.

We talked constantly and I found out that she came from a nice, apparently reasonably well-off family in Farley, just outside Slough.

We exchanged telephone numbers and soon Shirley was visiting me at weekends. This led to me going to Slough and meeting her parents.

I appeared, at last, to be putting thoughts of Pauline out of my head. I was getting to like this girl; she was nice, she had a refreshing manner and a relaxed attitude to life. When I was with her I began to feel at ease and very relaxed.

I do not remember how the question of marriage came up. I just cannot remember. Shirley was two years older than me and perhaps it was she who yearned for a taste of married life. I certainly became a willing partner to the idea. Her mother and father seemed to agree and when my brother and his wife visited Shirley's mother and father it gave even more respectability to everything. I started processing my own marriage paperwork. Was this something that deep down I had yearned to do all this time?

It may also have been that Ken West was having yet another 'sod it' day!

The papers came back exceptionally fast, within two weeks which was very unusual. The wedding banns were read and called at the appropriate places and the wedding day arrived with Dave, returning the favour, being my best man. My brother Derek and his wife came and several friends of Shirley's and mine. It was a nice day and this must surely be what life is all about! Had not my own mother and father's marriage been the original Darby and Joan? Yes, this is it, now is forever! We can work at it. Rome was not built in a day! It did not last forever either!

Dave had seen Pat, the girl who lodged at Pauline's house, and had told her the news that I was getting married. She in turn, of course, told Pauline. Pat later remarked to Dave that evidently Pauline had a face like thunder and said she did not believe it. When Dave in turn told me this, I suddenly felt happy at the thought of her reaction. I did not analyse my own reaction then, but getting married was maybe a case of getting one's own back. It would show that I no longer cared! If this was true, it was certainly a very drastic and unwise thing to do.

Shirley and I started married life in a nice suburban detached house that I had rented just outside the base. Shirley seemed to settle in quite nicely, apart from the visits back to Slough now and again. I did not notice at first that the word home was only used when she planned or mentioned visiting Slough. I did not complain, as I knew she missed her mother, but I was soon to find out, to my detriment, to what extent. It came to a head three months into the marriage. I came home one evening to find Shirley, looking a bit embarrassed, with her suitcase packed. Also there was and even more embarrassed Derek, my brother who had just come in for a flying visit.

'I want to go home for a while,' Shirley remarked, almost coldly. 'As he's going back to Reading, I've asked Derek to drive me there so I can get a train to Slough.'

Derek took me to one side and said, 'Ken, I just don't know why she's doing this. She asked me as soon as I got in the door. She had already packed her suitcase so it looks like she had already made up her mind to leave'.

I looked at Shirley's resolute face.

'Go ahead,' I remarked in my usual bullish manner.

Derek took Shirley all the way back to Slough and I remained in our home. I must admit I was hurt and just did not know what was going on. We had not even had a disagreement; she had seemed to enjoy our new life together. We had visited Dave and Gloria (who lived close by) and all had seemed well in the new West household.

I went to Slough a week later to see Shirley and to find out what was going on. Shirley just sat on the edge of her mother's chair as if she was glued to it. She would not comment or answer any of my questions other than to say she wanted to stay there with her mother. I was perplexed! John, Shirley's father (who happened to be a local magistrate), was there and he suddenly suggested that he and I should take a walk. I did not want to walk anywhere at that time but perhaps I might learn more about what was going on.

We went to John's golf club and, with a couple of golf clubs, started walking around the course, putting as we went.

'Ken, please do not take this the wrong way but you are better off out of it!'

I could not believe what I was hearing. This was not a father trying to put his daughter's marriage back together. John seemed more intent on driving us apart. I looked at him and he noticed my amazed expression.

'Ken, you saw how it was back there, Shirley almost sitting on her mother's lap. Why do you think I spend almost eighty per cent of my time on this golf course?'

'You like golf, John!' I replied.

John smiled. 'No, old son, I am better off out of it. I love both of them but sometimes I feel like I am a stranger in my own home. I suggest you give it time, let things cool off and then we can talk again.'

I finally agreed and, upon returning to the house, I got into my car and without even a goodbye from Shirley (who refused to come to the front door) I started my long drive home alone. I looked in my rear mirror, back at the house and, deep down, I had a wretched sense of hopelessness. I realised that perhaps my gypsy lady was not quite the traveller I had previously thought.

The journey back to Oxford was very emotional; my feelings were a mixture of loss and disappointment. As the miles went by I reflected on almost every moment of the short time that we had been together. I thought about the trips home which Shirley had taken; I wondered that perhaps I had been a little too understanding about the number of occasions on which Shirley had announced that she was again going to visit her mother. I could not find any reason why she felt the need to leave. Her explanation of 'a while' had obviously been a lie and she was not happy with our marriage. As I neared the air base, quite suddenly, I experienced a strange sense of incredible relief! I was greatly surprised by this reaction within such a short time. Was I also admitting something to myself; that just perhaps I was not up for the marriage. Perhaps, just maybe, I had only been living a dream – a dream brought on that it was a tradition to get married, as my friend Dave had done and also my numerous mates who were filling in the forms almost weekly. No, I concluded that I was in love with Shirley but what was this sense of relief that I had briefly experienced?

I moved out of our village house to a flat in Oxford. I could have moved back to the base but one, I did not want to broadcast the breakdown and two, I wanted time to think. My brother acted as an intermediary like big brothers do. He met with Shirley's father and they agreed that Shirley and I should split the considerable off-base allowance and that John would assist Shirley in any possible shortfall.

The off-base allowance was quite good so I do not think he had to assist much in that way. Time went by and then I received a letter from Shirley at my new address in Oxford. It was very short, saying she was sorry that it did not work out and by the way she was pregnant; she did not want the child and, if I wanted it, I could have it! This was not a letter from a reasonable person and I knew deep down that she most likely did not mean what she said about the child.

I started divorce proceedings at the base and was upset to learn, from one of the affidavits that Shirley sent to the base, that she admitted going out to the local dances when she had visited her mother's home. Dave's wife Gloria also confirmed that Shirley had mentioned going out to dances while visiting her mother. Upon hearing this, I just lost all interest in the marriage and any baby that might be coming. If there was ever a reason for another 'sod it', now was the time.

The English divorce laws came into effect and it was not long before the court hearing came through just after the baby, a little girl, was born. I reckon the courts wanted to ensure that Shirley and the baby's interests were protected while I was still in the country. A lot of US servicemen disappeared back to the USA when they 'got into trouble' or, even worse, when their girlfriends did. Shirley's father, John, said in court that 'they' did not want any support from me in any way and likewise they would trust that I would not make any claim for custody of the child. It was interesting to see that 'he' had become 'they' and I guess that, at that time, I did not wish to be involved in a legal battle for a child I did not know for certain, at that time, was mine.

The final decree absolute came through just after I had returned to the States, many months later. I did, however, eventually receive a picture of the baby, a little girl called Deborah. It would seem that conception happened almost on the wedding night, which must have meant at least some true love was present, perhaps, even if it was for an extremely short time. God moves in mysterious ways.

This particular episode did have an enormous effect on my life, as had the break-up with Pauline. I now had another reason to cut this time of my life out of my mind and to accept that this was a period that had just not worked out. Derek, bless him, kept up the contact with the family in Slough and was to let me know of any news that would affect me. There never was any and it seemed I was a no-go for everyone including the baby.

My Bucket's Got A Hole In It...

Hank Williams
My bucket's got a hole in it
Yeah, my bucket's got a hole in it
Yeah, my bucket's got a hole in it
I can't buy no beer.

WITH A NEW DETERMINATION TO seek out new ventures and to try to put a very trying time behind me, I started venturing further afield than Oxford and the immediate surrounding areas. I visited places such as Newbury and High Wycombe. It was at High Wycombe that I met Amanda, a very striking young lady with beautiful reddish hair. We seemed to click straightaway and, although it was a fair distance from Oxford to High Wycombe, after a few romantic encounters, I started planning my life to include regular visits to see her.

It was only two weeks later that Amanda volunteered some additional information that she had not been revealed to me before: she had a two-year-old child. Oops! Not married, but never the less a little bit of baggage. Lovely as the baby was, I guess I did not have enough goodwill left in me at that time to even start thinking of continuing the romance any further. After all, I was only 'window-shopping'!

With S/Sgt White apparently calling the shots on base with regard to my advancement to the next stage of my career, I began, for the first time since joining, to get a little peeved with the Air Force. I knew my work was being appreciated, but still no one could outvote Sgt White, or change his mind, when it came to the final decision of whether or not to promote me to Airman First Class. Nowadays, I guess I could have shouted discrimination and things would have changed.

That would have been a hoot, a white guy having a go at a black one! Unheard of!

One thing I used to marvel at was how the catering staff on base used to feed so many people, day and night. It was just amazing to see the hundreds of hungry airmen lining up with their trays for food; very good food at that. You always had several choices and the usual juices, milk and soft drinks. I guess the booze was restricted to the officers as one cannot have the lower ranks getting a bit tipsy – can one? It is strange however, that you do carry on with traditions such as eating with a fork in the right hand and always having a slice of bread in the other hand. This is something I acquired while in the Air Force and it seems correct to do the same even today. I guess I can blame the bread for the excessive waistline I have today! That is my excuse because I just cannot say it's the beer – it can't be! It must have been the most asked question of the day: 'What's for chow?' 'Steak, oh well, I might just go.' I guess if you had fed the British people on good steak in the 1950s you may have had them fighting in the streets! Gosh, is that the reason today then? Every Friday and Saturday night, being fed too much steak? It beggars belief!

As I mentioned before, life in the American Air Force was getting a little bit tedious with Sgt White's antics. My enlistment was almost over and I had to make the decision whether to stay in the Air Force or resign and go back to the United States. I decided to extend my tour of duty by six months just to see how things looked at the end of it.

It is better for the Air Force to have personnel stay over longer in the overseas bases than to replace them (which of course has costs). You do get a small payment for this and an even larger one if you stay longer. I knew that I liked being in the Air Force, it was a nice life, but now, especially with Dave getting settled into married life, it was not quite the same. Perhaps I was beginning to feel kind of left out – even with a wife?

The financial arrangement continued with Shirley but I felt no compulsion to visit her or the baby. It is very easy to write things off in one's mind if you so desire. Baby not really mine, too busy, afraid of the response if you did the right thing. I was later informed by Deborah herself that her mother admitted it was all down to her and she said I was a nice guy. Small words of comfort, but nice to know.

Shirley never married again and remained with her mother until her mother passed away.

I would often daydream about the differences in my two worlds: the comparative safety of the air base and the laid-back way of life in England at that time. The ladies in my life, whilst in England, had made my time in the 1950s and 1960s quite interesting. I would remember my first meeting with Pauline and the bombshell she gave me about being married and how I dealt with that. The meeting up with Doreen and the extremely wild kind of love she brought me, not to mention her mother who caused a laugh when she jumped into my bed the first time I stayed over. I would recall the early moments in my life in the Air Force in basic training, the bad toes and the dreaded needles. These memories are gems that can only make you smile whatever the trials and tribulations you find yourself experiencing.

Some of the delights of Oxford, apart from the extremely nice walks beside the waterways, were the many public houses that they had in the city centre. Certain pubs did not welcome the GIs (Government Issue) but, fortunately, others did. Two such pubs come to mind: 'White's Bar' and 'The New Inn'. Both of these public houses were known as 'American' haunts and normally local English guys rarely entered. I cannot remember too many problems between the English and American guys.

I often wonder why we now have so much trouble on the British streets between races and colours. I know drugs are now more available and consequently are more common. It is very sad that, in the last forty years, life on British streets has become more dangerous than in my time in England in the 1960s.

I remember with affection the closeness of my family in the 1950s; we used to sit down together to eat. My father and mother talked, we would listen and learn and we all knew they wanted only one thing - for us to be happy. We certainly were happy so, therefore, we felt secure. Even the reading material now seems to have changed, not necessarily for the better.

Enid Blyton's books about the Famous Five and their dog always had the heroes showing respect to their elders with 'Yes, sir' and 'No, sir' the norm.

Any gangs were restricted to cowboys and Indians with no real scalps being taken and the only hitting being when you tried to break your opponent's conker, not his head!

Richmal Crompton's 'Just William' books encouraged dens to be built and occupied for a small time until you could 'afford' a tree house. The dens were never used for the taking of drugs which has become the normal practice these days. The nearest one came to vandalism was the cutting down of a yew branch, which was carefully hewed into Robin Hood's bow. The arrows were fashioned but care had to be taken because no one really knew what direction the arrows would take when they were fired at the approaching Sheriff's men. Needless to say there was an endless supply of your opponents who only seemed to die for the one minute or so!

Perhaps the person who invented the saying 'stop the world, I want to get off' had it about right.

Nobody's Lonesome For Me

...

Hank Williams
Everybody's lonesome for somebody else, but
Nobody's lonesome for me.

For the first time since my arrival back in the UK, I was lost for female companionship of any real meaning. I guess it was about that time that I realised that I was definitely not a 'man's man'. I always preferred to be around ladies than hang around with men. There were exceptions to this, like going to Bedford and Hyde Park for days out. It seemed that, although there was always the chance of one-night stands, so to speak, I still genuinely longed for a meaningful relationship with one special lady. Me, I was still lonesome and nobody was lonesome for me! Until, that is, Maureen came along.

Maureen was from Gloucester and was in the full flower of youth. Looking back now, I can understand why her father viewed my appearance on the scene with outright suspicion and much apprehension.

Maureen, however, had no such hang-ups when it came to our relationship. As I stated previously, Maureen had that English rose look, a damsel waiting to be plucked of her virginity. I guess agewise she was eighteen and by now I was twenty-four years old. I had been around the mill, in the moat and nearly drowned while she was still most certainly hoping to start out on her first adventure. My past life crept up on me; I was the tormented one for a change and I felt like I was the one being stalked. I was getting old! I was in sympathy with her father. Knowing me, I would not trust me either! Talk about chickens coming home to roost!

Maureen seemed very disappointed, her first Yankee love affair and she had to meet a Yank with a conscience!

This personal revelation did nothing to quell the need for a solid relationship, one which could possibly keep me on the straight and narrow and at the same time give some meaning to my life. I then made my decision not to extend my service time in the UK again; I decided to go back to the United Sates to re-assess my life. I promised, of course, to return to the UK, when I was able to, and sweep Maureen off her feet. This is where I came in four and half years ago at Croft Air Base. The only difference now was that I was 'permanent' and planning to be 'temporary'. This Limey's time in the Court of Uncle Sam (UK-wise) was quickly coming to a close…

Having made my decision to quit the Air Force, I then had to tell my squadron commander that I would not be extending again. He was rather surprised as he knew I had been very enthusiastic about being in the Air Force. I had to wait until the orders were cut and then the arrangements were made for my return to the USA. I, of course, informed Maureen of my decision and made the usual promises that we would be together very soon. In fact, I did not have the slightest clue what I was going to do in the USA when my enlistment finally ended.

The papers were processed and I was given a leaving date in approximately three weeks' time. After some rather sad farewells, I left the Brize Norton Air Base and flew to Mildenhall Air Base, which was now the base selected for all returning airmen. We arrived back at the Base Camp in the US and I started processing out of the Air Force. We were informed about our rights, one of them being an official guard of honour for our funeral when we departed this mortal coil. Good God, they were already lining up my funeral and I had not even reached my twenty-fifth birthday!

As I signed the final papers, which meant that I became a civilian again, I had very mixed feelings. I could not help wondering if the reason was really one of wanting pastures new? Perhaps the truth was just that I was in a really bad mood and apparently wanted to blame the Air Force for my state of mind? I knew deep down that any blame must lie a bit closer to home!

Too late, ex-Airman West, you have made your bed and now you have to sleep in it and on your own again! I was to remain in the Air Force reserves for a further three years which meant that I could be recalled at any time in the event of war. Just so long as they did not send me back to the UK, I would not be too worried. The 'sweet memories' that had been sung by Dean Martin all those years ago; well, they just did not match up anymore!

In the words of Hank Williams: 'Why Should We Try Anymore?'

Wilmington, Delaware was now the home of my parents and I found it easy to settle back into civilian life there. I discovered that there were plenty of guys my age living in the locality and I was invited to join the numerous drinking sessions which took place and to join the bowling team. I enjoyed this immensely and even won the 'most improved bowling average'. This was, of course, mainly because I was so bad at bowling when I started - I could only get better. I found that pubs as I knew them in England did not exist in the good old USA and drinking hours normally extended well into the early hours of the morning. Guess I could just about manage that!

Across the road I had a couple of good mates called Joe and his brother Mike. They were sports mad and always talking about different baseball games and football heroes. They used to ask each other questions to see who knew most.

One night, in the early hours, Joe turned his attention to me 'Limey, who won a certain title in 1960?'

I had only heard of one team, and that was the New York Yankees, so I offered this forward in vain hope. You should have seen Joe's face.

'How did you know that?' It was nothing, Joe, ask me another! Thankfully Joe never did! Welcome back to the real world, Limey!

As the days slipped by I was expecting, and soon received, a nice 'Dear John' letter from Maureen, informing me that she had met someone else and, of course, would not be writing to me again. I guess that just about concluded my last real romantic connection with the UK.

I soon found that the weather in the United States was extremely varied with the summers being very hot and the winters very cold.

In the winter I would normally have to dig my car out of four feet of snow and, after putting on my snow chains, I would just go about my business. The snow had to be extremely deep before you stayed at home. I cannot understand the chaos that seems to occur in the UK everytime it experiences even the smallest falls of snow. Where are all the snow chains?

Weary Blues From Waitin'...

Hank Williams Lord, I've been waitin' too long.

For some weeks I chilled out but one thing I had to acquire was a car. My father came to my rescue as usual. It was decided that he would lend me the money to purchase one and I would pay him back ten dollars a week. There would be no interest to pay but I had to ensure that the ten dollars was paid every week. That was Dad coming to his logical conclusions about saving money and choosing the most economical way. Typical Dad, but I had no problems with this arrangement in any way. Dad and I went to the local car lot and I chose a nice Ford Fairlane. I also had to take, and pass, a driving test to enable me to drive in the USA. The driving licence that I was given in Oxford by the base Provost Marshal was not deemed to be legal; I wonder why?!

    I missed the Air Force; I missed the comradeship of my fellow airmen, the easy-going lifestyle that I had entered into without any fear. Had I done the right thing? I knew also that I missed Pauline, not that I would ever admit this to anyone. However, I guess my parents were pleased to have me home as they encouraged me to seek out new friends. Not that I needed much encouragement by then. I did try to get a job working as a representative for DuPont's, the largest employer in Delaware. I went with a friend to an initiation course and what did we find? Nice young American ladies who loved to talk to new conscripts such as us. I was singled out due to my English accent and soon I found that the way to my new friends' 'hearts' was to 'act the goat' as my dad used to do.

    What was I doing there? Had I met the Queen? All normal questions that nice American girls needed to know but, as usual, I would normally take it that much further.

Yes, I had met the Queen and, of course, taken tea with her. I had also just popped over to the British Embassy over in Washington and would be popping back there in a few months! Of course you had to give yourself some time for the magic to work! Prince Charles, eat your heart out!

For a while it seemed to work and I took out some fantastic-looking ladies, one of whom, Nancy, was very similar to Pauline: very cute and petite. I arrived to collect her at the huge house where she lived in one of the nicest neighbourhoods of Wilmington. Upon being shown into her house I went to greet and meet her parents. Her mother was fine, however her father was missing. We finally found him laid out on the luxurious carpet in an equally luxurious lounge watching TV over his head! Strange, but then with his money I guess he could afford to watch the TV from whatever position he wanted to. Nancy was nice but, as usual, I seemed to attract a certain type of lady. One day, on the way back to her house, she suddenly blurted out that she thought she loved me!

I of course responded with 'Don't be daft, we've only just met.' This, of course, hurt her feelings and when I did call her a few days later she would not speak to me! I guess she was a twin to another young lady in Oxford who had started in the same way and look how that finished.

Parallel universe!

I imagine that most of the young ladies I met in this way had just used me for their own edification, taking me around perhaps as a freaky boyfriend. Oh well, Airman West had been used to performing like a seal. Well, I had certainly jumped through a few hoops!

I was also soon to learn that real Americans can be rather cliquey and that, in particular, those of Italian and Greek descent like to marry within their own race if at all possible. We lived opposite a Greek family with two very attractive girls, the older of whom, Helen, was rather special. Teddy, another Greek friend, knew the girls and we used to go over for drinks and a chat. Helen and I used to talk a lot, with Helen asking me all about my time in the Air Force and what I did in the UK. I did not cover up all the truth but told her most of it, well, not really most of it, actually, hardly any at all, I guess. I was attracted to Helen a lot but was rather put off by the heavy influence of Greek family life. However, I did live with some hope.

By the time I did get a phone call from Helen, asking me if I would like to accompany her to a special 'do', I had started going out with a very nice English girl and, with some reluctance, I had to decline.

'Helen of Wilmington', you could have launched a thousand ships and perhaps you might just have been the one to have given me that extra something. Now we will never know.

I found the drinking habits of my newfound friends were much more extended than I was used to in the United Kingdom. I found that when we went out we stayed out! It was not unusual to go out Saturday lunchtime and still be in the same bar at twelve o'clock the next morning. Sometimes we actually left at five in the morning which, at that time, was the law. The bar would close so that they could clean the toilets and so on and then reopen at six in the morning again. Daft that!

We almost invariably ended up in an all day and night diner and would order our breakfast. One of the favourites with the lads was six eggs, lightly boiled, in a bowl with toast. I tried this and found I actually loved it. Mind you, when you had been drinking for many hours you would eat anything, but the six eggs and toast seemed to hit the spot - everytime!

Drinking laws were more relaxed then and that suited the drinking habits of my new friends; they seemed to have endless thirsts and long legs. The booze had to go somewhere!

I do remember Joe driving his Dodge car into a packed car park at two o'clock in the morning, driving down the rows of parked cars and suddenly turning into a space that seemed to appear from nowhere at a speed that not one of us could comprehend.

'How did you do that, Joe?' gasped Teddy, who was sitting next to him in the front.

'Easy,' replied Joe. 'I opened my eyes and there it was.'

Oh great, Joe, but no one else asked to drive; we knew a good thing when we saw one.

I saw an advertisement in a Philadelphia newspaper for a Dance Instructor wanted by the Arthur Murray School of Dancing. I applied and was asked to attend an interview in Philadelphia which was, of course, in the next state to Delaware. I arrived at the dancing school and met Ryan, the boss, a gentleman in his thirties. He had a lady instructor and he asked me to dance with her to several tunes in order to ascertain my dancing abilities. I, of course, was able to dance the normal four dances such as Waltz, Quick Step, Foxtrot and Tango. He was quite impressed but asked how I was on the Latin Dances. I had to admit that I had not fully mastered them as I had left England before I could progress to that stage.

He said not to worry as he could teach me the Latin Dances; then he asked me if I would like to join the company. I did not have any firm prospects so I accepted, if we could agree terms. He said that the job would entail me having to set up my own customers, who he would introduce to me, then I would be able to earn several thousand dollars per month. It sounded good as long as I could survive the initial period; I would not be earning much money at the start.

I did have some obligations such as room and board which I paid to my mother and father, plus of course, paying back the ten dollars a week to my father for the purchase of my car. However, I had a little money left over so I decided to have a go.

The following week I reported to Ryan at the studio, which was quite lush in real terms, much more swish than my old dance room at Reading. I guess it did not have Maureen either who had managed to stir emotions in me that I never knew existed! I was a little concerned that something like that might happen when I started dancing with the new ladies who would evidently arrive to receive my personal instruction.

Ryan explained that the American people were really not interested in learning to dance and if we could give them a pill that enabled them to dance afterwards they would be happy to pay for it! In other words they would rather not have to do the hard graft of actually learning the steps. It was a social thing. I started a revival course with Ryan and within a few weeks he said I would good enough to receive my first client. Mary Ann was a really nice person; she was dying to learn to dance and she had said on her application form that she would be a willing pupil. I was quite pleased to hear from Ryan she was quite rich! I was really excited at the chance of my first client and with it some badly needed influx of cash, what with my usual nights out with the guys, the bowling, the drinking, and of course the payments to my family.

I put on my dancing shoes, straightened my hair and waited. I could hear Mary Ann's steps coming up the stairs leading to the dance school. Were they a little firm? Mary Ann entered with a flourish of a film star, her long blond hair cascading down onto her shoulders. She was under no illusion that she looked good, she had obviously been to the hairdresser, the beauty parlour, and most likely had purchased a new dress. I guess Ryan had done a good job informing her that he now had on his staff a 'young Englishman' who was keen to show the Americans just how to dance properly!

I greeted her with a smile but was a little concerned about the fact that Mary Ann was about fifteen stone: about 210 pounds!

She had a really nice face and probably she was a nice person socially as well.

I tried to put my reservations behind me and started my first lesson which fortunately did not involve me having to hold Mary Ann. Would I be able to get my arm around her waist? The thought of trying to get her to do what Julie my dance instructress, in Reading had made me do: place my arms in the air and push her around by my hips! Even that was beyond contemplation and I knew that perhaps I might just cut that important part out of any future lessons. If Ryan took pictures of that he would make a fortune selling the prints to Candid Camera or somewhere like that.

I went through the basic steps and I found that Mary Ann, bless her, was a very quick learner; she really was. I tried to spread it all out in order to put off the inevitable moment of having to guide her around the dance floor. I knew I would have to face up to that sooner or later. At the same time I was conscious of the fact that people were paying to come here to learn to dance and if I was going to take any money from them, I should do so with some grace and not judge anyone on their physique.

After all, years ago, I had been looked upon as a beanpole by my parents and told to put some fat on myself. All on a 1950s diet.

The hour-long lesson came to an end and I booked Mary Ann in for another lesson the following week. Sixty dollars, not bad for a start. Ryan would be taking a small percentage from that eventually but for now he said I could retain all that I made until I managed to build up the 'pot'. I had one hour to wait until my next pupil arrived so I was put through a lesson myself, this time for a Latin dance, the Malaguena, American-style.

My poor feet were taking their toll and I realised that I would probably not be going out drinking and carrying on that evening or perhaps the rest of the week.

My next lady arrived; it seemed that the majority of my clients would be ladies as men considered themselves natural dancers.

Some hope, that is all I can say.

Jeanette was a lot lighter in the 'poundage weigh-in' but a little older; in fact a lot older. To me she was really old but I guess in real terms she was only around fifty-five or so. I could tell at a glance that she was more interested in me than the dancing because everytime I led her into a position she just seemed to latch onto my fingers as if she was going to fall over. I knew from Ryan that she was not a beginner in any way and she had been before several times. I was to learn from Ryan later that the instructor before me had to leave suddenly when Jeanette started calling him at his home. His wife was more than ready to deal with any amorous ladies that zeroed into her territory. I said to Ryan after the first lesson he should put warning notices on the booking-in sheet. He replied he just wanted to see how I coped. 'Yes, thanks a lot, Ryan!'

Ryan then took the wind right out of my sails when he said that my next booking I would have two to teach: Lorraine and Doreen. By now I was getting to wonder just whether and if the ladies really wanted to dance because that first week alone I had had many offers to provide some private teaching but I did not want to go down that road. Ryan had been good to me and I knew that, by the ladies coming to the dance studio, it would be much safer for me.

Lorraine and Doreen were just a little too hot for me to handle. I had to put up with a lot of innuendoes but when faced with me being asked to collect the cheque from their apartment, I just had to ask Ryan what I was expected to do about the latest peaches and cream episode. He just laughed and said I could always write a book about the Confessions of a Dance Instructor. I laughed it off with my mates but really I found the trips up to Philadelphia, the actual dancing, the dance instruction just a little too much for my poor feet to handle and the last thing I wanted was a repeat of my ingrowing toenail incident which I had had in Texas! Not the big guys again with the enormous needle!

I said to Ryan I would do just one more week while he advertised for my replacement. I left that week, although I did receive a phone call from

Ryan asking if I was sure I wanted to quit as he said I had gone down well with the lady clients and could have a good future at the dance school. I thanked him but replied I had already just got out of one frying pan and I did not wish to get into the fire!

I guess the tales of my adventures did keep my mates laughing and I was certainly the butt of their jokes for the following few weeks. Still nothing ventured – nothing gained!

My father, with his friend Al, liked to go to the Trotter track to watch the horses racing while pulling small carts. The horses looked very grand as they trotted out onto the track, their heads sporting large plumes of feathers. The jockeys would hedge their carts into the best position that they considered would enable them to win the race. We sometimes wondered if it was kosher as the most unlikely horses seemed to come from behind to win at great odds. It did look as if it might be possible to hold a horse's head back just a little to prevent it staying in front. Still, it gave pleasure to many people, including Al and my father, so who am I to cast aspersions on the art of Trotter horse racing. The tracks were designed for close proximity to the punters; the horses would gracefully trot past you with their heads held high, nostrils flaring as they sought to draw in fresh air for their encounter ahead. It seemed to set the scene and add to the excitement of the waiting crowd.

One day I did not wish to go, so I gave my father two dollars for the 'daily double', which consisted of a bet to forecast the winners of the first two races. I asked him to bet 8 and 8 and they actually won. The only problem was my father assumed that 8 and 5 would stand a better chance, so he bet those numbers. His face was quite red when he came back with much less winnings than I should have received. I quickly forgave him, after all it would take some time before I could ever pay back anywhere near the amount of money and support that he had given to me in my life.

I will never forget the call that went up at the start of those exciting races. All the racers would approach the start at a canter and as they all arrived at the starting line the announcer would cry, 'Here they come – there they go!' Almost like the coming and going of my past ladies…Talk about winners and losers!

It took some time for me to get used to the heat that greeted me when I arrived back in the United States. Perhaps my time in England with its much cooler temperatures was something I had taken for granted; the high temperatures I was experiencing in Delaware were something else. I guess the air-conditioning helped but so did the many cans of Budweiser my father and I consumed whilst sitting on the outside porch. Nice that.

My father's negotiating powers came in useful when he was elected as one of leaders of his union. Everyone seemed to call him Art which of course is short for Arthur. I reckon it would have been more appropriate for it to be short for Artful after Dickens's Artful Dodger because when completing the final documents for the new pension retirement scheme, my father, noticing it would exclude himself (as it did not come into effect until after his retirement date), brought forward the starting date by one year. The new changes were accepted and apparently went through unnoticed. This meant the first person to benefit from the new scheme was my father. As mentioned before, prudence was one of my father's best attributes, but cunning, well I guess he had that as well. I would prefer to call it shrewdness!

With every day that passed I tried to put behind me all thoughts of Pauline, Shirley and also the new baby who I had now conveniently put right out of my mind. I guess that is what I believed was the right thing to do at the time. I wonder how many men and women are forced to do this at some time in their lives.

My father and mother were a little concerned about the failure of my marriage but my father, after going over the details of how it all happened, came up with his usual down to earth approach and told me to get on with my life but not to forget I still had some responsibility for the new child whatever its mother said at the time.

Myself, I just wanted to sample the delights of drinking, bowling and any new ladies in whatever order they arrived. Ken West just wanted to go window-shopping again. His father's words of wisdom and good sense did not really register; after all, I had done nothing wrong!

Settin' The Woods On Fire...

Hank Williams
Comb your hair and paint and powder
You act proud, and I'll act prouder
You sing loud and I'll sing louder
Tonight we're settin' the woods on fire.

About this time, with the tenpin bowling going reasonably well and the drinking sessions with my newfound friends, I had to start looking for a proper job. I was offered one in the Quality Control Department at the Ludlow Textile Company. It was interesting work and I found some new friends but I also found a few people who acted like my '90 day wonder boys'. If you did not have an American college education you never quite fitted in. I was invited to sit with the bosses in the management meetings as I worked closely with most of them but I knew I would never reach the level of remuneration that they were receiving. I was about to leave when a colleague suggested I might like to meet a fellow English lady who was staying with her sister. Her name was Claire. I agreed and soon we had struck up a relationship which we both enjoyed and meeting her sister and brother-in-law seemed the correct thing to do.

My divorce papers had come through but I did not want to even think about marriage again at that time. However, this changed when we started having even stronger feelings for each other and I knew we would certainly have to make some decisions and sort out things if we were going to continue with the relationship.

My sister and her husband were still with the American Air Force and at a base in Michigan. We decided to go and visit them but before we could do that it was mentioned by Claire's sister that perhaps an engagement ring might at least be appropriate! So we got engaged; a nice ring but when I mentioned it would be a good idea for her to wear it in her nose, she declined, - why I can't imagine!

Claire did, however, put my love to a severe test when she asked why I had so many photographs of Pauline and when I protested that they now meant nothing to me she called my bluff and proceeded to tear up each and every one. My face with the gritted teeth spoke a thousand words. It was certainly an early test which I apparently passed but not without some heart-wrenching!

With the family's approval, we started making plans for our trip. I guess we were both romantics because, when we found that we would be passing reasonably close by Niagara Falls, we decided it might be appropriate to tie the knot there and make it a nice occasion. Yes, all good things seemed 'nice' to do at the time but, unfortunately, Claire soon had a terrible case of conscience and we found that the happy event was marred by her worrying about what her mother and sister would say.

Either way, we had an enjoyable time viewing the thunderous falls; it was an awesome sight. After a few days, we went onto Michigan and spent two weeks with my sister Coral and her husband (they were also visited by several tornadoes while we were there - maybe a sign of things to come?). I was pleased to find that being with Claire helped me to put the thoughts of Pauline and Shirley (that used to flood back into my head at odd times of the day and night) behind me. It is said that in the wee small hours of the morning, that is the time it affects you most of all. I can only agree with that.

The trip back to Delaware was a little apprehensive but, as my sister had phoned ahead and already broken the news, we found congratulations more in order than recriminations. At last I, Airman West, had done something right and found a girl who would be a good wife. Claire was nice-looking with real blonde hair and, as my family were a family of blondes, it was obvious that any children would be blonde and they were.

Our married life did not really get started as Jim, Claire's father, suddenly became seriously ill and it was decided that Claire should return to England to be with him. It would also give her a chance to prepare things for her return to the States where we both planned to live. Claire flew back and was soon reunited with her mother and father (which also gave her the chance to make amends with her mother for missing the wedding). I was glad to miss out on that particular encounter. Call me chicken, but as I mentioned before, I did not take too well to meeting the older ladies when courting their daughters!

As promotion was not forthcoming, I decided to leave my job at the Ludlow plant and looked around for a replacement in order to earn more money. I had an English friend called Jerry who had worked as a waiter. He duly informed me that lots of money could be made waiting on tables at a nice restaurant he knew. He said all you had to do is to pretend that you are Jewish and to say you worked on the Queen Mary, sailing across the ocean…

'Yes all right, that sounds reasonable,' I said, forgetting the knock on my head years ago had even happened. Now the problem with waiting on tables is that you should know the basics of the job. You also need quite a good memory as you should at least try to remember who orders what. We arrived at the restaurant and Lewis (the Boss) knowing Jerry soon agreed to give us a 'start'.

The restaurant was situated just inside the state of Pennsylvania and was a fantastic seafood restaurant with many dishes including no less than twenty-four starters - all à la carte! Soon after I started I found that the reputation of chefs being temperamental was not an idle notion but really true. The shouting was similar to the drill sergeant years ago in basic training and woe betide you if you missed your place and did not collect the meal prepared by one of the many chefs.

I was standing there in my usual spot, congratulating myself; everyone was busy eating, the boss seemed pleased with my work. I had been given twenty-four covers, six tables, and I had even received a few tips that would be given out at the end of the evening. I suddenly found several pairs of eyes seemingly bearing down on me. What was the matter with the silly people? I had taken their order and I could not get the meals out any faster than the chefs could cook them! I glanced down at my pad. Yes, everything seemed to be in order and going well and then, oh god, what was that top copy sitting in the middle of my pad? Six orders, six of everything, starters, main course and sweet.

Oh God, the bloody chefs would kill me if I tried to jump the gun and cut in…but what about the customers? Jerry managed to add it to his order which did help a bit and finally the meals came out and hunger settled for my 'not too impressed' customers. Well, the waiter was strange, wasn't he; he talked funny! Perhaps the size of the tip should show their displeasure. A dollar! Blinking heck, in England that would have been about seven shillings - not bad for a cock-up!

Lewis ran a tight ship and if you made a mistake he would deduct the missing amount; say, for example, fifty cents for a portion of peas, off your wages that evening. No messing, YOU paid for your mistakes! He would not!

He took me to one side at the end of the session. 'You haven't done this before, Ken, have you.'

'Er, no, Lewis,' I replied lamely. I tried to look as apologetic as possible.

'Are you a Jewish boy?' he asked.

'Er, not quite,' I answered.

Lewis looked at me with an extremely bewildered expression on his face. It said it all, how the bloody heck could you be 'not quite Jewish!' I guess the look of pure desperation on my face and the fact I had only managed one mistake made him relent and he booked me in for another session. He had not heard, of course, about the half-hour enforced wait that some of his customers had endured earlier that night! I worked for several weeks at the restaurant. I worked hard and even began to be quite efficient but never quite managed to become completely Jewish. I guess no one would have let me even if I had wanted to.

The tips improved and I started to enjoy my new position, learning at least something about the catering game. One day I received a phone call from a company that I had visited soon after leaving the Ludlow Textile Company. I had visited the Steel Company of Pennsylvania and left an application for a job, something you were allowed to do then in America. My past experience interested them and after a long interview I was offered a position as Production and Quality Control Analyst.

This turned out to be a fantastic position and soon I was earning very good money and the prospects were good, very good. This, together with my work at the restaurant in the evenings meant that I started saving quite a bit of money to put away for Claire's and my future.

I then received some startling news from Claire: her father was not doing at all well and his condition might even become life-threatening. Oh, by the way, she was pregnant. Oh my God, the timing was incredible.

We had been hoping that everything would be settled in the UK, her father's condition might improve and Claire might be able to return to the USA. The only intermediate solution was for me to go to the UK and when everything was better we could return to the States.

I was rather sorry to resign from such a good position but, with promises that I might well return, I left the steel company and booked my passage on the new Queen Elizabeth cruise ship which was then the fastest ship available. It would take five days and travelling by ship suited me as I could take more suitcases.

While staying with my parents we had acquired a pet dog, a German Spitz, who came to us as an adorable white ball of fluff. He had grown over the short time I had been back to a reasonable-sized pooch. Not one of those large dogs that seem to grow very large and you can put a small barrel on their collar. Either way, Spitzie, as he was called, not very original as you can imagine, had been accepted as my dog. At least it was always me that had to clear up his poo!

The family had all been discussing my return to England and a certain amount of packing had been completed. I must admit I am not very good at farewells and I certainly had not discussed anything with the dog called Spitzie. I was sitting in one of the armchairs the day before I was due to set sail for my return to England, when a very strange thing occurred. I was suddenly nuzzled by Spitzie who then proceeded to make his way onto my lap, not an easy feat as he was now quite a large dog. The family all looked on in amazement and my mother remarked that the dog instinctively knew that I was leaving. I sat with the dog on my lap for the next two hours and realised that perhaps we do tend to underestimate our pets' intelligence.

My first encounter with the sea all those years ago, on the TSS New York, had been a bit of a disaster. Perhaps this shorter trip on a larger ship would be an improvement? It was nice to relax after all the running about which had been unavoidable due to the sudden return of Claire and now me. I was going back to England even sooner than expected and without any prior warning.

I was returning to my old haunts but what would I find when I got there? Would old wounds open up and would I bump into any of the ladies from my past? It was only a relatively short time since I had left. Claire lived in Bristol, so it was arranged that once I arrived at

Southampton I would get a train to Bristol where I'd be collected at the railway station by her brother Jim.

Firstly however, I had to endure five days on the open sea with people I did not know. Arriving on board and getting settled I soon saw that it was going to be a 'hard' trip. I met several guys that obviously liked to drink, (so I was kind of forced to join in with that). However, drink and chat only attracts persons of the opposite sex!

I had no desire to even talk with any persons of the female sex. Had I not been down that road before with such drastic and heartbreaking results? I did very well until the last night when everyone seemed to be in a demob mood, drinks were aplenty and soon everyone was kissing everyone else, except me, I was keeping out of the way. Some nut decided that we should go up to the top deck to see if we could see France (which was the first port of call and where some of the passengers were getting off).

I went up with the others and without warning I became detached from the main crowd and found myself with a young lady called Andrea who seemed pleased that at least she was not on her own. It was a bit spooky on the top deck and the weather was not the best. We sheltered from the wind which had blown up and as we sat and talked I guess things could have gone further, such as kissing and the like. However, I resisted all temptation. When we finally found the rest of the party, Andrea seemed to be content to exchange telephone numbers and addresses with everyone who had been at the gathering of passing souls that evening.

Although I had done nothing to be ashamed of I gave my brother's address. It was a good job I did so because a month later, Andrea arriving in England from France wrote to me and wanted to meet up. My brother later read the letter out to me over the phone. He went into hysterics with laughter; evidently Andrea wanted to know why I had not been there to see her off when she disembarked in France. Would it have been too much for my heart?

What was this silly girl saying? We had not even kissed or touched in any way for goodness sake and I was a married man. Did I not tell her that? No, oh well, she should have seen it in my eyes!

I left the ship, caught the train for Bristol and Jim collected me from the train station as planned. Claire was pleased to see me but I was not sure that her mother and brother were that keen, due most likely to the sudden marriage and perhaps they felt a little left out.

Claire's father, Jim Senior, was not getting any better; in fact his problems had become more serious. He was a fantastic guy though and would often take me up to the public house 'The Hen and Chicken'. We used to play skittles and get quite 'happy', but not too happy as Claire's mum did not take kindly to too much drink.

Jim was a great character and an ex-Bristol dockworker. He must have been one of the original 'Del Boys'. He could obtain anything you wanted from the numerous docking ships. He knew everyone, including the dock police, who just seemed to take to 'Old Jimmer' as he was affectionately called. He always cycled to and from work and normally wore a large overcoat, whatever the weather. His pockets were always bulging with contraband that old Jim had orders for!

I guess he would have gone on for years except that he had a very bad smoking habit, smoking over forty non-tipped cigarettes per day. This of course had a bad effect on his lifestyle and later on in his life he unfortunately developed leg thromboses and, after removal of both his legs, he died. What a brave man; even with one of his legs removed he remained cheerful and would always be telling jokes and thinking of everyone else, especially those less well off than himself. I had a lot of respect for my new father-in-law.

For a while we stayed at Claire's mother's home and then we managed to get an apartment on the other side of Bristol. I obtained a position at Charles E Ford (Bristol) in the sales department supporting a chap called David Cavender. A really nice guy who loved statistics and, me being a bit of a chart whiz kid, I developed a chart showing all of the sales figures so David could see at a glance just how much he had paid a year ago for the grain commodities he was buying and selling. I guess it was similar in style to the old Squadron Recall Plan I devised all those years ago at Brize Norton but this time I would not be called to account about where I was at 2 a.m. in the morning. I was home with Claire and by then we had our first child, Kim-Ann, who was a delight to us. It was now 1963 and I had left behind the disappointments of my past romantic episodes and was at last apparently building a new life. I did like my job at Ford's but, with David Cavender well entrenched as the only salesman, I had no way to progress. So when my brother suggested I start to work with him in Porthcawl, South Wales, I readily accepted.

My brother had worked hard in his profession as an architect and had now progressed to be a master builder. The houses my brother designed were brilliant and looked just like doll's houses with large roofs which really made them stand out from other houses. I was to handle the office side of things, do the staff wages and assist with the sales. I went on ahead and stayed at my brother's house which was situated just as you entered the 'Devrow Estates' building site.

It soon became apparent that my brother's marriage was in some difficulty and after several intense meetings with his wife Vera I learned that my brother had been carrying on with a lady called Joan, a local police lady. I could do nothing to make her suffering any easier and, as I had to inform her, I was the last person to be in a position to throw stones! They do say that blood is thicker than water! What a horrible saying….

Claire and our daughter joined me and we settled in and started to enjoy the village of Porthcawl and the surrounding countryside.

We were able to purchase a house through the company and soon we had a nice three bedroom semi-detached property. Things went well until my brother went to the US to visit my father and mother. He was gone for six weeks and, upon his return, he found that the 'boss man' everyone wanted to talk to was Ken West not Derek West. Even his highly paid foreman used to come to me asking for directions on how to proceed with certain matters affecting the building of the houses. Why, I am not too sure.

It is funny how the same name can confuse things! Derek did not seem to like it a bit. He was paying me just under the tax level, I was certainly not getting anything near the correct remuneration for the job I did. Years of brotherly love seemed to disappear overnight and it was soon obvious that the site could not sustain two brothers. I had no problem with Derek being the main man as he had much more experience than me. It appeared as if he thought I had overstepped my position but it was a position I had been forced into when he had departed on his extended holiday to the States. Unfortunately, just like years ago with Sergeant White, I was not calling the shots. You could only have one Top Gun on site so after hearing no more money was available; I looked around and obtained a position with the Steel Company of Wales at nearby Port Talbot.

The countryside around Porthcawl and Port Talbot is fantastic and with the sea close by, you can have many lovely walks and visits along the coast. I was soon earning good money. This went on for several months until it was decided that we would all go from two shifts per day to three which of course meant working nights. Claire and I decided that, due to the situation which was developing with Derek and his wife, it might be prudent to look for somewhere else to live. Maybe back to Bristol? I guess I had no fear about getting a new job and when one of the site electricians suggested I worked for him in Bristol installing immersion heaters in houses I readily agreed. One thing did bother me slightly: I was not a trained electrician, but, given firm assurances from my new boss that it would be easy, I said okay, I would do it.

We moved back to Bristol and managed to rent a nice apartment near the centre of Bristol. The pay was good: £18.00 per part-wire per job and £30.00 for a full-wire. I found that the part-wire jobs were very easy but I hated installing new immersions (which meant cutting the tanks) and routing the cables back to the main electric box . I was soon making enough to keep Claire and Kim-Ann in the manner they richly deserved. I found a good electrician who knew more about the job and I used to give him all my 'full-wires' which he seemed happy to do. This could not go on forever, however, as I did not want to get into a situation where I might have caused a fire without knowing it. So I eventually resigned as the agent in Bristol.

I started looking for a new position. At least we had some money left over from selling the house in Porthcawl and this enabled us to purchase another property on the west side of Bristol. Life seemed ideal when I obtained a good position with British Aircraft Plastics Division earning good pay and with the arrival of two new babies, Natalie and Tanya, life was pretty good. We settled down to normal family life in a nice house, in a nice neighbourhood; what else could a man want?

What indeed. One problem however was the travelling from our house to my new job at Filton (which was a long distance from where we lived). Not having a car meant that I had to leave the house at 5.30 a.m., go into the centre of Bristol and then another long bus ride up to my workplace at the factory at 8 a.m. It was a long day and I never managed to get home before 6.30 p.m. each evening. It was nice to get home but it could not go on. Who could have foreseen that a decision to change my job would lead to a major change in direction that would affect not just our whole lifestyle but, even worse, the very fabric of our apparently successful marriage?

Looking in the Evening Post newspaper one evening I was attracted by an advertisement for a 'Trainee Entertainment Manager' offered by the Top Rank Club. Top Rank operated a very successful chain of Entertainment Centres throughout the UK. I applied and, after an interview at the Top Rank Suite in Bristol, I was offered the position of Trainee Assistant Manager for Top Rank. What a mouthful.

The pay was excellent but with one snag: I had to go to Southall in Middlesex (near London) to complete my training. It would be for twelve weeks. I could come home after every ten days for three days which would help. We both decided it would be best for me to accept the position and within a short time I left the security of our home in Bristol and left for London.

I'm So Lonesome I Could Cry...

Hank Williams
Hear that lonesome Whippoorwill
He sounds too blue to fly
The midnight train is winding low
I'm so lonesome I could cry!

THE SOUTHALL BOWL WAS A cinema that had been converted into an entertainment centre with twenty-four bowling lanes, a snack bar and entertainment bar.

It had been open for three years and was situated close to the town centre. I walked into the centre and I found myself in a world that would not only excite me but would turn my life upside down. It would also allow me eventually to use some of the talents that I had acquired over the past years. Some acquired in the American Air Force, some at the bowling centres, and others while at the restaurant with Lewis. I was instantly seduced by the excitement of fulfilling customer's needs.

I was introduced to the Centre Manager, Wayne Benson, who would be my immediate boss. He was reported to have connections with royalty. The bowling centre was laid out with the twenty-four tenpin bowling lanes spread over two floors, with a large snack bar located at the entrance of the centre. Upstairs there was a large bar which had plenty of room for entertainment. We had around forty staff, some full-time and some part-time. My immediate task was to shadow Mr Benson and learn from him how to run the complex and very busy entertainment centre. The first amazing thing I learned from Mr Benson was something I did not choose to adopt. Every time he drank a beer he would place his rather large tongue in the glass as he swallowed the beer. It was simply amazing; I was transfixed every time he did this. The staff seemed to accept this as a normal event as no one commented about it. Poor Mr Benson; it was soon apparent that he had no clue how to handle the sort of people that used to come into the centre. He had a nice educated voice that did not seem to communicate in any way with the rather rough local clientele.

Across the road was the White Swan, a large pub that was frequented by most of the undesirables in Southall at that time. It soon became apparent to me why there had been a vacancy at the Southall Bowl – the clientele who used the pub across the road were not the type that would offer anyone a nice congenial atmosphere. Mr Benson did not particularly like them and seemingly they did not like Mr Benson.

I was oblivious to all of this of course as I walked in Mr Benson's shadow and I guess, looking back, this gave Mr Benson some Dutch courage, shall we say. We were up in Mr Benson's office and he was informing me just how well he ran the centre and what he expected from me. I would have an extensive training course over the next twelve weeks and I would eventually be expected to look after the centre when he was not present. I could not be expected to do this until I was at least six weeks into the training period.

'Fine, that's okay with me, Mr Benson,' was my response. Suddenly the phone rang and with a stern voice Mr Benson informed me that we were required downstairs. We went down the private stairs that led off from Mr Benson's office and went into the snack bar where we were presented with the spectacle of two rather scruffy black guys. We were informed by the manageress of the snack bar that one of them would not pay for his coffee.

'Why won't you pay for your coffee?' enquired Mr Benson.

The black man known as Raymond looked at Mr Benson.

'Don't like it, not strong enough,' Raymond replied.

Mr Benson's answer could only be described as feeble: 'But you've got to.'

Raymond spoke with even more authority (which wasn't hard to do when compared to poor Wayne's response).

'Make me!'

It could have come from a Clint Eastwood movie except that it was ages before such movies were made.

What happened next was a blur to me, never in my life had I witnessed such a spectacular vanishing act. One minute Wayne was there, the next he was gone! I could not believe my eyes; where had he gone? He just turned tail and went up those private stairs two at a time. I looked at Dora, the catering manageress, who was seemingly unperturbed by this amazing turn of events and she continued to wipe the countertop like everything was normal. After what I had witnessed I realised Raymond already knew just how far he could push our local General Manager. I was left looking straight into Raymond's eyes which had that kind of non-committal look, waiting for my response.

I looked at him wondering what I should do next. It was almost another high noon situation.

'Where's he gone?' enquired Raymond as if he did not know.

'Well, I would imagine he has gone to call the police,' I offered, not having the slightest clue. I could not imagine for one moment that Mr Benson would do such a rash thing. Too humiliating, and overkill for such a small amount. Still needs must, as my old friendly medics informed me, when they removed part of my toe all those years ago. I still had to deal with Raymond, and to deal with him now or I too would lose face, an option I did not want to consider.

I carried on with my false appraisal of the situation: that Mr Benson had gone for the police.

I looked at Raymond and he looked at me. Who was going to crack first? I knew I would have to stand my ground or I would most likely fail my first test. Was this my first test? Had Mr Benson, scourge of the local hard men, deliberately left me to deal with this 'easy' task?

'Raymond, surely it's not worth getting arrested for such a small amount?' I offered hopefully. 'Look, please have the coffee on us but it'll mean you will not be allowed in again and that would be a shame for everyone.'

Did I really believe what I was apparently saying? I did not have a clue who would keep this rather large and unpleasant individual out but was he being that unpleasant? To me, having sampled the coffee on offer, I would most likely have had to agree with his opinion of it.

As we were attracting more than the usual interest, I decided to offer a solution that was best for everyone.

'Raymond, have the coffee on me,' I said. 'You had better leave now but I will not bar you if you promise not to come in and drink the coffee again.'

Raymond looked at me and laughed. 'Hey man, I could get to like you - maybe!'

I was quietly relieved that the situation had been defused and Raymond left with his honour intact. We had managed to quieten down a situation that had not been dealt with properly in the first place. I called on the intercom phone to Mr Benson and enquired politely what he was doing, (just to see if he had called the police) and perhaps if he was coming down again. He replied he was 'tied up with paperwork' and did not even mention poor old Raymond and his cup of coffee.

I now knew I had the full picture of Mr Benson's resolve and I also knew that the next twelve weeks would be anything but boring. To what extent even I, with my worldly wanderings, would be greatly surprised. I guess the word went around the bowling centre that the new Trainee Assistant Manager had more about him than the previous lot had (whoever they were) and I was treated with some respect and above all kindness. Perhaps they were hoping for some changes in the establishment that might just make their working environment a bit more pleasant. I am sure that not one of them could ever have dreamt that such changes would actually occur in such a short period of time.

It started innocently enough with a phone call informing our office secretary that Mr Benson had a price on his head! This was laughed off by everyone except Mr Benson who, understandably, received the news with some unease. I was two weeks into my training and was already looking after the centre most nights (which was certainly not in line with the procedure laid out by Head Office). The phone calls continued until they actually named a price of £100, a tidy sum in those days. I could see Wayne was fast losing the will to manage! He was absent more than he was in and I soon had to shoulder most of the responsibility for the centre.

Fortunately, I had some good staff and we settled down to a routine which seemed to run quite smoothly, even if I do say so myself. I had just returned from my first visit home, which I had to take rather later than I had envisaged. I had the evening shift and, when the phone rang, a lady informed me that the price on Mr Benson's head was now £200. I thanked her and said that Mr Benson would be pleased.

Next day I was informed by Julie, our secretary, that Mr Benson had phoned in and informed her that he was going to London to see Mr Fancourt, the company controller.

I thought Mr Fancourt should know about the last phone call. So I rang him at his office and I informed him that (although I thought it was mainly just bull) I felt he should know the price was now £200. He thanked me and told me Mr Benson was about to see him. Mr Benson arrived at the office and was ushered into the office of Fanny, as the staff used to call him.

'Mr Benson, what can we do for you?'

'Mr Fancourt, there's a price of £100 on my head!' replied Wayne

'Oh no, Mr Benson, it's £200 now,' replied Mr Fancourt.

The story goes that Mr Benson almost had an 'accident' and it was shortly after this that I received a phone call from Fanny asking me would I like to take over the Southall Entertainment Centre in the post of General Manager forthwith, with of course a pay rise to match the extra responsibility.

'With pleasure, Mr Fancourt, I would be pleased to do so.'

I was now General Manager of a Top Rank Centre, with forty staff and after completing just four weeks of my training programme. A bit of a swank, better than winning a jingle contest but surely a bit 'too easy' and at what cost!

At last 'Top Gun', the man in total control and I was loving every minute of it. My training looking after the officers and the office at the air bases came in handy and, with my own personal secretary Julie, I had nothing else to do but to supervise. Oh yes, and possibly deal with the bunch of bums that were gathering nightly across the way outside the White Swan. It must have been the local pastime with everyone joining in…baiting Mr Benson every night! I had seen the gathering before but over the last few nights before Mr Benson – eh – left, it seemed to have got worse. After consuming a large quantity of alcohol the clientele would assemble on the pavement outside the public house and start their chanting. This normally amounted to shouts of 'Benson out' or similar.

My first problem was how to deal with this lot. One of the best things Mr Benson had done before he left was to engage a doorman or bouncer. We called them doormen more for public relations; it also looked good on the payroll. Desmond, or Des, as we called him was a really nice (ex-military) coloured man and we soon became firm friends. This was mainly due to the fact that we spent every evening of the first week at the front door with a baseball bat each. Des was an ex-boxer, but two men against around forty or so morons? Anyway, there we were, baseball bats at the ready. We did put these out of sight when the genuine punters came in, all of whom seemed to take these extraordinary happenings as normal, would you believe!

We always had the old cinema doors on the catch in case of a charge, it was that bad. It fortunately never came to that but, to the young newly-promoted General Manager West, it was quite real and it was happening just four weeks after arriving from my safe and dependable office job far away in Bristol. I decided not to inform my lovely wife sitting in our nice safe house.

There was, it seemed, one really hard man that everyone in the neighbourhood treated and talked about with respect: Tom Roberts. I had heard the name many times and it was put about that it was he who had first started the vendetta against poor Mr Benson. .

It was a complete surprise to me to receive a message from the snack bar that a Mr Tom Roberts was downstairs and he would like to see me. Oh heck! It was bad enough to view such people from across the street but to meet him in the flesh, in person. Not that I had actually seen him. I am sure he had created more of an effect with Mr Benson by remaining in the shadows; what on earth am I saying? What shadows? The only Shadows I knew played with Cliff Richard! What was that song I had been humming? 'I'll never get out of this world alive!' Suffering succotash, to think I had volunteered for this!

I walked down the private stairs with some trepidation; what would our mystery hard man look like? He would obviously be an ugly, hard-looking character who would have tattoos on all his arms and maybe even on his forehead, indicating that he would normally have new 'green general managers' for breakfast! I was amazed; he was well groomed, slim and even rather handsome, and seemed quite friendly, (if you like hard men as friends.) I greeted him as normally as I would anyone else.

'Hi, Tom, what can I do for you?'

Tom looked me up and down.

'I'd like to come and use the club upstairs!' he said with ease, as if he was asking for a cup of tea (not the coffee which we all knew was not that great).

'Well, Tom,' I was trying to be as nonchalant as he appeared to be, 'the problem, I understand, is that some of your "friends" have not behaved themselves previously,' I remarked, careful not to include him in the past misdemeanours.

Tom then said an incredible thing, a statement that endeared me to him straightaway: 'I'm not worried about that lot. I just want somewhere to bring my wife to have a quiet drink.'

I looked at his face and I could tell that this hard man might just be telling the truth. I realised I now had the chance to change things to my own advantage and, by association, the club's.

I knew once I had let in one of the group others would try to follow. I also knew I would be taking one heck of a chance even with Tom. I had not met this mystery man before but my gut feeling was to trust him.

'I'll tell you what, Tom, you come in with your wife and if everything goes well for one month and we get no problems, we can give you a proper membership.'

Tom readily agreed and we shook hands. He never even enquired about the 'membership' which was something I had just dreamt up that moment. We had never had a membership but we did now!

Oh well, Ken West, Top Gun, had just made his first executive decision and one I hoped and prayed I would not regret. I was on a roll, so I then suggested that, if things worked out okay, Tom's immediate friends could also come in (with their wives) as long as Tom would vouch for their behaviour. Tom also agreed to this. I informed the staff of my decision and I must admit received many a strange look. Des seemed to understand and respect the solution and he used his calm relaxed manner to welcome Tom and his wife when they turned up the same evening (as if to test the arrangement).

It was an incredible sight: there was Tom around 6'2" inches tall and his wife, who can only be described as tiny (around 4'2" inches) walking arm in arm into the centre and up the stairs leading to the club. It was most likely one of the best decisions that I would make in my early months at the centre; just how good was proven within weeks.

One evening I was upstairs in my office, which was close by the club entrance, when I heard some shouting (even above the noise of the jukebox). Des had been answering a call of nature when two men had taken advantage of this and quickly walked in and up to the bar. I hurriedly walked out to see Des who had just arrived after seeing the two undesirables scampering up the stairs to the bar. Des was asking them to leave and a stand-off had occurred. Before I had even got to where Des and the two intruders were, Tom came up to me and asked if I needed any help. I declined but felt greatly comforted that I had the backing of most likely the hardest man in town. I joined Des and was about to join in the verbal exchange when Des, sensing that things had gone past the talking stage, let fly with both fists at the same time.

The two men did not know what hit them, such was the speed of Des's punches. Years of boxing experience came into play as Des showed that he was in charge and, if he said leave, it was in one's best interest to do as he suggested! The two men stumbled back, turned around and ran, noses puffed up and blood cascading down into their mouths, which had opened in surprise at the speed of Des's lightning actions.

Down the same stairs they had previously hurried up, thinking they were in and cheating the system. Des in full pursuit, they did not even stop to open the closed doors; bang and straight out into the street. Des had spoken!

We learned later that one of the two had just come out of jail the day before.

Some bars have good atmospheres, some do not. Even half empty, the club bar atmosphere was tremendous. The jukebox with its 50s and 60s music added an even greater atmosphere to the friendly crowd that came to use it. I was pleased to include Tom and many of his friends who had asked to join. The music of the Beatles with such tunes as 'Penny Lane' and 'Strawberry Fields Forever' were firm favourites and I came to love the great feeling of congenial fun which emerged in the club. The clientele, along with the bar takings, grew steadily as news of it being a great place to visit spread.

I knew that I had been hired to do a job and I set out to do this with some vigour. I knew I had to stamp my own personality on the centre and made sure that I did my rounds every half-hour so that all the staff knew (and expected) that I was around, whatever the time of day.

I must admit I had to apologise many times to Claire for the delays that frequently occurred in my coming home on time. I had a job to do and I wanted to do it correctly. At last I was in charge and seemingly master of my own destiny, no Sgt White to keep me down.

I stopped the group of hangers-on that used to congregate in the snack bar by introducing a minimum charge of one pound, even for our lovely tasting coffee or tea.

Regular price of course for our regulars and if we did find some clients who persisted and stayed longer than our manageress wanted, we used the old standby – a fire drill. This was used quite well until one day, after two in one week, (I used to allow Dora free will on this as long as she recorded it in the book), I received another request to visit the snack bar by my old friend Raymond, who calmly requested that if I wanted to get rid of them to kindly ask them to leave rather than this old crap with the fire alarms. I said point taken, but reaffirmed that once Dora asked them to move on they should do so.

Another problem apparently solved by a normal level-headed punter who had shown more common sense than the resident 'Top Gun'.

We had a tremendous group of multi-talented staff and when asked to perform in promotions, even when it meant dressing up, they readily agreed. Slim was our 'large' Chief Engineer and was always ready to show willing by getting involved with the many events we put on to increase the centre's turnover and profit. One of my first promotions was the staff performing in fancy dress on the lanes, to the sounds of 'Grocer Jack' by John West.

We even had Slim in a ballerina dress with one of the bar staff in rather tight-fitting tights dancing to the 'Sugar Plum Fairy' which proved a great hit. The profit of the centre rose as many more punters came to play this new exciting game from the States. With Head Office approval we reduced the charge from four shillings a go to two shillings and six pence, all day up to 8 p.m. The centre was full most days and nights. We started new leagues with other bowling centres and the extra revenue soon took effect. We were pleased to find (with some amazement from the staff) that we had climbed from near bottom of the performing centres to within the top three. I guess looking back we could only go up, not down, such was the poor performance of the centre before I took over. You could always tell if you were doing the right thing because you had more visits from the Head Office bosses. Normally they would keep away from 'badly performing centres' in case the manager in charge decided to throw the keys back to them. We always said that, if such a thing happened, the area managers would hand the keys to the janitor rather than do it themselves.

John Teasdale was a good area manager; he would come in without warning, check the toilets and say that if they were alright then the rest of the centre would be too. When we rose to the top of the league table we knew we were doing something correctly. Top Gun had a bit of a swank on that day but I never forgot the staff that had made this possible and trips up to London were normal when rewarding key members such as Slim and Julie (who actually ran the office in such an efficient manner that it was great for me). One day I was out with John Teasdale and we had visited the Croydon Bowling Centre to see if we could tie up some more inter-bowling competitions. Upon arrival back at the centre we drew up in the car and found two men about to load one of our large cigarette machines into a large van. When challenged, they ran, got into the waiting van and sped away. I was not at all pleased that the staff on duty allowed this to happen in the first place but such was the climate we all worked and lived with in the 1960s.

We had to bolt every vending machine to the wall to prevent such occurrences happening again. It made life interesting though!

I employed another employee from the Top Rank Cinemas, John Butterworth, as my assistant manager so now my team was complete. When not returning home I used to stay at a very nice lodging house not far from the centre. It was booked in for me by Julie and I found it very nice. I did however have to share it with another guy for a short while. I didn't see much of him though as I was working the long hours my new job required.

I normally came home in the early hours to find him already in his bed. I woke up one day to the sight and sound of him scratching like mad. Straightaway I thought he must have fleas! The poor guy seemed to be in agony, and I wondered where he had got the unwanted arrivals. I knew the landlady kept a spotlessly clean house. He left shortly afterwards but to my dismay I soon found myself scratching like mad! I quietly told

John my assistant manager about my displeasure and not in Julie's young tender hearing because the itching was in a private part of my body which was – well, private! My 'cojones' as they say in Japan. John, a bit more worldly than even I, suggested I might have caught 'crabs'. In all my years of travelling, even in the Air Force of all places, I had never, and I mean never, heard of 'crabs' other than those you had on your dinner plate.

He suggested that I seek medical assistance and get some 'blue ointment' which I duly did. It seemed to take ages for the itching to stop and I spent many hours having showers, anything to resolve this embarrassing episode that had descended on my life or rather on my poor cojones. I was reliably informed that these little 'peskies' can jump over ten feet at a time. No wonder my old room-mate had left so quickly. He must have known he was missing a few by the time he left! Yes, I had them!

I, of course, had never been mad on hospitals since having the episodes with the toenails and the smack on my bum when I caught 'strep throat' but what was to happen next was even more embarrassing. Just as I thought I was out of the woods, I was dismayed to find when showering that a large swelling had appeared on my left testicle.

It did not look at all good and I hastened off to see the local doctor who, upon seeing it, announced it was a 'goitre', and sent me off to Hillingdon Hospital to have it removed. What did he mean, removed! Did he mean my left – everything or what? There I lay on a trolley with my blue hospital gown just about covering my essential parts and why, oh why, do they always leave you in the draughtiest of corridors!

I just managed to phone John to inform him that I was detained in the hospital and to keep it quiet! I did not inform him just what I was in for because I know that bad news travels fast but 'embarrassing' news (especially concerning the 'top gun' of the local centre) would travel even faster! I was taken down to the operating theatre and my poor little 'swelling' lanced. I had a local anaesthetic and soon I was in recovery which happened to be a side room with no windows. Then my recovery took a turn for the worse. Not that at that time I could imagine things could get any worse!

They seemed to come in their hundreds: the lovely young nurses who came to check on my well-being. Of course, this was only in my imagination, but fair's fair; a man's got to keep what a man's got to keep and, under other circumstances, I would have welcomed, shall we say, the intimate attention! They informed me that I would be staying overnight, longer unless I had someone who could collect me and bring me back every day for new dressings.

John came in to see me and after the usual dry remarks about me having to walk lopsided I managed to get him to agree not to divulge such delicate information to anyone and I meant no one! Under the fear of death! If the staff did learn of it they certainly kept it very quiet but it would not have been normal for John to keep such a good titbit to himself!

I did however walk a bit like John Wayne again, similar to how I walked that day in the dance hall after dancing with Maureen! After a while, the nurses that came got over their giggling and just asked me to move the larger part of my anatomy out of the way so they could dress the affected area. I told them once that, if they would care to move it themselves, it would probably stand up on its own! I only did this after I got to know them because I did not want to upset any of them – not with all those enemas at their disposal!

I never did see my old room-mate again and I knew that if I ever came across him again he would end up tied to the end of my tenpin bowling lanes with me throwing the first ball! Balls, what am I saying?

Not all the clients that used the club bar were hard men. We had a character called 'Poppy' who was a known fence. He seemed to handle anything (but not drugs which were, fortunately, not as freely available as they are now). He used to come in and ask me to lend him a tenner. Within days he would be back with the money and possibly a large piece of beef or something like that. He was a great character and when asked if he had any cash, would normally answer, 'Yep, plenty of poppy in the bin.' He seemed to go on forever, never ever being pulled in by the CID who also used to frequent the club bar. Then one day I heard that he was in jail.

'How did that happen?' I asked.

'His girlfriend wanted something out of the shop and it was half-day closing…so Poppy broke the window and took the item out.'

I did wonder after that just how high Poppy's tolerance level was for alcohol.

The local CID were also drinking buddies of mine. They used to ask me why I allowed so many of the hard boys in the club. I replied that if I banned everyone in the town I would have no custom and anyway they all behaved themselves while in there. The CID boys used to respect this and never ever pulled any of the boys up while in the club. It was like a neutral zone in the middle of the town where the 'boys' met the 'Old Bill' on level terms (if that was ever possible). I do know many of the 'Old Bill' used to chat up the many young ladies that frequented the club.

Claire and I used to laugh at the antics of the children; we had three girls by now, and with Kim-Ann growing fast, she had the responsibility of keeping an eye on the other two, Natalie and Tanya. When I came home once, Tanya nearly caused an upset when she started talking about her big daddy and her small one! It took some time before we worked out she was referring to when I called on the telephone (when I was her small daddy) and of course when I came home, I was her big daddy!

More promotions were aimed at the bowling side and I persuaded a local travel agency to offer a free holiday. It proved very good business for them so they agreed to supply an even better package of free holidays. We even raised cash selling 'Manx Kippers' which we flew over from the Isle of Man fresh every day for three days. The local mayor came and, selling kipper suppers, we managed to raise quite a bit of cash for the local charities. Everyone seemed to enjoy the kippers; that is, if you enjoyed eating kippers at lunchtime. I guess when we first advertised them we were not sure if the event would go on through the entire evening. As it was, it normally lasted about four hours depending on the clientele. We used to send out invites to raise money and interest in the travel business as well.

When raising money for charity it was sometimes a problem to include all the departments of the centre; for instance, you had to see if the promotions could somehow involve everyone. I found the section heads were quite protective about the part they and their staff played in the overall performance of the bowling centre, whether it be the bar, the cafeteria or the actual bowling itself.

It was something I tried to encourage but getting new people through the door was the main priority for the centre. It was always seen by Head Office as a bowling centre and improving figures on number of games played would, of course, justify the huge investment the company had committed.

It was for this reason that many times I had to excuse myself when engrossed in a conversation with the bar clientele and spend time with all the other section heads. I think it is called 'making your presence felt' and it also kept the staff on their toes. I quickly discovered that the best people to work on lane control were people who loved the game themselves. It was also important that they kept a close eye on the punters and this included the idiots who tried to smoke on the lanes while bowling. Some people never seemed to realise that just one spark from their glowing cigarettes could quickly set fire not only to themselves but the whole centre itself.

The oils that are used on the actual bowling lanes are highly inflammable and Chief Engineer Slim always kept them in an excellent well-oiled condition.

I did take on a Chief of Staff briefly but had to terminate the position suddenly when I found him sitting in the control section dictating some of his daytime work to the female control clerk. If there was any dictating to do, I would certainly do that!

With the centre showing good results every month it was nice to receive friendly visits from the Head Office staff. They would always drop in unannounced to have a coffee, such as it was. They were as artful as I was, always coming in and talking to the staff to get their reaction on how the centre was running. I guess the comments they received must have pleased them because I did get an unexpected pay increase which was very welcome. It certainly pays to have the staff on your side, but it is possible for people to get bored if some of the excitement is taken away completely; after all, this was the entertainment business and everyone needed some excitement. Even General Managers!

Your Cheatin' Heart...

Hank Williams
Your cheatin' heart will make you weep,
You'll cry and cry and try to sleep
But sleep won't come the whole night through
Your cheatin' heart will tell on you.

It was only a matter of time before I became distracted from the duties of Top Gun of the centre. I was too professional to be silly enough to chat up the many attractive lady staff that worked for me. It just was not right and I obeyed the unwritten rule of non-familiarisation with the female staff. However, what was I expected to do about Maria?

The guys at the travel agency, Mike and Peter, were always coming into the bowling centre for meetings concerning the new promotions which had now become quite regular. I could not help noticing Maria, a young New Zealand girl who was very pretty and dressed in very bright attractive clothes. She was always the one who had to make me a coffee when I visited the travel agency which was close to the centre. We used to have a few laughs but nothing more.

I really do not make any excuses for what was about to occur. I can only put forward that, by now, I was completely immersed in my new exciting way of life. There is no excuse for any kind of cheating, call it what you will, but the euphoria of running a successful centre, perhaps being alone for long periods of time, even knowing you have a loving wife and family, cannot be enough to stop wayward spouses. It was soon obvious that Maria had told her employers that she was attracted to me and whenever I came into the agency, the standard joke was who was I coming to see? At first I did not catch on but with a few nods and winks from Mike, I knew that any attraction I had for Maria was certainly being reciprocated and I was flattered, really flattered. Old feelings of desire, the excitement of a possible new conquest, the excitement of the moment, no excuse can be adequate for the betrayal that was about to happen. Ken West did what he had done years ago. Sod it! He shut his mind to the happy family life that he had in abundance in Bristol and took the easy option for him …he took a mistress!

Maria was the perfect mistress, she would come into the centre with the guys, stay around without making a fuss and, when it suited me, we left at separate intervals and I used to take her home. I just neatly placed my two worlds into two time portals; I used to enjoy family life on my visits home to Bristol but I suddenly found myself longing for my return to my entertainment centre. Ken West, the man who had his feelings mauled at will in his early days in the Air Force, was now turning his back on the first good thing that had happened in his life! Claire was oblivious to all this and continued to do what she loved to do: play house and bring up our family. The love that she freely entrusted to me was misused and compromised and once this happened, there could only be one direction for true love and that was down! A great man once said, 'It might not be the end of the beginning, but it certainly is the beginning of the end.' I am sure old Winston Churchill never had such problems, but then who knows?

With Maria in tow I managed to get out and experienced some of the delights that the West End of London was offering. I took her to see Fiddler on the Roof staring Topol. 'If I was a rich man' was not lost on me as at that time; I did feel I was getting more than my fair share of riches. Well, if you can include the love of two ladies at the same time, both of whom seemed to be happy with what I was able to offer them. I guess it is easy to shut your eyes to the moral side of your actions when you are just being your usual smug self. Maria lived in South Kensington in a nice flat but I never had the time to spend more than an occasional night there. I was too busy being 'Top Gun' at the centre but not without some humility.

I was just playing the part that I had learnt in the American Air Force which did encourage you to work at will on your own – just as long as you followed the correct US Air Force procedures.

I was given an additional assistant manager from time to time and, although I found this to be convenient for me to take my time off at home in Bristol, I still preferred it when I was totally in charge. It seems that the company used the Southall Centre for training of the 'new boys'. I guess they thought that if they can survive at that centre they can survive anywhere. I suppose it was a compliment but with the destructive influence of Tom Roberts and his associates from the Swan Pub seemingly now resolved life at the centre became settled. The family were about to move from Bristol to the Southall area when fate took a hand and the company suddenly asked me to take over the Bristol Centre which had been experiencing severe financial problems. As the request made good sense with my family already living in Bristol, I had no choice but to readily agree. Maria was heartbroken at the news and I guess I had very bad misgivings about leaving the first love of my life - the Southall Centre. I had had many a good time there and the staff had been terrific but with the lapse of good personal behaviour on my part I felt perhaps a new challenge might be on the cards. After a memorable send-off I packed up my belongings and headed back home to Bristol. I had made my name at the Southall Centre but at what cost to my family life?

What else was I bringing back to Bristol with me? I had already compromised the marriage I had sought for so long. I was no longer window-shopping so why had I started again? Why had I had betrayed not only my wife but my little family? I made the decision that I would be good from now on and not let what had happened all those years ago with Pauline and Shirley spoil what I was blessed with now!

After all it was their fault – wasn't it?

Mind Your Own Business

Hank Williams
If my wife and I are fussin', brother, that's all right
Because me and that sweet woman got a license to fight
Won't you mind your own business cos
If you mind your own business then you won't be minding mine.

We duly arrived back in dear old Bristol and I assumed the position of General Manager of the centre. As it was converted about two years before the Southall Centre, the Bristol Centre was not as in good condition of repair as the one I had just left. It had a tired appearance and it showed in the staff's attitude to working there. I was not at all impressed and immediately started trying to get them on my side. Following a few well chosen promotions we soon had a nice working relationship which seemed to perk up everyone up. Claire of course was pleased to have me nearer home. I for my part was happy to see more of the children and they had to start getting used to having the 'big daddy' home more. The girls were growing up fast and soon we found we had three very attractive young ladies on our hands. I guess we would have to keep an eye on the boys in a few more years; after all, did I not learn about the birds and the bees when I was seven years of age. Memo to me: 'Must look out for any character that looks or resembles Blackie!'

Claire also found that she had some adjustments to make as she had obviously made things her own and was used to running the house and of course all the finances that went with that responsibility. We had a few heated arguments and I found myself retreating back into my safe haven – my world of entertainment.

I loved getting my bowling shoes on and showing the basic techniques to young and old who wanted to master the art of tenpin bowling. I soon found that even with my previous time spent in the USA bowling centers, I was by no means 'Top Gun' when it came to bowling. A lot of guys had mastered the art and were able to obtain good scores on the lanes. 190-230 were common scores when it came to the league competitions which we set up. I started to work on improving the takings of the bar but not without some opposition. I informed everyone I was going to start charging on the door on entertainment nights. Soon an unofficial committee had been formed by one of the local councillors Roy who had his usual followers. Moans and groans whenever it was mentioned. I quickly realised that this suburbia of Bristol was quite different from the suburbs of London; they were much more parochial.

I met one of my customers who had not been to Bristol for ten years. I did not believe him.

'Dave, you must have been,' I said, 'it's only six miles from here.'

'No,' replied Dave, in his deadpan voice. 'Never had the need to.'

That just about summed up the attitude that some of the locals portrayed. We had rented a house close by the entertainment centre so I did not have far to go to work, actually just across the road.

I persisted with the idea of charging on the door for entertainment nights. If people wanted bands and singers they would have to contribute something towards the costs. At seven shillings per pint of beer, and two shillings and sixpence for spirits, there was not enough profit in the bar takings in general to enable the company to cover such costs. Any opposition was soon quelled when the first act I booked was the 'Black Abbots' whose lead singer and comedian soon became extremely famous: Russ Abbot. At £75.00 it was a good booking. I had discovered yet another possible solution, buy cheap but make sure they are the best. After the show finished Roy was the first one to come up to me and state he would pay his half a crown (two shillings and six pence) for acts like that. I guess the penny had dropped, although I could understand the argument against paying anything, but needs must!

It was quite obvious that the company needed maximum effort to get punters through the door and for them to spend money on everything, not just bowling. So I put on promotions which had one purpose only: to get people through the front door and entice them to spend money.

With this in mind we put on a fashion show featuring 'Miss Selfridge' who agreed to supply the latest clothes and a few of the models. We had to supply a few extra ladies to make up the numbers. I guess I never really saw her coming - Patricia the vamp of the west. Patricia had everything: glamour, she was flirtatious, pretty and very, very curvy. She was a very close friend of my secretary (yes I had one at this centre as well) and she used to drop in for coffee while out shopping.

Patricia was also married but one can only say she acted single - extremely single. I of course was oblivious to all these charms - I have always had a larger than normal size nose! I had put my secretary Jane in charge of soliciting some attractive girls who looked good and would of course be happy to prance down the catwalk looking – well, glamorous and sexy. I was happy for Patricia to join the attractive group of girls that offered themselves for this happy event.

About ten days before the event I was having a lunchtime meeting upstairs in the bar with my friendly bank manager when Jane and Patricia came in for a drink. No problem with that until later on, when my bank manager left, I found myself alone with Jane and Patricia. I was not oblivious to the attention that Patricia was paying to me. I decided to play my evergreen favourite tune 'Penny Lane' which always reminded me of past times at Southall. Suddenly Patricia was at my side at the jukebox and within minutes I felt her presence - extremely electrifying. It seemed quite normal to accept her invitation to join her one night for a drink! The next few days were a personal nightmare of thoughts for and against such a meeting taking place. All my previous good intentions seem to disappear and I knew what I planned to do was very unwise, to say the least.

I met Patricia at the agreed meeting place and we went for a drink as planned. We had a great time and many laughs. The evening was drawing to a close and we drove out into the country and parked in a secluded place. Patricia suggested we would have more room in the back of the car so, after agreeing, I was soon in the back seat with this new lady who seemed to be very much in charge.

It was January and decidedly cold, very cold. I could not believe what came next. With 'two' seemingly effortless actions, Patricia completed a 'strip-naked' which should surely have been worth a mention in the

Guinness Book of Records. Good God, I could not believe that Father Christmas was still delivering in January!

I soon found out how Patricia handled difficult situations if anyone queried her actions at any time. She would say, 'Deny it!'

I found just how she viewed this reaction when we were out with my secretary and her boyfriend. We visited a pub that I had not been in before (can you blame me) and I went to the bar and ordered a gin and tonic and a pint of beer. As the landlord was dispensing the drinks he looked directly past me and said, 'Is that Patricia Jenkins with you?'

I looked blankly at him and answered, 'Another pint and an orange juice please, landlord.'

His look said a thousand words; he obviously knew Patricia's husband and I was certainly not he! I went back to the table and hurriedly informed the waiting trio that the landlord seemed to know Patricia! I was imagining a quick exit but no, Patricia just picked up her drink and remarked, 'Oh, don't worry, I'll just say it wasn't me.'

Oh my God, now I knew I had with me a 'professional philanderer'! I guess that I also realised I was becoming a 'professional cheat'!

A similar thing occurred as I was putting the finishing touches to the catwalk for the fashion parade. I was bending down tacking some of the side parts in place, when Patricia came up and bent over to whisper something suggestive in my ear when suddenly around the corner came Claire and she could not help but see this buxom woman bending over her husband, showing parts of her anatomy (normally classed as big boobies) at eye level! She was understandably not amused.

'Who was she?' asked Claire after Patricia had done a very sharp exit right, as they say in show business!

'Oh, just one of the models, dear,' I answered lamely.

Education never really ever stops and in this life there is always someone to teach you that something extra and to fill in any of the gaps that you may be missing through no fault of your own! Of course you do not have to take advantage of this extra tuition!

I was however, and so it seems, a quick learner. I never did receive any medals for this achievement and almost certainly did not deserve any! Despite this betrayal Claire and I remained in a marriage only marred by my indiscretion which surprisingly never came to light at that time. Patricia was not interested in taking it any further than just what she physically gained out of the relationship. As for myself, after seeing the size of her husband, I decided to err on the side of caution and after a short period of time I suddenly became very busy and ignored future invitations. After all, why did I need to go window-shopping again!

Life carried on and we all settled down to the routine of running the club and pub and Claire, seemingly happy with the marriage, then managed to produce an addition to our growing family: a son who we called Curtis. At least one for the home side, having four girls in the house did make it a little lopsided! I went down to the hospital and to my dismay found I had just missed the birth by about ten minutes, trust me. They brought our son out to show me and informed me it was a boy and I stupidly asked the nurse was she sure? Was it really a boy? The meaningful look I received left me in no doubt that they had some experience in these matters. Either way I went back to the pub in considerable high spirits and handed out the cigars. The arrival of my son surely must have a good effect on my future behaviour!

I guess when things are on the up, something will normally happen which only levels it all out again. Again fate took a hand when the Rank Organisation suddenly sold off all its interests in the centres and we found our entertainment centre surplus to requirements. I was offered a move to Cardiff to the Top Rank Suites section which I declined. I had been down the Welsh road before and as much as I loved Wales, Claire and I did not wish to move back over the Severn Bridge.

I was made redundant and, with some cash in the bank, I started looking for alternative employment.

I was not out of work for long because, after being advised that the local brewery were looking for managers to do relief work, I started to work for them doing a relief position in the lovely city of Bath. Jim who I was taking over the pub from was a great character and I really was impressed how he ran his public house. He was always attentive to his customers, offered good food and, above all, he kept a good pint of beer. This is something I sought to continue and I enjoyed my time there. I was rather surprised to receive an invitation from the company to take over my own public house which was located just outside Bristol.

The West family moved to the new pub and with the children settled in the local school we tried to see what we could do to improve the takings of the pub.

I had purchased a 'black box', one of the first stereos with a nice sound. I placed it in the lounge bar and turned down the public bar jukebox – just a touch.

The effect was amazing: people came in just to listen to the nice and easy music, such as Ella Fitzgerald, Ray Conniff and his music. One of the customers who switched bars was a chap called Frank. I viewed him with some scepticism as Frank looked more like a prizefighter than a music connoisseur. I got to like Frank a lot and he became a regular customer every evening and we had great times talking and listening to the music. He was probably the most intelligent person I had ever met; he knew just something about everything. He worked as a technical representative and travelled all over the South-West which was his territory. He knew Torbay very well and it was decided that he and I would go down there for a few days off.

With Claire's approval we set out our plans. I had made another friend in the same town called Gerry, and he and I had become good friends as he ran one of the local pubs in the high street: The Royal Oak, an old but nicely situated pub right opposite the bank where we used to deposit the company's money.

This became a regular watering hole when I went to the bank to deposit the company takings which was at least three times a week. The company had found out to its disadvantage that sometimes past managers had treated the takings as their own so they insisted on the minimum three times a week rule for everyone's benefit. I guess that these watering hole breaks became rather longer than normal and it was not unusual for the 'banking time' to last well into the late afternoon. Claire accepted this as normal as long as I was back in time to open up the pub. Introducing Frank into the inner circle just ensured this occurred at least three times per week.

When he was told that Frank and I were going down to Torbay, Gerry invited himself. Not a worry though, as he volunteered to drive. Gerry had an old Volvo saloon and in those days, although speeding was not frowned on as much as it is today, it was customary to try and keep four wheels on the road when driving. Gerry was a good driver but even Frank with his considerable mileage every week commented that perhaps Gerry might slow down a bit so we could at least enjoy the countryside. Talk about Stirling Moss!

It was a sunny day when we arrived at the resort, we booked into a B and B, and then went downtown to have a coffee or two…Well, perhaps there was a brandy in the coffee.

It was twelve o'clock midnight and we were in one of the several clubs that we had managed to find, - surprise, surprise. Gerry and I were talking to two young ladies and I was giving them some of the old GI chat-up lines. I guess I imagined I was Robert Mitchum or someone like that; I leered at this delectable young lady, quite oblivious to what was going on around me. I glanced around; Frank was talking earnestly with some bloke and Gerry, well, he had collapsed in a heap and was taking no more interest in the two young ladies.

'Have another drink,' I offered in my best Robert Mitchum accent. Good God, that's how bad I was. I don't think many people can understand old Bob at the best of times.

'Oh, I'll have double vodka and my friend will have a gin and tonic,' replied my delectable girlfriend smiling sweetly. I was in like Flynn!

Poor old Gerry, he had missed the boat, couldn't handle his Canadian Club, which of course we were now all drinking. My young lady leaned across, placed her hand on my knee and breathed lightly in my ear. I could only imagine that we would now make our plans to leave the club, I would get a taxi for us and we would go back to their place and, goodness me, I might have to keep up the side on my own.

'Thank you, Ken, for the lovely drinks but I would like to mention just a little problem.'

'What's that?' I asked. 'Oh no, not the wrong time of the month!'

'We're both lesbian.'

I just sat there, crying in my glass! Claire would have loved it! Frank arrived back on the scene and asked how I was getting on.

'Don't mention it,' I growled.

Waking Gerry up was not easy and we had to half carry him back to the bed and breakfast hotel. The problem was that the hotel was right at the top of some forty odd steps. Frank looked at Gerry and suddenly, with one heave, he lifted him onto his back, just like a sack of coal. I admit Gerry was slight in build but this surprised me even in my bemused state. We started the climb with me holding Gerry's legs which most likely made things even harder for poor Frank as I am not sure if I was actually taking the weight or perhaps just holding on!

We reached the hotel, fortunately his room was unlocked, and Frank plonked Gerry onto his bed. Suddenly, to our complete surprise, Gerry sat up, put his legs over the side of the bed and took off one of his socks. He proceeded to take out all his money, notes, change and keys and put it into his recently removed sock, placed the sock under his pillow, and then went straight to sleep without a thank you. Frank was amazed as Gerry had appeared completely out of it. I guess Gerry, being a Jewish boy, was just not taking any chances with his cash and one thing was certain: Gerry's stashing his money in his sock became Frank's favourite bar tale upon arriving back at the pub.

There was a rumour about Claire and the window cleaner that I put it down to gossip that went around the pub circuit. A window cleaner! I knew he was quite handsome but Claire could do better than that. Now Richard the local hairdresser certainly fancied Claire and I guess Claire liked him because at a local party at his hairdressing saloon just across the road I caught them just about to kiss. But wasn't it true all hairdressers are gay? I accepted this interlude as a normal event - why shouldn't Claire be chatted up! People in glass houses – don't throw stones.

We put on many shows such as 'Roaring Twenties' with me being the Godfather with my false Italian accent, what a donut! Girls were dressed as Dolls and the Guys portrayed by male customers. We had several of the hard customers who also joined in. At least the machine guns they carried were not real, or at least I hoped they were not. The highlight was a large birthday cake for me, the Godfather, and at the selected time out popped Nancy, the wife of one of the real local hard men, Kevin. I did not make any effort to keep Nancy not just because of 6'4" inches Kevin but I guess Claire wouldn't have let me. Nice thought though!

We had good staff. I continued to do what I did best and laid out a congenial atmosphere the customers appeared to want and they came in their droves. With every session we improved our takings and, with it, our standing with the company. One of my local customers also worked for the brewery as an area manager and he looked after a large entertainment house at a seaside resort. He asked me to consider taking it over as it also had a large entertainment room. Claire and I agreed and we were soon making arrangements for the change.

Moving there we found it to be a large hotel situated nicely beside the beach and it was similar to my old haunts with Top Rank but without the bowling side. It had a large bar with a stage, which enabled us to put on shows that proved a great success with the locals. I started writing my own Christmas pantomimes such as Oliver Twist, performed by the staff and, with me playing Mr Bumble, it soon showed that perhaps my waistline was getting a little larger.

We had a couple of 'hard boys' in the area and when confronted with several of them one evening we managed to throw them out. However, one guy, named Charlie, did a strange thing as I was marching him out of the front door (by his neck under my arm): he bit my tummy. Strange man. I of course remonstrated with a bang to his left eye and out he went. I understand that, shortly afterwards, Charlie had to appear in front of the local magistrate. Charlie said that he had received his black eye from a taxi driver who had beaten him up after he had refused to pay his fare. Charlie had an iron bar with him at the time. Nice kind of guy!

This did not stop him tapping on the window after close, late one summer night when I was alone in the bar doing some paperwork. Charlie wanted to know why he could not come in to use the bar, etc. Good God, I had been down that way before. I knew that as far as he was concerned he was not there but for any other reason than to get his own back. After some small talk I waited for his move, and it came very quickly. Attempting to grab my shirt he tried to pull me to him for the customary headbutt. It was fortunate that we had the open window between us because I instinctively fell backwards grabbing his extended arm as I went. Although I was not a trained martial arts expert, I managed to hit him across his exposed throat. He released his hold on my shirt and fell back gasping for breath. He left hurriedly after that and later I heard that he told everyone I was a trained karate expert and an ex-policeman. I realised my action had not done my reputation any harm with the local villains. It was just as well for me that no one came to challenge the latest hard man on the block. Thank goodness!

It was by no means all trouble at the hotel; we did a lot of charity work which we managed to get many of the customers involved in. Rolling barrels down the outside slopes might have been a bit dangerous but when you are trying to raise money you seem to be able to get away with a lot. One of the daftest things we did was to take over the brewery dressed as SS German storm troopers. We hired the costumes from a local fancy dress hire shop and ten of us arrived at the brewery head office which was located in Bristol. Getting out of the cars, I noticed an old lady who was cleaning and sweeping her front step. I wish I had taken a picture of her; it would have been worth recording the look on her face. She was a typical Mrs Mop of the day: headscarf, fag in her mouth, shaking out her mat; the Mrs Mop who loved her housework and a chat with the neighbours. She just froze, the cigarette seemed to hang suspended from her mouth, she was not sure if she was witnessing an armed raid or what. I mean German SS, at 10 a.m., admittedly a really tatty looking lot at that.

We entered the large entrance hall and I went to the receptionist who immediately started screaming which was something I did not expect. We had planned for all the 'Germans' to surround the hall, so they all positioned themselves in a circle in the reception with their 'guns' at the ready. I mean a kid could see it was a laugh but this lady must have really been taken by surprise and I had to calm her down and ask her to get my area manager down from his office.

She rang him up on the phone: 'Mr Stevens, please can you come down we have some Germans in the hallway.'

Goodness knows what he thought of that! Upon his arrival he laughed and then allowed us to go all around the offices, even to the big boss, collecting money for muscular dystrophy. The only problem occurred when one of the 'troopers' trod on one of the open-plan telephone points and put out most of the telephones of all his colleagues. Oops! Hitler would have loved that! Daft sod!

We raised a lot of money and it was well received by the local charity office. I guess that did raise some eyebrows in Head Office but I was to find out later our antics did not do me any harm.

Claire, the children and I used to enjoy the walks down the promenade when we had time. The old pier was certainly quite an attraction even though half of it had been blown down in a gale some years previously. Years later the locals did raise a lot of money and it was finally restored to its former glory. I guess the old attractions of yesteryear still hold great affection for many folk.

From time to time, being in the pub game, we were offered some items which had been 'left over'. We had a guy who worked for a cheese factory who would come in with 'leftover' blocks of cheddar cheese, something we used quite a bit of. We had a block now and again but I did not like to make a habit of it.

However, one day he came in and asked if I wanted any cheese and, as I had recently been to a managers' meeting and been asked by some of my fellow managers to get them some, I reluctantly agreed and ordered six blocks. Claire and I were going out so I informed my assistant if the cheese arrived to put it in the cold cellar. Upon arriving back at the pub my assistant told me the cheese had arrived and it was in the cellar but did I really want that much. I went in the cellar and was aghast to see six packs of cheese each holding six blocks. I could not believe it and we spent the rest of the night calling up my mates asking them to collect their order (and some) right away.

We had over the next twenty-four hours an almost continuous procession of managers coming in to collect their booty and I for one decided that would be the end of my trade in dairy products forthwith! Daft bugger!

We did have one sad occasion: a small boy came into the hotel early one morning and said there was a lady lying in the children's paddling pool. We went out and found an elderly lady fully clothed lying face down in the swimming pool, which was adjacent to the sea.

We called the police and they discovered that she had several hundred pounds in her coat pocket and her false teeth in her hand. I guess she had just had enough of life and she had walked out into the pool and had just laid down. It upset nearly everyone including the children.

I wondered if she had found that perhaps living without her husband had been just too much to bear and had decided to join him. I felt very comforted that evening when Claire and I sat watching the television and for once she held my hand. I guess she must have felt she was pleased that we were both alive with our family and not in that cold water world.

Claire and I were invited to the newest addition to the Courage Empire. A public house situated at Frenchay, Bristol, had been changed into an entertainment centre with a boy meets girl nightclub at the back. It was a grand affair with the resident manager apparently very pleased with his newly acquired addition to his premises. The pub had two bars, one lounge and one public, which were normally used by the darts teams. The new club area at the back had a stage, dance floor, a large bar with an area for serving chicken and chips, sausage and chips and the usual hamburger and chips. There was seating for around one hundred people, and it had plenty of room for people to stand and drink at the bar.

We enjoyed the night and, as we drove back home to the pub, I did feel just a little bit envious of the manager, a chap called Martin.

I was amazed next day to receive a telephone call from the Head Office manager looking after the Snuff Mill pub asking if I would be interested in taking it over? I was speechless for a moment and asked if I had heard him correctly? After all we had just been to the grand opening the night before! It appeared after waiting for one year for the conversion to be completed the manager had decided it was not his 'cup of tea'.

'Yes please,' I replied.

Three managers were asked to attend the interview and after an intense interview with the company taking into consideration my past experience I was asked to assume the mantle of General Manager of the new exciting project. We were on the move - yet again.

Moving to the Snuff Mill had several advantages: it meant that, as a family, we would be that much nearer to Bristol which pleased Claire. Even so, Kim-Ann our eldest did not like the idea; she had made a lot of friends at school and liked living by the sea (if you could call it sea) and she played up so much that she ran away down to the end of the long promenade and Frank, Kevin (who happened to be visiting) and I had to go and look for her. I had to explain that it was a good career move and she would just have to put up with it.

'Okay,' she replied, 'but I'll not forgive you' and she did not for some time. I guess some of the old West stubborn streak was showing even at her young age.

Even living in a public house did nothing to dampen the girls' enthusiasm for the shops of downtown Bristol. Having been born in Bristol, Claire had no problems finding out about the local schools for the three girls and our son. Bristol is a city with a very historic past which goes back to Saxon Times and was at one time actually spelt 'Brisfol' which goes way back to the times of the slave trade. Even now you can see traces of the historic past when you visit places such as Corn Street with its four flat-topped pillars called the 'Nails' used when trading all those years ago. Merchants would strike one of the 'Nails' when a transaction was agreed giving rise to the expression 'to pay on the nail'. I wonder just how many lost souls from the Africas had been bartered for and at what price. It has been said that the Queen's Square, a lovely crescent of houses in the centre of Bristol, had been built mainly from the profits of such a trade.

The Docks now have long given up their trading of silks, and of course human cargo and now the whole dock area has been converted to bars, restaurants, museums, and pleasure trips, all of which give an added attraction to the visitors and residents of Bristol. A more recent addition is the SS Great Britain, the world's first iron-hulled, steam-powered ocean-going ship. After an illustrious career which included a transatlantic passenger service, a troop ship taking service men to the Crimean War, trips to Australia taking the English cricket team, and later used as a coal hulk taking Welsh coal to San Francisco, she ran aground in the Falkland Islands and it was from there in 1970 she was salvaged, refloated and towed back home across the Atlantic to Bristol. It took thirty-five years to complete the painstaking conservation and restoration everyone can now enjoy. It is possible to get married on the ship and to hold exhibitions.

As we drove into the large car park of the Snuff Mill public house to start yet another new 'lifestyle', I thought to myself, I guess the 'Ramblin' Man' is still ramblin'.

The front part of our new pub was already very busy and we were soon able to add considerably to our finances due to the fact that we had the catering franchise for the food. I started looking around for another formula for the club at the back. I did not really like the club name (which also included the front part of the pub) 'The Snuff Mill'. It was not catchy enough; it seemed to lack commercial appeal.

I cannot remember how exactly how we arrived at its new name, but I believe it was finally named after one of the children's pet rabbits which had been called 'Snuffy'. It was a name that would become a household name in Bristol and the rest of the country, well at least with clubgoers.

I arranged a meeting with John, an entertainment agent friend of mine. We decided to try to go big and selected several new acts and also some oldies such as Gerry and the Pacemakers. Advertising was via the local newspaper and the first show which was with Billy J Kramer. Looking out of the pub window at 6.30 p.m. on the Saturday we were surprised to see a long line of people lining up outside the closed club doors. As we never opened before 8 p.m. we were just amazed at the sudden amount of interest.

We opened the doors promptly at 8 p.m. The room was filled within ten minutes, we had no spare seats and when called suddenly into the club I was confronted with approximately thirty large and rather irate ladies who demanded in no uncertain terms that they required a seat! There were none left in the club anywhere. I sent in the staff and we raided the front part of the pub taking all the spare seats available. Needs must!

It was a sell-out and this continued every weekend. Panic set in at Head Office and they quickly arranged some extra seating for our newly acquired clients. Our new clients also were much more selective when it came to eating and soon we had changed the menu to include steaks and much more enticing meals. I managed to get the company to change the name to 'Snuffy's' and we then started opening more nights to suit the demand that came with our newfound fame.

Gerry and the Pacemakers, Joe Brown and his Bruvvers, even The Platters, with Herb Reed (the only original Platter) nevertheless packed out the club, all the week. Bernard Manning was another top draw and even with his sometimes risqué sense of humour the Snuffy's punters could not get enough of him. These acts were a guaranteed box office draw.

Claire and I had the franchise for the catering and we found that we were obliged to take one pound out of the entrance fees to go towards the catering costs. This proved quite a good earner for us because when we put on Dave Lee Travis, a well-known disc jockey, we had one hundred pounds basically for nothing as most of the younger clients did not wish to eat.

We had however been aiming at the older clientele who preferred groups from the sixties so we finally relinquished this arrangement in return for a smaller catering rent charge which suited us much better. The company were taking the risk for the payment of the groups due to the VAT so it was only fair that they took all the entrance money. Fair dues!

Changing the room from a long bar to two smaller ones and larger restaurant area with lights on each table gave our little nightclub a nice intimate feel. People who came added to the atmosphere which was tremendous and when the acts played Snuffy's they received always the best of receptions. I obtained the services of a local professional compère, and with his help we managed to take the old Snuff Mill public house to one of the most talked about 'Nightclubs in the West'. It became a very good profit earner for the company. Roy, our compère was excellent, and we were always playing tricks on each other. One night he was singing 'Singing in the Rain' and asked me to join in! Big mistake on my part because, as soon as I started singing, Roy and the band unleashed several soda siphons on me. I was drenched, and as I squelched off the dance floor to much applause I was silently crying, as I had just purchased the darn suit that day! There must be a better use for soda! What do you do for a laugh?

Crazy Heart...

Hank Williams
You thought she cared for you so acted smart
Go on and break, you crazy heart.

NOT ALL MEN BEHAVE BADLY all of the time; sometimes one gets a good feel for life and what is happening around them. Ken West with his new surroundings, the new challenges which were presented to him, soon found that he could act in a responsible manner. If you give something you generally receive things back two or three fold. I knew we had a chance to not only improve our standard of living but to improve our family lifestyle which could only be for the better. New responsibilities brought with it many hours of hard work, early rises getting the cellar ready for the days work, preparing food for the clients who came in like clockwork ready to be fed and watered: clients who brought us their wants and we were ready to grant their every wish.

Claire not only managed to look after the children, get them ready for school and keep them clean and reasonably happy, but still assisted with the running of the pub. Life can be great especially if you enjoy what you are doing and we really enjoyed the routine which became normal in the West household. Rising early was a must and after the chore of getting the beer cellar ready I could then think about breakfast and perhaps a quick cup of coffee before we had to plan the rest of the day. This generally involved the cash and carry about three times per week as the turnover of food was incredibly fast, but it was a chore that became second nature to us both.

The girls and our son joined an excellent local school and soon we found that our move from the sea to downtown Bristol had certainly been a good one.

No regrets - not yet anyway.

For the first time we were able to work as a team and we worked well together. We even had time to go out some evenings, to events such as the Licensed Victuallers' Balls, which occurred each year.

In addition to this we also had the NALHM which was the National Association for Licensed House Managers. All nice and friendly, well at least while you were within earshot. I remember one of my friendly fellow managers informing some of the other managers that I would last only three months at Snuffy's. After my first three months was up I mentioned to him that perhaps I was on borrowed time and would he like to tender another leaving date I could work to. I enjoyed the look on his face but after that we became firm friends. We found days became weeks and weeks turned into months; the time seemed to fly by, and soon we had our first Christmas at the Club.

I had long ago managed to get the children to act in a similar way that my father and mother encouraged me to do: wait for your presents until after tea and the only change was they could have one present to open on Christmas Day morning. Hard? Not really because they knew that one thing I was generous with was my gifts for everyone, and they certainly got used to receiving nearly everything that was on their 'Father Christmas' list. Not that there was total belief – well none really; with the children being twelve to sixteen years of age, it would have been difficult for such a nice dream to still exist. As for myself I did not have a repeat of the late Christmas present which I had received all those months before with Patricia and her sudden strip tease! I still felt very strange when I infrequently drove past her house; Patricia was not a girl you could forget altogether. However, the past was the past and when the water has gone under the bridge it is gone and no one can bring it back and one should not even try.

The wealth of the family improved considerably and it reached the point when any special occasion gifts were not that small and normally took the form of a new car or a nice diamond bracelet.

When I had a guilty conscience which was often, and when such feelings surfaced, the whole family, especially Claire, benefitted and who, knowing the full circumstances, would have denied her anything.

I had been encouraged to be a manager and that meant one had to actually manage! Top Rank, like the American Air Force just expected you to cope with the normal things which came under the job description that you signed up to.

While we had good staff we needed key personnel who could, and would, step in and take control when Claire and I were absent. Richard, a family friend, was such a person. He was a natural leader and even being connected to banking I guess he enjoyed just being involved with the entertainment and getting involved with us running the centre. He would become a key person in our lives as time went by.

We had many indoor romances taking place at Snuffy's: we had two chefs Terry and Sandra, who met over the hot plate and then decided to take things further and kept things sizzling after hours. Many wedding receptions took place at Snuffy's, but theirs fortunately did not, which made it easier for us to attend. Later this specially conceived 'Hot Plate' marriage is still going strong; well at least they are still living under same roof which is more than can be said for some of us!

A lot of people think that running a large entertainment centre is difficult due to the amount of people you need to run it. If you are able to manage correctly and plan it well, it is much easier to run than the normal sized pub or business. Not a lot of people know that - thank you, Michael Caine. We used to open the club at 8 p.m. and I, in my dress suit of course, was the 'mine host': if you ensured the staff worked well, no problems!

The 'bigger' the act the more 'friends' you seemed to have as they arrived suddenly to see how we were getting on! They could never have free seats though; they were only for the paying customers, and if you did not balance the fees of the entertainers you would not last long. There are things that are important in the club business – good nights and bad nights. Good nights equal full houses and of course bad nights – ugh.

As long as the week's takings balance out everything is okay, with the exception of the amount of drink you tend to absorb. I was of course, a master of absorbing drink – well, Canadian Club, that is. Was I getting to like it just a little bit too much? The hours in running a pub and club are considerable and it must be acknowledged that bringing up a family does not help and Claire did get tired a lot. I found that many nights when the club had been exceptionally busy I would be the last to climb the stairs only to find the rest of the family were already in bed. This was understandable but nevertheless I began to feel just a little bit alone. No one to talk with about the night's events and it became normal to have to recant what had happened the following morning if you had the time, which in many cases we did not have. Occasionally we were able to sit down and watch TV with the children but these times would invariably be interrupted by staff who wanted answers to customers' enquiries.

It must be said that Claire always put the family first and the job second.

Me, I was still a person eager for the excitement of entertainment and all that went with it!

The after-hours drinking increased with me and the staff who stayed late with the acts, which was customary to do after a good night. We were just finishing off after most of the staff had gone home and I was playing spoof with the doorman. Carol, one of the barmaids, was serving and, while giving me some change after I had lost at spoof, pressed my fingers at the same time. I looked at her and she smiled: a smile which was to set me thinking.

I was wondering why she had done this; after all she had worked for me for over a year without any inclination that she liked me particularly. This should have been the end to it but no, I needed to know more, so when she came in the next evening I asked her to explain the night before.

All Carol said was, did I fancy a drink sometime outside the club? I just replied, 'Maybe' and left it at that. I was quite flattered at this sudden attention. Carol was married and had worked for me for over a year and had always been a quiet and seemingly respectable young lady with, if I remember rightly, a daughter about two years of age. Was she getting a three-year itch? Either way, I was not window-shopping, so why was I even thinking about making plans to meet this quite delectable young lady who, when she walked, had a wiggle that could only be described as sexy! What am I saying? Had I noticed this even before the hand squeezing event had taken place?

For years I had conveniently put the blame for everything at Pauline's door, and also I had blamed Shirley for opting out of our previous marriage, hurting poor Airman West's feelings and dumping him. I just could not go on making excuses for what was quickly becoming a serial occurrence. Even I, in my ever self-deluding sense of betrayal could not make any more excuses for my actions. At last the penny dropped and one might say it was about time too, but that is life and one can go through it making all the convenient excuses imaginable but one day you just have to admit to yourself that you have become a not very nice person. However, what was about to happen next would not be to my liking!

Carol and I started an intense affair that can only be described as very physical. We met twice a week and always in the afternoon. The local hotels were always handy for such trysts and seemingly with money to burn it was nothing for me to pay for my extramarital pleasures. I enjoyed the excitement of the intrigue and of course all that went with it. It went on for a few months before the inevitable happened. Carol started getting serious and when a wife stops allowing her husband conjugal rights something has to give. For my part I had no such problem after returning from my day out. I just had a bath before the night's work and literally washed my sordid actions out of my hair! Could be a name for a song, that one!

I was having a great night. I was standing at the bar being the usual 'mine host', drinks were aplenty and had been all day. All the staff was working well; it was Saturday night and we were buzzing.

I suddenly noticed that Carol seemed upset and, taking her to one side, I found out that she had had a few words with her husband who happened to be there. I was rather concerned, was it about us? No, not really, he was just fed up with her actions or lack of them maybe. Who could blame him?

I guess fate took a hand then which is often the case when worlds appear to fall apart and I then did one of the most stupid things I had ever done in my life! It was just about the end of the evening and Richard came up and said he would pay the staff their wages which I had made up earlier. Good old Richard, always dependable, never drunk or even tipsy – ever.

Me, I was filled with goodwill and most likely, as I was soon to realise, Canadian Club! Carol came up again she was rather tearful; her husband had gone off home in a foul temper.

I then did an amazing thing and one that I would live to regret, maybe for the rest of my life.

'Don't worry,' I said, 'we'll go for a drive' and led her out of the back entrance to where my car was conveniently parked. Carol looked at me questioningly, she was stone-cold sober. What on earth was I doing or suggesting? We got into my car, drove out of the car park, turned left, to go God knows where. I did not have a clue. I had left the club on a Saturday night, admittedly by now almost empty, I had left my wife upstairs awaiting my return, and my children asleep, so I could expect that someone might just start wondering where the boss had gone and, for goodness sake, Carol as well.

Evidently no one at that time thought anything was amiss. I continued driving up the road which would eventually lead to the M5 motorway. If I had just gone around the roundabout and returned to the club no one would have been any the wiser. Even if someone had seen us return, I could have just passed it off as taking Carol to pick her car up or something daft like that. After all, we would have been gone less than three minutes. No, Ken West was just being his usual stubborn self and would show everyone that Carol and he were apparently above any reproach and he did not like his 'lady' being upset. He did not even consider just how many people even knew about their little secret. Now, through his own stupidity, his lack of ability to realise right from wrong, he was about to make an announcement not only to his wife and family, but also to the staff and Carol's husband, so that the affair with Carol was soon to be public knowledge. Alcohol had apparently taken over his senses completely, and now he was proving a point but to whom? No one was pushing for answers at that time. The small divide between drinking sensibly and drinking out of control had been breached! To say the least!

Within minutes we had reached the roundabout which would become a crossroad that was to become a thorn in the Top Gun's side. We actually hit the roundabout and turned towards the motorway entrance leading south.

Carol spoke quietly suggesting that perhaps this was not a wise thing for us to be doing.

I just laughed. 'Serve them right, see their faces when they wake up and find us gone!'

Wake up! They had not even been to bed. For the first time in my life I was completely out of control! My befuddled mind was in overdrive, I didn't care what I was doing, I was escaping from the rat race, I was almost hysterical as I drove at high speed south on the M5, laughing like a maniac and just enjoying my own personal demented state.

Carol was not at all sure about it, she still questioned the wisdom of our actions or rather mine. I guess that she wanted this to happen eventually, but surely not this way, which was madness in the extreme. She realised that I was at the very least drunk and not in complete control of my senses. Here was her lover who was showing quite a different side to his normally controlled self. As the miles sped by and the club got further and further away, the chance of averting the inevitable crisis disappeared with the spent miles. Ken West, the man who knew all the answers, had apparently lost all his marbles!

Arriving in Exeter we found a convenient motel and booked in. I was doing one thing and that was sobering up, but rather slowly!

We woke up to just about the worst morning of our lives. Carol was now worried about her daughter who had been conveniently forgotten by both the runaway lovers. It was decided to contact home.

It appeared that Carol's husband and his three brothers had taken up residence in my top floor apartment the night before and of course by now all parties knew of the whole sordid affair. Claire and Richard, the husband in question, compared notes and even worked out the exact days the trysts must have taken place.

Of course, not a pretty fate was waiting for us back in Bristol, but what on earth were we going to do? I had, of course, access to cash, but walking away from what was most likely the best employment I had ever had in my life was clearly madness!

The full realisation of my actions came home to roost: why on earth had I done this stupid and utterly crazy thing and for what reason? A night of passion! What passion? Passion had not even been on the agenda when we left!

We got up at dawn, 5 a.m., and in the early morning sunshine we got in the car almost as if we were in a dream. We drove even further south, as if we were searching for an alternative direction to take. I almost expected Claire and Carol's husband to appear at anytime. We finished up at a small seaside town called Brixham, a lovely seaside town, the beauty of which at that moment was lost on the both of us. We sat, talked, and watched the water swirling around the rocks on the nearby beach. If it had been any other time it would have been idyllic but now this lovely scene did not register in any way to either of us. It was almost as if we were in another time dimension; people were getting up and going to work as if it was just another day. This was certainly not just another day for us; it was a nightmare. If only we were both asleep, then we could just go about our normal day's work: looking after the pub and club, going to the cash and carry or, in Carol's normal life, looking after her two-year-old daughter. Not to mention her husband. . This unfortunately was for real and we suddenly experienced great fear and unforgettable remorse, but it was a bit late for all that!

We both realised that we had no option but to go back and face the music. This meant facing an irate wife and an even more irate husband, and his brothers, who had all joined in the hunt for the wayward wife and her lover. Good God, West, the man who apparently knew all the answers was about to find out some real home truths. We drove back to Bristol scarcely saying a word to each other.

Carol's car had been collected by her family, so I dropped her off at what I must admit was a safe distance from her house and I drove back to the club to face the music. I did not know what to expect; perhaps the husband or the odd brother. I closed my mind to the possible connotations. It was still relatively early and I quietly let myself in by the side entrance only to be confronted by a very evil-looking Claire.

She was quite calm about it, just stating that I would be receiving a visit from the clan and I should prepare myself for that. Crazy, I never expected this calm response. I started working, but not without some apprehension, I must admit, waiting for the entrance of the hurt parties. Nobody came; it seemed Carol had gone home and somehow calmed her husband down with a tale that I had a weak heart! It was perhaps lucky for me that he even believed it.

Then a strange thing happened: Claire became attentive and very affectionate! I could not understand her reaction to my disgraceful behaviour! I, for my part, was relieved to say the least. It appeared I had got away with my stupid behaviour without a good thrashing, or too many recriminations from Claire, and I still had my job. Of course rumours were abounding, with the doormen spreading the news to anyone who would listen.

Many of the staff arrived and were greatly surprised to see me in situ and Claire still talking to me. I guess they just could not understand it if all that had been said was true. For my part I was being the ideal husband and Claire was, for her part, a dutiful wife, or so it seemed. I just ignored the looks and the questions that were asked of me and laughed them off saying that we were just messing around. God, what a fool, what an utter fool! Claire did ask what an earth was I thinking of, what had possessed me to do such a thing. Was our marriage that bad? All I could come up with was that I felt alone! She replied, 'How could you be alone amongst all these people?' I could only reply, 'Exactly.'

I did not quite get away without some reaction from Head Office. Shortly afterwards the area manager came in and suggested we walk around the outside of the premises as if to do an inspection tour.

I knew what was coming, so when he asked if the rumours were true I just remarked that it was a misunderstanding and obviously Claire and I were together – people just made things up to be spiteful.

I refrained from drinking other than the occasional glass of wine and things soon settled down to as normal as they could be under the circumstances. Claire took it to heart that perhaps if a man strays it could be for a reason. That, however, did not make me feel any better.

I guess that Carol's phone call also did not help matters when she rang me on the private phone to see if I still felt the same way? I was of course in full remission with Claire and had to tell her I did not want to rekindle our affair. Claire came in while I was on the phone and I had no choice but to give the phone to her, or rather she just took it from me and gave Carol a few well chosen words.

Carol, understandably stung by my rejection, related back to Claire that I had of course been involved with other ladies before. I guess I should not have told her about Patricia: that did shake Claire, and of course we had a few rows about that! Goodness, what do they say about a woman scorned? Talk about chickens coming home to roost. About time too, many would say!

I was a cat with nine lives and, according to my own calculations, I had exceeded more than was lucky for me!

Move It On Over

Hank Williams
Came in last night at half past ten
That baby of mine would not let me in
So move it on over, move it on over
Move over, little dog, cos the big dog is movin' in.

The atmosphere at Snuffy's on a cabaret night could only be described as electric – most nights. The Platters were just sensational. Herb Reed was the only one left touring from the original Platters who had stormed the 60s with such melodies such as 'Only You', 'Smoke Gets in Your Eyes' and, of course, 'The Great Pretender', just classics. Their manager was a unique character: Chic Murphy, a handsome man with all the trappings of show business, gold medallion and all, who would always accompany the group wherever they played.

One night he arrived along with John the agent as the group were having a soundcheck. We all had dinner together and after the show Chic departed, back to his house on the Thames at Windsor. The Platters were playing for four nights so on those nights we were always late getting to bed, normally around 2.30 a.m. I was surprised when the phone rang and a voice sounding very secretive asked, 'Ken?'

I recognised the voice immediately, softly spoken with a London accent. 'Yes, Chic, what's up?' I replied.

'Got a nice baby grand - interested?' asked Chic.

'You've got a what?' I answered, still a bit sleepy as it was now nearer 3 a.m. and I really wanted to get to bed.

'Baby grand, fantastic condition, burgundy, you can have it for a grand!' came the reply.

Now I did not know much about pianos especially baby grands, but I knew they were not cheap. I was a little bit on the spot as I had told Chic earlier that Claire and I collected antiques etc and like to buy and sell.

I passed the buck and asked Claire who was by now wondering what was going on.

'Chic's got a baby grand for sale; do you want to buy it?'

Claire thought and replied, 'Well it would be nice for the children.'

So I said, 'Okay, Chic, we'll have it.'

Just like that - we had purchased a piano at 3 a.m. from a guy we hardly knew and without even seeing it. It was just like buying a can of peas!

'Great, I'll send it down, just pay the man readies, OK, mate?'

I replaced the receiver and, with a bemused look at Claire, asked her where the heck would we put it. I did not want to put a baby grand in the club; it would not last five minutes in that atmosphere. We decided it would go upstairs in the lounge and then perhaps the children could practise on it. Ha, some hopes!

At twelve noon the next day, a large truck arrived at the club with two large men who lifted the piano out and took it upstairs just as if it was a crate of oranges. It was a lovely piece of furniture if nothing else, absolutely fantastic.

We paid the man the money and got a receipt (just in case) and after a couple of beers they left. I was rather taken aback by our actions. We had not even mentioned buying anything like a piano but there we were looking at a piano that was taking up a fair bit of space and looking right out of place in our present lounge arrangement. It should really be in a classy house, perhaps with some chandeliers hanging above it. I guess it had been hard to say no to such a character as Chic, which was unusual for me as I had always prided myself on speaking my mind. Still, there was no way I was going to be able to send it back!

We were at Blazers Nightclub a few weeks later when my mobile rang. It was Chic who informed me he still had the piano seat that went with the piano and could I collect it straightaway. He would be at a motorway exit four miles away. It was 11.30 at night. What a time to call up!

John Mills agreed to go with me. We arrived at the motorway exit and I said to John, 'Funny place to meet.'

John was about to answer when a huge black limousine drew up in front of us. I expected Chic to get out but instead two huge men in black overcoats emerged and opened the car boot. It looked as if they had stepped out from the 1920s; all that was missing was a couple of tommy guns slung over their shoulders. They proceeded to take out what we knew was the seat but anyone else who might be seeing this strange happening on the lay-by of the M4, almost in the middle of the night, could be excused for thinking it might be a coffin or something.

The two men put the seat in my station wagon and, without a word, just got back in the car and left. John and I looked at each other; only Chic would grandstand such an event. I was a little perturbed with the theatrical setting we had just witnessed and I did wonder if any part of this was 'dodgy'?

Going back to the club, John and I discussed it briefly and put it down to Chic's born showmanship. We could only trust this crazy, very likeable individual who was now part of our 'showbiz' lives. I know that John shared my belief that Chic, as loveable as he was, had an air of being a 'Gentleman of the Night!'

About this time Claire and I took a stand in the Antique Market at Bristol. We both loved the thrill of buying and selling and were fortunate to have been taught many things about antiques by Marlene, a lovely lady with much experience in the antiques field. All our spare money went into our newfound business, and it was a business.

You cannot play at antiques, you need to keep at it almost daily and feel the buzz that grasps you when you see lovely old items which have been passed down by long forgotten families. You get a feel for nice items which, in a lot of cases, seem to be looking for a new home. Problem was, of course, we were there to buy and sell, not buy and keep! Marlene taught Claire and me for some time, and then she would test us on certain items that came into the market. What would I pay for this and that? I guess I must have been a quick learner as usual because she said I had a good eye for a bargain. The problem was, that was the story of my life to date; I just loved old things and unfortunately new acquisitions as well, and whatever 'shape' they came in.

Claire and I continued to work at our stall, which was just inside the front of the Antique Market, so we normally got first choice for any items which were offered, although, of course, the rest of the stall owners had their own suppliers and regular customers.

We purchased rings, porcelain and clocks, well, just about anything that we fancied. Our stock levels grew almost daily. I started dealing in clocks and would buy just about any clock that was offered. I found a good clock repairer who lived and worked in Clifton and after a while I found it best to purchase from him at a good price and 'sell on' in the market. David, the repairer, could not get over just how much more I could make on the clocks he sold to me.

One day I was on the stand when a gentleman, who I later found out was German, came in and started looking at my collection of clocks.

He indicated, 'May I?' meaning he wanted to look closer at some of the clocks.

He came onto the stand and proceeded to place one clock after the other on the outside of the stand. I just sat there mesmerised, what was this strange man doing with my stock; he can't be meaning to purchase all these clocks? He finally finished sorting out his wants and then said, 'How much?'

I worked out the total cost with the customary discounts of course. It came to £750 which was a lot in those days. In fact, it is not too bad nowadays.

At 6.30 p.m. and end of business I decided I needed a drink and with all this money burning a hole in my pocket I went to see Ali, owner of a local wine bar that was just a few doors up.

Ali was a great character who was Persian with many of the gentle ways of his race. He was about six feet four inches tall and very athletic.

He was extremely skilled in karate and such like and when he walked it was almost as though he was walking on air. We had several drinks together before I returned home to a not too pleased Claire. Where had I been? What was I doing coming home at this hour? It was only 7.30 p.m.

I was filled with horror at what she was saying; rightly or wrongly she had destroyed my entrance with all this money in my pocket. I was crestfallen, the moment had gone. I pulled the wad of notes out of my pocket and threw them in her direction.

The notes cascaded down in front of her and for a moment I enjoyed the look of amazement on her face. I had made my point but why did we spoil a moment that should have been a happy one for us both. I guess, having said that, with my past history of betrayal, who could blame her for thinking that I might just be up to my old tricks! Oh well, comme ci, comme ca.

One day I was sitting in my little perch in the front of the Antique Market just enjoying the peace and quiet of the moment. Claire and I often competed to go to the market and I had managed to bribe her with some new shoes. Never fails, does that! I guess that both of us used the work as a pleasant way of relaxing. Suddenly I was startled by the movement of two men running past the shop with Ali in close pursuit.

Ali was running like a gazelle, he seemed to run just like we had seen in the movie 'Chariots of Fire' but certainly not in slow motion.

I ran to the front entrance and looked in the direction that Ali and the two men had gone. He had caught the two men who had realized the game was up, well at least the running part. He did an incredible thing; he had approached the men from the rear and, as if by magic, he placed both his hands over the top of each man's head and put two fingers from each hand up the nostrils of each of them. He then just lifted the men up from the pavement! Absolutely amazing! The men had done a runner from his wine bar without paying and Ali, like the two greyhounds that had run and seized my poor cat years ago, had just proven too fast an adversary. He frogmarched them both to his wine bar where they meekly paid up. Well done, Ali.

The Antique Market became an integral part of our working life with one of us working a few days at a time at the stand. Eventually we were making enough out of this business to employ one of the professional ladies who were connected with the market. Many of these were married ladies who were just interested in being part of the buzz of working at the market rather than the payment they actually received.

We continued to run the pub and nightclub and even managed to enjoy the social life that went with it. It became second nature to book the acts and get the club ready for the evening's entertainment. The set-up with the club was rather fixed when it came to numbers of seats available: some could easily be changed with a stool added here and there but if clients had expressed a desire to dine we had to allow a lot of extra room for this to occur.

Roy, our resident compère, always managed to do a magnificent job compèring at the club. He used to sing all the old favourites: 'Down at the

Old Bull and Bush' and such like. He had the clientele swaying in time with the music, singing to their hearts' content. It was always essential to set the scene even for the biggest acts and Roy, who was a local guy from Bristol, had that gift which he always managed to communicate with his audience.

It was with great sorrow that I learnt some years later that Roy passed away suddenly without any apparent prior illness. I can honestly say I can never not think of the club without thinking and admiring just how Roy set the scene for many of the most successful entertainment evenings at Snuffy's. A great talent sadly missed.

I'm A Long Gone Daddy...

Hank Williams
All you want to do is sit around and pout
And now I got enough, so I am getting out.

I HAD THE CHANCE TO take Claire away to Paris, with John Mills and his wife. I booked the flights and we set off. We both enjoyed the break and even went to the Moulin Rouge to see the ladies with the big boobies. Three days with nothing to worry about and to relax from the pressure of running a busy centre and perhaps get away from the few rumours that still persisted but which we hoped would eventually die out.

The children were growing up fast and doing well at school and Kim-Ann started courting one of the local boys.

They seemed to get on well and Richard was generally accepted as her boyfriend by all the family including Claire. I quite liked Richard; he was a hard-working lad who worked for the husband of one of the staff, Margaret, who had became firm friend with Claire and they would often have a chat and a cup of tea.

It was about this time that my mother and father decided to return to the UK from the USA. They arrived at Southampton. After a brief stay with us they went down to Pencoed where my brother was still building his houses. By now he had separated from and divorced his wife, remarried and was living in Pencoed. Claire and I had made up our differences with him, blood is thicker than water, and we had visited him and his new wife. We had no problems with her as she was his choice and what will be, will be. I had heard that before somewhere.

My father arrived at the right time for my brother. He was short of money and my father lent him six thousand pounds which he used to bridge the gap and three thousand of this was going to be for my father and mother for Derek to build a new house for them.

I was a bit disappointed with my father and mother at being so far away. However, things took a turn for the worse when my mother and father fell out with my brother over his reluctance to give up the actual deeds of the house they had bought and paid for. It was then decided that they would sell their newly built house and move back over the Severn Bridge to Weston Super Mare, a seaside resort which was nice for them. My father summed up things in his normal way stating that my brother was an 's....' and he would have nothing more to do with him.

Same old Dad, nothing came before his sense of what was proper. He must have wondered where he went wrong, what with Derek, me, and then Coral, who also had got divorced from Hank.

To complete the circle my other sister Rosslyn also got divorced and stayed over in the States with her new husband. Gosh, the West family were getting in a state when it came to marriages or rather staying in them! My mother and father liked visiting the club and they enjoyed many evenings having dinner and watching the shows. It was a nice time of life for part of the West family and one I always like to recall.

I owed a lot to my mother and father and with them approaching their senior years I still had much respect for them. I wonder how families lose this respect so quickly today. I was very grateful that Claire never discussed or informed my parents of my midnight ride down south. In her own personal distress, she as usual, had shown real dignity.

I could not in all honesty have explained to my mother and father how this had come about because as far as my father was concerned I knew his opinion would be that I was completely out of order and needed my head examined! Dad's view of right and wrong would never change.

For me, I must have missed that lesson and could only put my hand up for acting not only like a louse but also a bloody fool!

Claire and I decided to purchase another house which was situated close to the beach at Brean Down. We called it Fawlty Towers due to its castle-like turrets. We both loved its quaintness and we spent a lot of money doing it up, building an extension and installing a modern kitchen, all in keeping with its old style. I managed to acquire a 1934 Daimler, and we spent many hours restoring this lovely car to its original state. The children loved sitting in the back using the Speakeasy tube to call the driver's seat at the front. It gave you a brief sense of being royalty.

We purchased an Edwardian chair and many other antiques to put in the house. It was to be our retirement home, and a place to visit and relax when we found the time. The children, of course, after the initial interest, soon found other more interesting things to do and we found that often we spent our spare time there on our own.

The club still took up much of our time and we made many friends with the acts. We met some crazy guys. One in particular started his act with a car bumper which he held up and said would the owner move their car as it was in the way. Daft sod! 'Bright and Breeze' were also great favourites with the punters and when poor old Elvis died, the 'Bright' side of the partnership sat down and wrote a song that asked who had got Elvis's guitar. I told him if he sang it at the next performance he would certainly be lynched. He never did sing it in the club but I know he did record it on tape. We also had a great night once with Bernie Clifton who used to have a great finish to his hilarious comedy act. After taking a lot of stick from him, Roy, the band, and I decided to get him with small flour bombs on his final spot.

As the spotlight narrowed just to show his face, we hit him from all sides. He was of course smothered in flour all over his face. He then exclaimed, 'Right – war' and proceeded to use his fire extinguisher (which was part of his act) on all of us. It was all in good fun but after the show had finished and the audience had gone home he came back to us with a few 'borrowed' flour bombs that he had got from Claire. We of course reciprocated and a flour war broke out; everyone was smothered with flour again. Of course, I decided to go that one step further and got a new two-pound bag of flour from the store room; I chased after Bernie, missed him completely and hit the wall of the club. I then realised that as usual I had gone that much further and had to spend the rest of the night cleaning flour off the walls.

Another 'told you so' from my mother would have been very apt!

As another year ended we went into the New Year with the usual celebrations. Our New Year's Eve parties were always great. We were hoping that the good times would continue, but rumours were circulating about yet another brewery takeover. We heard that, just maybe, a company who dealt mainly in catering was interested in taking over the Brewery's larger venues, such as Snuffy's. We started worrying that our golden goose was about to be hijacked and we would be excess to requirements – again. Either way, nothing happened for a while, but I did ask the area manager to let me know what was happening; if they did want to dispose of the building I would be interested in making an offer to rent it as a tenant licensee.

At about this time we had a bit of luck on the football pools, not a lot as it goes, but still a win. Claire and I had been away on holiday and were on our way home when Richard, our friend looking after the family, had checked the pools for us and found we had won over four and half thousand pounds. Claire decided she would like to visit her sister in America again, so we made plans for her visit which would be for six weeks or more. My share was going to go on paying the VAT! Nice one!

I was envious. I wanted to return to the US, I wanted to relive some of my youth and sample again the American cheeseburger and experience some of the old feelings of excitement. (As if I had not had enough over the last couple of years). Either way, after putting Claire on the plane at Heathrow, I did feel more than a little disappointed but I could not justify any more time off. Claire was a different matter; as she was officially only hired (part-time) under different terms of employment. I returned to the pub, back to work doing what I liked to do: entertaining people, but who would entertain me!

It was about this time that I received the distressing news that my father had suffered a stroke and was not at all well. He was taken to Weston Hospital and stayed there for several weeks.

Returning home, he managed to recover his speech and the hand movements he had lost after suffering the stroke. I suddenly realised that my parents, especially my father, were entering into most likely the final stages of their lives and I would eventually lose a vital part of my life, a thought that was most distressing to me. I did, however, start to visit my parents more often and was pleased when my father seemed to recover all his faculties. My only concern was that there was a distinct possibility he could suffer another one within a very short space of time.

As the days grew into weeks I found myself missing Claire and almost envying some of the staff as they made their way home to their prospective spouses. They seemed so eager to return home after a busy night's work. For my part, I just went upstairs to the darkened apartment and after a cup of coffee went to bed on my own. It was silly really, but how can you be so alone with so many people around you. Ken West was starting to feel sorry for himself again, which really was quite a silly thing to do. The warning signs were showing, but as usual I ignored these.

Claire extended her visit in the United States and I found myself wanting to seek out some light relief. I think that is what a man or woman does when they want to make excuses for what they are about to do.

Rachel had a nice walk and was always flirting with all the male staff. I liked her a lot, but being a reformed character I had just looked on; well, you know, just taking a friendly interest in my staff. Rachel had joined the staff nearly three years ago with her friend Lisa. Both had the most amazing hair that seemed to glisten in the light. Both also had nice figures but up to this time I really had not taken too much notice of either of them. Poor lonely Ken, left on his own and no toys to play with! Lisa had left to have a baby so was absent for part of the three years from when they had first joined the staff.

I guess all my good intentions, all the good sense of well-being, and not risking my family, would soon to be put into jeopardy - again. Rachel and I started going out for an occasional drink and then things developed into an affair similar to what I had started in my London days. However, this time with a member of staff, one of the self-imposed rules that I had adopted many years ago. We even managed a trip to London to see of one of the shows – Fiddler on the Roof - with Topol. Again! It was almost as if the leopard was returning to his lair again. It certainly was not shedding any of its spots.

Oh, the old times came back with a vengeance, memories of Maria flooded back, but now here I was in London with another girl, same show. Staying over in London was only made possible through a few well constructed lies by me to Richard. Why I was hell-bent on pursuing this disastrous way forward, even to the copying of going to the same show. A psychiatrist would have a field day observing and commenting on such behaviour. Why I needed to relive the past in such detail! I liked the show immensely but twice in such short time? Was it just that I needed to share the good times again? Was it not true I already had the good times that I had apparently yearned for all my earlier life?

Rachel had actually split from her husband due to illness; him, not Rachel. She was not at all ill and she certainly enjoyed her time in London with special attention to our spacious room and bed. Rachel was more than window-shopping; she wanted more. Shortly after the trip to London, I had to tell her that I was no way able to take the relationship further. We had agreed from day one that our relationship would only be on a casual basis but of course a lot of ladies do get romantic notions, and they have to be acted on.

With the door firmly closed, she started to look elsewhere for her way forward. I, for my part, could understand this and consoled myself by dating her (newly returned) friend Lisa.

The extremely lucky escape that I had experienced a few years ago seemed to have been dropped conveniently from my memory bank. The near miss of receiving a possible beating by an irate husband and his brothers seemed to have faded like the March wind. Perhaps Ken West had just neatly filed that away as being part of his personal good fortune that went with his present state of well-being. Ken West, the man of the moment, could do no wrong. Didn't past events prove it?

With the writing on the wall, with danger signs already for everyone to see, Ken West continued on his merry way.

The weeks continued to slip by and I just shrugged off my latest actions as 'just a bit of a fling'. I did not however, continue with this latest 'fling' without feelings of guilt taking over and I found myself breaking dates and 'working' a lot. The relationship nonetheless seemed to survive these bouts of conscience on my part and when Claire eventually returned I was still having a 'bit of a fling'. Would this person never learn? I guess Confucius summed it up correctly when he said parts of your anatomy have no conscience, to put it bluntly.

Why Should We Try Anymore...

Hank Williams
What's the use to deny we've been living a lie?
That we should admitted before
We were just victims of a half-hearted love
So why should we try anymore.

It should have been quite apparent to me by now that I had lost the plot. I was completely in free fall, easily adopting a way of life which was certainly the direct opposite of what I had been taught.

The youngster brought up in Reading, to know right from wrong by a mother and father who could not be faulted, and the time in the Air Force, which although not without its emotional problems did not differ from the teachings of the correct way of doing things. I would never have dreamt of going out of my way to hurt anyone, well, not without being attacked first. I know I had neatly dodged the responsibility of having a child all those years ago, but could I be blamed for that? I was asked to comply with the mother's wishes and I had agreed. I had obviously taken the easy option that day. I had continued for years to blame everyone with the exception of myself. It seemed that I had adopted a gung-ho approach with my newly found position of centre manager in London and, certainly with the newfound success, I had steadily become extremely arrogant. This did not explain however the complete deceit that started in London and continued almost unabated over the coming years.

I had found a good partner in Claire, we had produced four great children who we both loved, but suddenly even this was apparently not good enough for Top Gun West!

Claire arrived back and rather surprised me when she said she had missed me terribly. The children were pleased to see her and after a few days rest to get over the jet lag she soon became immersed in the running of the family and helping with the pub and club. It is strange; when you feel that you are doing quite well fooling everybody then you come down with a bump! I had sold some furniture to Rachel (just before we split) and got a good price (I thought) of forty pounds. Claire suddenly announced that she thought it surprising that I had sold it to her and I must have had an ulterior motive for doing this. She all but accused me of carrying on with Rachel, which of course would not have been too far short of the truth. Perhaps she had received some information from a friend or someone but I could not understand this as Rachel had not told any of her fellow workmates that she was even seeing me.

Perhaps Claire had had a sixth sense but as Rachel had already left our employment it nevertheless made me rather nervous.

I remember Claire coming down to the club one evening and standing beside, of all people, Lisa, and when she started remarking it was strange Rachel had left so suddenly and perhaps I had been seeing her, Lisa must have turned all colours as she was by then very much involved with me. Not a nice thing to happen to Claire, but as they say ignorance is sometimes bliss!

We received some news that we had secretly been dreading. We were to have a visit from a group of architects who wanted to look over the premises, front and back! They arrived and within minutes they left just as quickly as they had come. They had seen enough. What did it mean? We learnt soon enough. Imperial Inns had been taken over by a large company and they were intent on one thing, turning places like Snuffy's into family eating houses. It was the latest fad which was now sweeping the country.

We were informed that in a few months we would all lose our employment and would have to re-apply for a new position, (if your face suited).

I could not wait for this so I started looking around. I was informed by a friend of mine that the owner of a cabaret club in Usk wanted to sell and I went over to see him. I liked what I saw and found out the asking price. It had six hundred seats, which was twice the size of Snuffy's, a large bar in the front, and it also had ten chalets for renting out. It had a built-in disco, large stage and of course a large dance area and catering kitchen…I liked it immediately and set about arranging the finance for the purchase.

I went to see the managing director of the 'free house' side of the brewery and, as luck would have it, he knew of the work I had been doing at Snuffy's. With a barrelage of over five hundred barrels of beer per annum he was very interested in doing business with me and offered over half the purchase price with a very good price for further supplies.

It was a very good deal; perhaps at last we could make the natural move from being a manager to being a tenant.

I was deep in these negotiations when I had a surprise visitor: my brother Derek and he had just arrived (on crutches) from Canada where he had gone to live when he sold up his business a few years beforehand. I had heard something about it but since I had not been informed directly I was unsure of the details. He informed me that he had been quite poorly with a hidden abscess between his back and his stomach! Only a proper scan had revealed his problem and now fortunately he was on the mend. After a few hours he learnt what I was intending and asked if it was possible to come into the deal.

I must admit I really liked the idea as it would mean less cash injection by me and not so much being borrowed. In addition to this, my brother's building experience would be a fantastic plus for the business as I knew the club would certainly be needing repairs now and in the future.

We shook hands and I informed my bank manager of the changes and he welcomed my brother's input into the business. We paid the deposit and started getting the final monies in place for the move to the club. My brother arranged for his belongings to be shipped back from Canada and put these in storage prior to the big day. As his wife Joan had family at Pencoed, in South Wales, it was handy for them to stay there and commute back to Usk and Bristol for the numerous meetings. It was a joint venture, I would be the director of the entertainment side and he would be financial director and in charge of buildings. Great on paper but would it work out. I could not see any reason why it should not.

At this time, my trysts with Lisa were restricted to the occasional night out, and it was agreed that once I moved then of course our relationship would cease. It would not be at all practical, not least because of the location. We both agreed that it had been a nice time, but like all nice things they do come to an end.

I used to go out for a drink sometimes with one of the doormen Luke, and in turn we both used to act as each other's alibi. Naughty, but nice!

I was sitting by the private phone, having just decided with Luke not to go out at all when the phone rang. It was Lisa asking if we could meet.

I was not happy; I was just about brain dead with all the financial meetings and visits to the new club.

I really did not feel like going out. I agreed, not with too much enthusiasm, but Lisa said we would soon be going our separate ways and it would be nice to have one last night out together. I left the pub with a sense of dread which I could not explain; just a sense of foreboding which I did not feel right about.

I also then made a major error: thinking Luke was staying in and not going out, I didn't check with him. Lisa and I went out for our last evening together and drove out in the country pub where we sat and talked and basically confirmed that we should and would end the relationship which we had been pursuing for the last few months. Lisa had too many responsibilities of her own and I would hopefully have a busy time with the new club.

We drove back to the meeting place, where she used to park her car. I kissed her good night and watched her car leave the car park and speed off into the night. I also noticed another car leaving as well but did not think anything of it. I returned to the pub and went upstairs. I asked where Claire was but my daughter Kim-Ann could not tell me as she had just come in herself. I sat and watched TV and when Claire came upstairs I just said the usual 'Hullo.' Claire asked me if I had had a nice time to which I replied, 'OK.'

'That's good,' she replied, 'because I've just sorted out your girlfriend!'

My mind raced but, without emotion, I replied, 'That's nice' as if I thought it was a game or something. Within minutes, what followed next would remove all doubt that Claire had realised that something was going on.

The doorman had come into the front bar for a drink! Oops! This, of course, exposed my usual alibi, because as always I had informed Claire I was going out with Luke for a drink!

I never tried to show any emotion but my mind was racing and I got up from my chair to get a drink and then, pow! Claire aimed a blow to the side of my head but unfortunately she had a glass in her hand. Blood cascaded down the side of my face; it was just luck that the blow struck above and to the right of my eyebrow. Blood was everywhere as it spurted out of the wound and down the side of my face. Kim-Ann grabbed a towel and after a few minutes managed to stop the flow of blood.

After shouting a few choice words at Claire, I hurriedly retreated from the scene and went into the bedroom to pack my suitcase. Of course there was nothing I could say; I guessed that she had done what she said and followed Lisa home and caught up with her when she was getting out of her car. I understand later it was more screaming than blows. At times like this you cannot actually quite understand how things take their course but as I finished packing my case I heard the sound of a prolonged car horn as a car rushed by the front of the pub. I guessed that it was likely to be only one person and that would be Lisa!

I went downstairs and got in my car and, while I backed out, I was conscious of Claire trying to stop me. It was still a nightmare of my own making and one which would have many more serious consequences than anything previously. I knew I could only deal with the problem in hand and anything else would have to wait until another time.

As I left the pub car park I knew I was being followed by Lisa who had waited close by for my response. Funny, I was leaving anyway, not really answering the honk of her horn. We drove a short distance away to a nearby park where we both parked and I got into her car. I found Lisa in a very emotional state. As for my own state of mind, I was in a state of shock. One moment I was returning from an evening out after making a joint decision to end a relationship, the next I was plunged into a nightmare of my own making. My wound was smarting like mad, and I could not think straight. It was all totally unreal and my brain struggled to come to terms with the turn of events which were unfolding before me.

The nightmare of two years ago had returned but this time I could in no way blame it on my excessive drinking habits, this time I had been comparatively sober!

In a distraught state we decided to put some space between us and the problem. We dropped off her car near her house, leaving the keys so that her husband could find them and we left the scene like two rats scuttling away from a fire!

We drove over the Severn Bridge and, with tears falling intermittently from Lisa, we knew we had just about blown it this time. The good times had come to a complete stop and I realised that the times ahead were not going to be, in any way, plain sailing!

The first thing to do next morning was to get my head wound fixed. The nearest hospital was in Newport. We arrived in the A&E department and we were shown into a cubicle for the doctor to see me. He took one look and remarked, 'Stitches.' Ouch! Why does everything hurt so much! Thank goodness it was not the same side as when Colin, my young friend hit me with that hammer on fireworks night all those years ago. All these years later and I apparently still had not had any sense knocked into me!

I guess the amazing detective work carried out by Claire must be looked on as a job well done. It was about time that I received payback for all the years of my deceit. It was ironic that the drama was carried out on the actual day we had already made the decision to end our sordid relationship! Lisa had already realised that she in turn had responsibilities with her children; the youngest was no more than two years of age. It must have been fate stating that enough is enough and Claire should have a say in things in future events. This was to be very apparent in a very short time with dramatic consequences for all concerned. I had no option but to confront the incredible situation into which my association with Lisa had plunged me. I had carried out yet another illicit affair, been caught out in very dramatic circumstances and now I had to face the consequences. It was not long before Lisa and I had to make the choice to confront our prospective partners.

Lisa would have to go home and look after her two-year-old daughter; I would have to face the winding up of my position in the club. I had already tendered my resignation and it was only a short time before the club itself was to be turned over to its new owners. It was also fortunate that, due to the children's schooling, the family would not be moving to the new club.

Kim-Ann would come with her boyfriend, as he was to work as security manager in the new venture.

We had already rented a house locally in Staple Hill in Bristol for Claire and the rest of the family. I knew that Claire must be distraught and there was nothing I could do or say that could explain this betrayal. I had burnt the bridge which linked us together and I knew I was solely to blame for this terrible break-up. I had taken one risk too many and been caught out but it would take several weeks and even months before Ken West would come to the realisation just what heartache it would cause his family. The end was in sight but the 'in between' would not be to his liking.

After a few tense meetings between the lawyers it was decided that Claire would look after the business in the daytime up to six in the evening and I would follow on with the now much reduced evening schedules. I retreated to the house at Brean Down. Of course we were lucky not to have finished up on the front pages of the local paper or, even worse, the News of the World.

Meeting with the bosses was just a matter of routine and while they must have shaken their heads, nothing really was made of the break-up, unfortunately it was not the first time such an occurrence had happened in the licensed trade.

I guess everyone took advantage of the situation because when I went to finalise everything with the bosses, I found that the very last stock check on the pub was considerably down and I lost my deposit of five hundred pounds. This was despite the fact I had never had a bad stock in the seven years I had been at Snuffy's! I guess Claire had been generous in her drinks to the staff, but then, who could blame her? In Usk, brother Derek had moved into one of the chalets, with the owner's agreement, and was trying to learn the club business about which, of course, he knew very little. I went over when I could and was a little dismayed to learn that he had already placed in the club his two daughters who were waiting at tables. I had no problem with that but upon hearing that they were compiling a list of which staff should be sacked, I was not at all happy!

Even though Lisa had returned home, rumours continued that she and I were going to get together, which at that time were completely untrue. Claire was not at all happy about hearing such news and apparently rang Derek up saying that she would come over and cause trouble. Joan, his wife, started panicking (being an ex-policewoman). She was already trying to get involved in the running of the club. Derek and I had already agreed that only the two of us would do this, and that none of the ladies, other than Kim-Ann (who would look after public relations) would be involved in any way.

I was sitting in the Brean house when I was surprised to see a car draw up outside the gates and Lisa get out. She explained she was not happy at home and thought that perhaps we should consider getting back together. I looked at Lisa and felt that perhaps things were after all meant to be so I agreed that we should give it another try.

This, of course, was my decision and like my brother with his wife Joan, it was a personal one, and one I assumed my brother Derek would accept. How wrong was that! I took Lisa over to the club just once and, after the meeting with the seller of the club, I was surprised to see Lisa in the car, upset. It seemed that Joan had been really nasty to her and had informed her she should not go over there. What on earth it was to do with her I could not imagine. When I tackled my brother about it later he just remarked that Joan was worried about Claire coming over and breaking a few windows.

I laughed at this because I did not think Claire would do such a thing; either way Claire would still own one quarter of the club due to the fact that we were using funds which belonged to us both.

Lisa continued living at home under what must have been quite difficult circumstances. We had no plans to move in together; it would not be a good idea to move in with me, not with Claire still owning half of the property! I finalised everything with the brewery and left with some trepidation; what would the future hold now? The club would be a challenge and, as I saw it, any future that Lisa and I had would have to be only in the distant future, if at all.

I was at my new residence at Brean when I suddenly received a phone call from Claire. Had I missed my brother and his wife? I said, 'No' as I had been busy doing other things, like trying to see a solicitor re our now pending divorce, and other things which had suddenly cropped up.

Claire went on, 'Well, they've been over with me and it seems that your dear brother wants to take over the Usk club on his own.'

I laughed, but after she repeated this choice piece of information, I started feeling really anger! This could not be right? What an incredible story! She must just be making it all up! No brother would try such a thing. After all it was my dream, not his! I called him on the phone and challenged him.

His reply was clinical: 'Well, you can't raise the money now because Claire has stopped her part in the deal.'

I could not believe it. I rang Claire and asked her if this was true. She explained that Derek had suggested that she could do this if she was not happy with Lisa and me getting together. Nice to have a brother like that! I later learnt from my solicitor that Claire could not have actually stopped anything as she had already signed the necessary papers. She technically owned a share in the club, once the final money had been paid.

Derek and I were at loggerheads, and only the fact that he was after all my brother prevented me from going and punching him on the nose! Either way, he still maintained that he had not told her to stop the deal going through. .

I was, however, more likely in this instance to believe Claire; she had no real love for Derek due to his past actions down in South Wales.

Derek, however, found that his treachery would do him no good, because the brewery explained to him that, unless he came up with a partner with my calibre and understanding of the club business, they would not back the project. Either way, I also found that he was actually relying on keeping my previously paid deposit which of course I wanted back. Derek, seeing his chance to take over the club for himself, had asked the outgoing manager if he would stay to help him run the club.

As my father had remarked years ago he certainly was a 'born-again s***'. When he had returned from Canada, Derek had informed everyone that he had seen the Light!

A born-again Christian? I reckon my father had it right the first time!

I was in total disarray. I lost interest in the project; it was a step too far after what had already happened. My own brother trying to cut me out and trying to be Top Gun again! Although the owner waited for a short time, we soon faced the prospect that neither of us could go ahead without the other, and we were in breach of contract and we had to withdraw. Our costs were tremendous; not only did we lose the deposit we had paid the owner, but we also had to pay many other costs. We lost deposits on groups, like the opening act, 'The Three Degrees' which I had booked from my old mate Chic! On that booking alone we lost two thousand pounds. The printing costs were also in the region of six hundred pounds due to the fact we had five thousand very glossy brochures printed. The total joint loss came to over fifty thousand pounds. Nice one, Derek!

The owner later sold the same club for forty thousand pounds more than we would have paid him. He was certainly laughing all the way to the bank with this extra money, plus the nice deposit that he had collected from us two feuding Wests! I did not talk with my brother again for some years until we met at my father's funeral, and I have not since. He was not my favourite person, let alone brother! My pain was not to end there; Claire beat me to the punch and cleared out the antiques at the market, including the jewellery counter which had at least four thousand pounds worth of jewellery in it. I managed to sell a few of the antique items we had at the Brean house which gave me some money to pay the mortgage and live on.

After the failure to complete with the purchase of the club I remained in the house at Brean. The divorce was going through, and of course, the house would have to be put up for sale.

I then had a further problem to settle. I received a tax demand for twelve thousand pounds which was due to the fact my accountants had not made a tax return or informed them of the divorce and the freezing of the bank accounts. I was now going to be investigated. My accountants explained that it was the tax inspectors' way that sometimes they choose ten individuals and investigate one of them thoroughly and I just happened to be that one. Nothing personal! Someone's got to be kidding!

It looked like I would, as usual, be the one to pay! I had no money coming in at all with the bank accounts frozen due to the pending court case. I was asked to supply the last five years' accounts, despite the fact my accountants had religiously filed my accounts every year on time. Did they know something I did not know? Everywhere I chose to look, there seemed a problem which needed my urgent attention and, for once in my life apparently, I did not have the answers.

I was like a drowning man who had taken a step in the wrong direction and now I was to pay the price of the deception. I had for years conveniently convinced myself I had got away with it. I chose to put on my usual arrogant stance,

I was not too concerned about all this; I would survive. Was it not true I was the one who could handle anything with a cool response? As the pressure built up on a daily basis, the only person being deceived was me. Pride comes before a fall; everyone knows that!

After all the startling turn of events, I did start to find life at the Brean house nice and quiet, and I often took the chance of walking along the beach early in the morning when I reflected what a mess I had made of things. I was not at all easy with myself now after seeing the effect that the whole mess was having on my children. Kim-Ann and Richard were staying with me at Brean; she had been disowned by Claire because she refused not to talk to me. This was this totally nonsensical as Claire and I had become friends, not best chums, but friends, enough to talk over the phone.

My other two daughters, Natalie and Tanya and Curtis my son understandably refused to see me or talk to me, which caused me considerable distress.

I found it heartbreaking that suddenly, when you are used to seeing your children around you every day, it becomes unreal when you are suddenly denied their company. It is just another risk you undertake when you cheat on your wife. I knew I had to accept this for the time being and hope I could resolve it later when things may have calmed down. I certainly hoped so!

There are certainly no winners in cases of divorce. Lisa and I came to the conclusion that perhaps we should again stop seeing each other. That did make sense; either way I had too much on my mind to worry about new relationships. Funny when you had taken all that time to go out of your way to see someone to plug the empty space in your life. Suddenly you find they may not be so important anymore.

With Kim-Ann and Richard I started going to the local pubs and clubs. As I already knew some of the local licensees I was able to visit and enjoy some of the acts that I knew. I would often visit one of the clubs to enjoy a Sunday lunchtime drink before I went home and cooked the lunch. Yes, I was not totally without talent. Well, Kim-Ann and Richard said they enjoyed the lunches.

I felt I had to do something, anything to calm the unpleasant feeling which I had in my stomach all the time. I continued to put on my usual brave face acting like I was not affected too much by this latest episode of my life.

A lot more people had been hurt this time and mainly those 'people' were my immediate family who I did love. You suddenly find that by not working you have considerable time on your hands which only causes you to dwell even more on your problems. I used to drive up from Brean to Bristol, just to see the children come out of school and it hurt me to see Tanya, Natalie and Curtis all leaving their school, sometimes deep in conversation but other times laughing with their friends as if they had forgotten me already. They never once saw me as I hid and observed from a distance; their hotshot father who apparently could not control his sexual urges and had now paid the ultimate price of losing the company of not only his wife but his precious children.

The self-destruct had started again and he could not talk his way out of this one. What a sad sack he had turned out to be!

I was soon to be hit by yet another sad blow which was the passing of my father who finally succumbed to yet another stroke. It was a wretched time for anyone to lose their parent; his passing just seemed to be the final straw and I lapsed into yet another period of depression. Meeting my brother at his funeral did nothing to heal the wounds and we both ignored each other and the only time we surely actually joined together was in our grief. My grief prevented me from observing yet another event which I was blind to, the sudden apparent closeness between my mother and my brother. It was understandable but I knew deep down my errant brother wanted to be in the driving seat again and, within the months that were to follow, comments from my mother confirmed that any faults contributed to our fallout were being placed at my door! I found I could not compete with this change of affection from my mother and I just did what I always did in circumstances that were distasteful to me: I walked away from them both.

I did eventually find out that by not having to worry about the deceit of things, not to mention the continuous lying, I became more relaxed. It was, of course, just relief that the intrigue of the sordid affair(s) was now over and out in the open. Whatever the terrible price we were all paying at least it was now up to the courts and maybe God! I was realising that I was at yet another crossroads of my life; for heaven's sake, Ken West, get it right this time!

It was during one of the trips to Bristol that I dropped in to see John, a car sales friend of mine who was always pleased to have company during his long vigil on his car lot. We decided to have a night out with some friends in Weston, a nearby seaside resort close to Brean.

We started a pub crawl which is the norm when men go out on a stag night, only this time it was called a 'divorce' night which was very funny for my co-drinkers but I had to admit I had mixed feelings, after all it was my divorce everyone seemed to be celebrating. We finished up early in the morning at yet another nightclub and soon some of the guys were chatting up a group of girls who were standing close by. It was quickly apparent that the girls were having a hen night themselves and as the club closed John, always ready to continue the party, invited them back to 'Ken's place' for coffee. Thanks, John!

I knew that meant drinking my limited supply of booze. It was a good job that Kim-Ann and Richard were visiting his home in Bristol.

Piling back into the cars I found that I finished up with Alice, one of the bride-to-be's best friends, on my lap. I guess you might say we were thrown together; either way a few kisses occurred but arriving at Fawlty Towers I was soon busy supplying drinks and copious amounts of sandwiches to the waiting party revellers.

Fawlty Towers was spacious with many rooms so my guests could walk about and as the house was situated by the beach they could if they liked walk straight out onto the beach. Alice and I walked out onto the small hill that rose behind the house, and she asked how I managed to cut the grass of this small hill. I told her 'with great difficulty' as the slope down to the house was very steep.

It was a bit unreal to have a conversation with a girl on the slope of my house in the early morning talking about daft things such as cutting the grass. As the party reached its closure the guests started thinking about going home. I sensed Alice wanted to stay on but that would cause a problem as she was one of the girls with the car. John came to the rescue:

he volunteered to drive the girls back in Alice's car to their homes in one of the nearby villages. Thanks again, John! This time I meant it.

I had found Alice rather reluctant to talk much about herself and I did not press it; she was about twenty-five years of age, dark hair and very slim. Not wishing to pry I never asked her any more questions and it was rather late in the proceeding to even attempt to do so. Alice had made her intentions quite clear and divorce-happy Ken was only too pleased to oblige; after all this was 'his' divorce party. Any excuse would do!

Next morning Alice remarked that she had to get back to her house and after a cup of coffee we set out for one of the villages close to Brean. She was rather silent for a while and then suddenly started a strange utterance which I found rather disturbing: 'Pink for a girl - and blue for a boy' as if she was picking an imaginary flower! I looked across at this girl seemingly reciting a poem and a very strange one at that. Oh my God, what had I got myself into? I suddenly felt rather nervous and I gave silent thanks that I had witnesses that would confirm that I had in no way coerced this lady into staying the night with me. We arrived at her house, a rather pretty house with roses around the door, and I suddenly had this feeling that perhaps, just perhaps, this young lady might not be single! She leaned across and kissed me and thanked me for a nice evening, she alighted from the car and, with a wave, disappeared into the pretty cottage.

I drove back to Fawlty Towers with many thoughts racing through my brain. Had it all really happened? Why did she go into this strange poetry in motion?

I then had a sudden realization; perhaps Ken West, sinner personified, had for once been used for someone else's need - that would be a first. I hurriedly put this notion right to the back of my mind and when Kim-Ann and Richard came back I had to own up to the fact that I had had a few people over for an impromptu party as I had to explain the numerous coffee cups, glasses and plates that were strewn around the house, the outside area, and even by the front door. Blimey, did ten people actually make that much mess?

It was a good thing I had owned up as suddenly I received a phone call from one of Alice's friends. Had I found her earrings? She guessed they were by the bed! I went and found the missing earrings and promised to return them that lunchtime at a pub in Alice's village. As it was the normal Sunday lunch drink I had to take Kim-Ann and Richard with me. I am not sure I could have done anything else because Kim-Ann had knowingly managed to extract from me mostly what happened. However, arriving at the pub, I was rather surprised when Alice's friend came in to collect the earrings and not Alice. Perhaps it was Alice's way of saying thanks but no thanks...pity, I would have loved to have seen her again – in the daylight!

I was about to find some additional comfort in a direction that I was not expecting, and for once I was not actually 'window-shopping'. I was in a bar and enjoying a drink with Kim-Ann and Richard when I was taken slightly aback by some nice smiles I was receiving from one of the barmaids. She had a lot of similarities to Carol and had lovely red hair; and when she pressed my change into my hand in a similar way to Carol. I could not believe it. Déjà vu! I could not be sure, as I was still getting used to my newfound freedom. Freedom, but at what cost? I had lost my job, my self-respect and, worst of all, my family.

I thought well, why not, and I bought her a drink and asked her out. Her name was Jenny. Jenny explained she could not come out that day, (she already had a date) but later she came up and pressed her telephone number into my hand. I was full of anticipation. Who was this very attractive lady? Would she too become trouble for me? I could only find out one way. I rang her and we went out for a drink; although previously married, she was now divorced and living with her two grown-up children in a nearby village. We got on well and soon Jenny became a regular visitor to the house.

The problem was that now I was the one with baggage: it was Lisa. She would not go away completely and would phone now and again and say she still had feelings for me and could not stay away. Worse still, I was not at all sure I wanted her to!

Jenny knew all about my past and, while she kept quiet about it, she sensed that I had not got over this tremendous upheaval that had occurred in my life. The new start was tampered by my Mr Hyde character emerging and I sometimes treated Jenny in a very off-putting manner. I would go to see her at work and then ask her in an off-hand manner if she wanted to come home with me, almost like an afterthought. Only Kim-Ann's intervention informing me that I was out of order made me apologise to Jenny who forgave me. She knew from experience that marriage break ups were not at all easy. Jenny then came up with an amazing idea: she suggested that we go and visit Tamar, a medium who resided in Weston Super Mare. She said that she had been there before when she needed guidance, and she thought that such a visit would help me. I was full of doubts and it took much persuasion before I agreed to see 'Madam' Tamar.

I made an appointment for myself and one for Jenny. I went in before Jenny. I was still cynical; I entered the clean but sparsely furnished room, and I sat and waited for the medium to inform me of my future!

If she sensed my scepticism she did not show it. Tamar was a nice lady in her mid-fifties just like your friendly grandmother. She informed me I could take notes if I liked but I could not ask her any questions afterwards because she would not remember what she had told me. Despite my previous reservations, I started to record what Tamar told me. The woman was amazing, without any prompting from me she told me my life story almost to date. She told me she saw a lady who talked with her hands and would help me over the bad times I was now experiencing. She told me about my family, she mentioned Curtis would do well, she told me things that, to me, were just mind-boggling. I had not even opened my mouth and she seemed to know everything. She informed me that Lisa (although not by name) my friend had a little girl, three years of age who had a terrible cold. I knew that Lisa's little girl was certainly not three years of age, more likely to be around two and a half. Madam Tamar then mentioned several things such as me travelling around the countryside looking at certain areas, but this did not mean anything to me and I thanked her and asked her how much I owed her. She said that she normally charged seven pounds, but I could pay her five pounds because I was not working! Crazy, it was just crazy.

I realised just how much Jenny used her hands when she spoke to people; and I knew that she was the one who would help me get over the problems I was having. This would happen very shortly when one day I was on my own. Kim-Ann had gone to stay in Bristol and I had been out drinking. I was missing the family, Curtis and the girls. I had a really bad headache and, suddenly feeling extremely depressed, I reached for a bottle of paracetamol.

I gulped down several of the tablets. I went to bed and when I woke again, took a few more. I had no idea that over eight of these tablets could be extremely dangerous. It was fortunate for me that I had wanted to talk with Tanya one of my estranged daughters. I called her on the telephone and talking to me she realised that I was not talking at all clearly. She became very concerned and, with her mother, drove down from Bristol to the Brean house. They came in and woke me up and made me lots of coffee and got me back up on my feet. I did not know how and why I did this; maybe it was a cry for help. I guess that I had had too much pressure and for too long! The hard man had cracked at last!

What occurred next was amazing. Lisa actually rang while Claire was there and she in turn got an earful from Claire. I realised again that perhaps I had married the right person, and that made my folly even worse, if that was at all possible. They invited me to return with them to Bristol but I did not feel right going back with them so I got her to call Jenny who collected me and I stayed with her for a few days.

I wonder still what would have happened if I had returned that day with Claire and the children. I doubt it would have changed much as I guess I had done just too much hurt to Claire; enough was enough. I knew she still had some love for me, but who could not understand her anguish. She could never put her trust in me again. It had to be a case of once bitten, twice shy! And she knew there had to have been others!

We finally sold the house at Brean and with the money we bought a freehold off-licence for Claire and the children. At least I was not going to be bloody-minded about how the money would be spent. After all, they were my children too and I had not worried about their welfare when I carried out my affairs. They all moved into the off-licence. I in turn moved into the cottage they had been renting. I assisted in the setting-up of the business with the VAT and getting the stock in. Claire and I had a strange relationship I knew she wanted me back, but everyone knew she had to do one thing: get rid of me as a husband. I helped with the initial running of the off-licence and even stayed overnight sometimes. My son Curtis hurt me one day as I was seeing him off to bed. He asked if we were going to be back together again as a family.

'Maybe; we'll have to see, son,' I said.

Claire had already gone to bed and I asked her if she wanted me to stay over.

'No thanks,' she replied.

I realized that she had heard what Curtis had said and I knew she could not put this last betrayal at the back of her mind again, and who could blame her.

I was now almost penniless; I had no job and no home, other than the rented house that I had taken over from the owners who had rented it to Claire. I also had to try to sort out the tax problems which would, of course, take some time. I still had a lot of trouble accepting exactly what had happened with the club and how my brother had acted. So much for brotherly love! I suddenly remembered visiting the club and when I was walking around with the owner I had bumped into Derek showing his wife and daughters around. They were laughing and joking and he suddenly raised his arms and declared in an almost hysterical voice, 'It's mine, all mine!'

Good God, how daft was I then not to have seen the danger coming, but not my own brother, not the man who had safely seen me through the hurtful events of my first divorce from Shirley!

Kim-Ann and Richard moved in with me again, so I did have some company. We then had another blow: the landlord wanted his house back for his parents. We would all now be homeless as well as penniless. Kim-Ann could go and live with Richard and his parents but me? Is there a doghouse available?

Rootie Tootie...

Hank Williams
Met my future wife today
And her name is Casio May
Rootie Tootie, you're my kind of gal.

I STILL HAD MUCH ON the legal side to sort out, with my tax liabilities and divorce. My accountants had not notified the Tax Office about the divorce, and the subsequent freezing of bank accounts. This prompted the Tax Office to launch an investigation. It took months, with my accountants having to prove the figures again. Fortunately I had good accountants and the trading figures at Snuffy's were not hard to prove.

However, when the inspector said he wanted copies of cheques going back five years, I said enough was enough and asked him what the bottom line was. I had no job, no prospect of one and no money.

He said, 'We'll do a deal, five hundred pounds per year going back seven years which would be three thousand five hundred pounds with no interest and no penalties.'

I guess he just wanted to justify the time he had spent on my case because he never came up with any firm figures. I had to agree as I could not afford any more representation by my accountants, not at ten pounds per hour. I agreed to pay one hundred pounds per month. Where I was going to get it from I had no idea. I could always go bankrupt though! I guess that would just about be the icing on the cake.

Going to the magistrate's court to agree the divorce settlement was not much better. After giving up all the monies in the kitty, and having put any money due to me into the purchase of the off-licence for Claire and the children, all I had left was a small endowment with a value of eight thousand pounds in my name that I wanted to keep to at least help with the tax burden, and perhaps get a new business going. The magistrat was very sympathetic…to Claire; he gave her the eight thousand pounds as well. Her legal team had offered half before the start of the hearing, but I honestly thought I was entitled to something at least as the cost of setting up the off-licence had been in excess of thirty thousand pounds.

My solicitor and I walked over the bridge from the court and he was shaking his head – we had to appeal, he said.

'No, I can't appeal against my own family,' I said. 'I just couldn't do that to them. Haven't I not done enough already?'

My finances were a mess: I had an overdraft of three thousand five hundred pounds which was up to my limit. My bank manager could not believe what had happened and he was very sympathetic. He had given me so much leeway and had been very supportive. He could not believe Derek's actions as he had met him many times before and had been impressed by his professional manner.

My solicitor also said that, at first, he had thought it was my fault. Then, when he found out what had taken place, he was disgusted with my brother's actions. He showed his support by reducing his bill to me by half!

I had no money coming in at all with the bank accounts frozen due to the pending court case. I sold my Volvo estate car to my car sales friend John. He gave me a reasonable price and a car which at least would provide me with transport travelling back and forth. I had just completed the deal when a man came onto the car lot and asked if the Volvo was for sale. John sheepishly said it was and sold the car there and then. Evidently the man was a wine merchant and he gave John some wine in part exchange. John in turn gave me a case as if to say, 'Have a drink on me.'

I guess that was the quickest sale John ever had. Still I was just pleased to have a car and some cash in my pocket for once, and cash that the courts could not take.

Then John Mills, my agent, came up trumps: he offered me a job looking after the Frank Carson Show at a seaside resort which would not only give me an income, but also the chance of getting away from all the pressure, and of course I would have somewhere to live. I had two weeks left on my tenancy and John's offer was a godsend; it would enable me space to relax and lick my wounds! I now had ten days left in the rented property and was already packing. Then I had a visitor; it was Claire. She wanted to have the brass fireside set which had been at the house at Brean and which was with me now.

'Yes, have it. You've got everything else,' I remarked gruffly. She gave me an old-fashioned look as if to say that I would not get any sympathy from her. I wondered just how much one has to pay and how long one has to continue to pay for one's indiscretions. I guess maybe a lifetime.

While trying to get another job in one of Bristol's nightclubs I met a young lady called Christine. I had asked her out and we were having dinner. I was again doing the bit: buying her a meal with money that I could not really afford, but I needed the company of a female who did not know my history, with whom I could behave normally. I was intrigued by Christine's own story; she had also been through a bad patch in her life but much more sorrowful than mine. She had lost her husband in an accident at work. Mind you, many people say divorce is similar to death. We had a drink and were enjoying each other's company; then we sat down and started our meal. We had just eaten the first course when, without warning, Christine suddenly went ashen, her face drained of colour. She excused herself from the table and went to the ladies room. The waiter brought the main courses but I had to send them back as Christine was still absent from the table. I was very concerned. She finally came back looking terrible and asked me if I would take her home as she was feeling awful. I agreed of course and drove her back to her very spacious home. She still appeared very unwell and I suggested she went straight to bed – on her own. God, what was I doing passing up a night with a beautiful lady? Had the sun gone to my head? No chance at ten o'clock at night!

I arrived back at my rented house and went in and, shortly afterwards, was surprised by a knock on the door. It was a bit late for callers. I went to the door; a car was parked outside and in the gloom I could just make out the shape of two females. I recognised Jean, who was Lisa's brother's wife, and the other person was... Lisa, a bit the worse for wear! She wanted to see me and told me she could not live without me! God, what was going on now? I said, 'You'd better come in,' and while Jean stayed in the car Lisa and I talked after taking a cup of coffee out for Jean. As far as I was concerned Jean could have come in as she knew all of our tragic secrets anyway but I guess she was just being diplomatic. Lisa and I discussed what we could do, we found we had still some strong feelings for each other and in the end she said if we wanted to be together I had to rent a house for her and the children. I looked at her and wondered what the best option would be. I could not accept that, after all that had gone on, all the money that I had personally lost, still we had not finished up together. I was quite forgetting that we were not planning to go off together in the first place, but now things had changed, hadn't they? Perhaps it was also just me putting a price on the result of my actions.

I said I would try and we agreed to meet again to look for the house. As time was short we went out next day and found a nice house to rent just outside Bristol. I managed to get a good reference from John, my agent, (on his letter heading) and after scraping up the money to pay the deposit, I prepared for my new job down by the seaside. I left it to Lisa to make her departure from her life with her husband. I was not interested in being a go-between again. I was just too tired, so very tired…Where this direction was taking me I did not know. I had been informed by Tamar that there was to be a future with Lisa, but by now I had put that down to an incorrect reading to say the least. What I could not quite understand was the sudden cessation of my evening out with the delectable Christine which, if we had completed our meal, would have most likely meant I could have possibly stayed over for breakfast! That would have been nice.

Kim-Ann and Richard were out trying to sort out their lives. Kim-Ann, fortunately, got a job quite quickly and Richard was rehired by his old boss which was good as it certainly was not their fault in anyway. Claire still refused to see Kim-Ann as she did not wish to have anything to do with her due to her association with me. Kim-Ann had been a rock to me and stood by me when all the doors were apparently closed to me as far as the family was concerned. While she had never condoned what I had done it came down to the fact that I was still her father and she did try to remain neutral if that was at all possible. Claire's continued cold behaviour to her made this almost impossible and was as far as I was concerned, most definitely out of order.

I now started to look forward to a new time in my life, but while my love life might have settled down to some normality, my work would be anything but not boring! Oh come on, God, please pick on someone else! Please let me be normal! With Lisa now living in her own house, admittedly only rented I took up my new post as bar manager of the Frank Carson Show which was playing at the seaside resort of Ilfracombe in Somerset. The first week it rained, and rained, for the four weeks of August. We did well out of the show because of the rain, but as far as the bars were concerned other than the pre-show drinks, it was very poor. The punters were certainly not about until the evening shows.

I kept in touch with Lisa by phone and was surprised to hear one day that Rosa her daughter was three that day and she had a terrible cold! Goodness, where had I heard that before? Lisa's other children had decided to stay with their father so we only had the small daughter with us. I went back now and again to see them both and we started to try to set up a normal family home, if that was at all possible. When Lisa's husband had his daughter, Lisa was able to visit me for the weekend and we had some nice times together, having a few drinks with the staff that numbered around twenty. I put on a few promotions which everyone joined in. It reminded me of Southall again and the team spirit we had there. I do remember Lisa feeling a bit tipsy and falling up the stairs one night which is quite the opposite of falling down.

Either way, the relief of the peace and quiet from the previous six months was very apparent for both of us. I had to laugh when informing the staff about my meeting with Tamar. Some of them booked a session with her and went up to Weston to see her. They came back with mixed results but one of the staff, an older lady in her fifties, had been seeing one of the stars of the show and Tamar informed her she saw her with a man in a tux and that it had been going on for some years! We all laughed until she admitted that it was true and not to mention the star himself - he was not telling anybody – in any way! She certainly was a dark horse.

I received a message from Kim-Ann that her mother had met someone and was getting married. That was nice and I felt happy for her. I must admit I was a little put out when she sold the freehold off-licence for ninety-two thousand pounds to a lady who wanted to turn it into a poodle parlour. Oh, the spoils of war!

I in turn was still paying off our tax liabilities which somehow the magistrate had completely overlooked. A little bit one-sided, these divorce settlements.

Finishing the six-month management position, I returned to Bristol and moved in with Lisa. I now found myself wondering what I would do next. John had no more work of that kind but I managed to acquire another pub manager's relief position. It was at this pub that I stumbled into something which would have a big effect on my life. I was at the bar when a man entered and said he had been asked to demonstrate a 'waste compactor'. I asked what that was and he brought one in to show me. I could not get over the fact that it could compact six large bags of waste into one. I was very impressed. Talking further with the salesman, I found out that the company was selling franchises for the compactors all over the UK.

After finding out more I found that I could purchase the franchise for the Bristol area for three thousand pounds. The problem was I did not have that kind of money; not with my present bank limit. Tongue in cheek, I went to see my 'friendly' bank manager in Clifton. He agreed to lend it to me as I had managed to reduce the overdraft level by two thousand pounds. He also liked the idea and I guess, more importantly, he trusted me! He probably also felt sorry for me.

There are such things as nice bank managers but he was exceptional. I went up to London, saw Toddy the boss and we completed the deal. I was now a franchisee for a compactor business. With a sample compactor, I started cold-calling on anybody who would talk with me. I became quite good at it. If they did not want one to start with, I tried to make sure they changed their minds before I left. I sold enough to pay the rent, and of course, live! I went into Lloyds Bank purchasing department and managed to get the buyer interested in the product. They were interested in putting one in every Lloyds Bank in the country, and I thought at last my ship was coming in. I took the buyer to London to meet Toddy who promptly went completely daft and promised them the earth. Driving home, I worked out my commission on the deal. I would earn an extra one pound twenty-six pence on each compactor. He had given away any extra I would have received. I was not happy and told the boss. Either way, the bank had trouble getting such a big deal through at that time, so we only managed to sell one hundred to the Bristol and South West area. This was good enough to pay back my overdraft and, with the bag trade I got from the use of the compactors, Lisa and I managed to live quite well for a while.

It seemed that my love life had now apparently become normal and I was relaxed with my new partner. There was a problem of visits with her children (her son would not talk to me) but we seemed to settle down to an acceptable routine. Then Lisa took it into her head that she could not get on with Kim-Ann. I guess we would never know the reason for this; possibly Lisa viewed my daughter as a threat! I could never understand this at the time and as time went by it never became any clearer. It gave me great heartache, and it was to be a problem that endured for some time.

My franchise was expanded when the boss imported some larger machines for shredding waste; I was asked to try and sell the new equipment in the Bristol area. I was out visiting a local waste contractor and while I was giving my spiel about the machines, the sales director suddenly asked me if I would like to come and work for him. I would get a retainer, a car, commission on all I sold, plus expenses. I now had a salary and, after moving closer to Bristol, Lisa and I were able to purchase a house between us, which gave us a bit of equity in the housing market. It was in Frenchay, just around the corner from the old Snuffy's that by now had been converted to the eating place previously planned.

I was employed by the waste company mainly to sell a service dealing with clinical waste. The company offered a complete service including the disposal of certain items. One of the places to call on were nursing homes for senior citizens but I eventually became uneasy when visiting these places. They give out a certain smell which perhaps, when residing there, you get used to but when visiting I was always pleased to leave after completing my business. I worked with different representatives at the company and when Malcolm was promoted to a more senior post, as sales director, I was able to transfer over to the normal waste disposal side which I found I was better suited to, both in attitude and, fortunately, a different kind of smell. I became more of a roving representative which enabled me to work in different areas when help was required. Waste not, want not! I suddenly remembered what Tamar had 'seen': that was me going around the country inspecting and looking at things. That is what I had to do: inspect companies' backyards and see how I could improve their waste disposal. Definitely scary!

With both of us now divorced it was not long before the topic of marriage came up and, in due course, Lisa and I tied the knot at the local registry office. Married again!

Shirley first, then Claire and now, Lisa. A total time of nearly thirty years, how time flies when you are enjoying yourself. Some people must be gluttons for punishment!

I enjoyed my work with the waste company but when I was asked to join another company I did so only because of one thing: I was offered much more money! Nice car as well. This, however, lasted only two months, when the second pay cheque bounced and the entire sales force were out of work. I could have worked on a commission basis but I would not accept that. I went to a sales agency and in due course was offered a position with a company at Corby, selling shredding machines and large compactors.

I was having a lie-in after coming home with my new contract when I received a telephone call from the director. He said that the sales manager for the Dutch side of the company had been stopped on the M5 at twelve noon and breathalysed: he had not only lost his licence but also, of course, his job…Would I consider taking that over as well. More money? Well no, but better commission. Nice one.

'Oh, by the way we've booked you on a flight to Holland. You have to go there next week to learn about the product.'

I was on the move again, to the land of canals, bridges and of course the red-light district. With my history that was maybe asking for trouble! I suddenly realised that I was going to have company in Holland when I made visits in the future. My daughter, Kim-Ann, had not only outgrown her boyfriend, she had outgrown Bristol and then in turn London. Kim-Ann had learnt all about computers, and had become skilled in office procedures. She had also spent her time in London developing good sales techniques with a large company and now she was looking for new challenges. With a girlfriend, she had plans to visit Holland to see what a new country could offer. She had also become a little tired of being on the 'outside' of the family; Claire was not a person who would go out of her way to forgive any offspring, who she considered had 'stepped out of line'.

Claire should have been in the Air Force, she would have fitted in quite nicely. I was not happy with this new venture but with Kim-Ann inheriting her parents' stubborn traits there was no way of dissuading her from going on this new venture. With some reluctance I could only advise her to take care. Holland, they wear a funny sort of shoes over there, don't they? Another shock came later when Kim-Ann informed me that she had gone to Holland on her own, her friend having pulled out at the last minute.

Was this now another generation of the West family going where no one has gone before? I had gone in the opposite direction all those years ago and now my maverick daughter was apparently following my example, all these years later! Kim-Ann later informed me that she loved the Dutch people and their lovely flat country, but before she could make good use of it, she had a cash problem. She had gone over with only one thousand pounds and she soon realised that she would not be able to stay long with her already depleted funds. Fate must have taken a hand with her future because, while sitting there waiting to book a taxi to take her to the airport, the owner of the hotel she was staying in asked her what the problem was and why was she going home? Upon receiving the explanation, he did a strange and wonderful thing: he offered to let her stay at the hotel at a greatly reduced rate so that she could look for a job in the coming weeks.

It was a start of an extremely close friendship that would last for many a year. It would also allow her a close look at the gay population of Amsterdam as Anjo was just one of the many gay people living in Holland. Kim-Ann, always being a good mixer, was soon making friends with the many intriguing and exciting people who populated the nooks and crannies of Amsterdam. Of course, that is another story but one which would have many humorous incidents in my extended visits in Holland. Kim-Ann secured a good job with an American company 'Times Warner' which gave her a good income and she started to really enjoy the delights of Amsterdam and the surrounding villages.

One of the requirements of my new job was to take clients over there to view machinery which had not yet been sold and available in the UK.

It would be my job to show the UK paper merchants the delights of Bollegraah machinery. I now realized, however, that I was going to have at least part of my family in situ when I visited Holland which would turn out to be quite often. One West in a foreign country is bad enough at the same time, but two?! It does not bear thinking about!

One day I received a letter from my old solicitor who I had not spoken to since the break-up with my brother. He informed me that he understood I had a daughter from a previous marriage to a person called Shirley, and now the daughter wanted to know if I wished to meet her. Oh my God, what an amazing trick of fate. I could not believe what I was hearing. My firstborn from all those years ago in Oxford now wanting to come back into my life.

I discussed this with Lisa and we made contact with Debbie. We agreed that she and her husband should come to Bristol and meet us both. They duly arrived and I was surprised to see what a lovely lady my firstborn had turned out to be. Simply stunning! They had no children but were still hoping, nevertheless. Debbie asked me what she should call me and as I knew she had always looked upon her grandfather as her 'dad' I suggested she called me Ken. She seemed happy with that.

I then asked her how her mother was and was deeply hurt to learn that she had passed away some six years previously. It was quite funny to learn that if Debbie had not made contact with me then she was going to try to find me via the Cilla Black show 'Surprise, Surprise'. Goodness me, that would have been a heart attack occasion!

We had a nice day and later when I was in the area I managed to travel down to the south coast where Debbie and her husband lived, and we both went out for lunch which was extremely nice. Lisa, Rosa and I managed to go down and stay with them for a few days, and I felt that at last I had some closure on a part of my life which had been a great disappointment to me. I was pleased that my daughter, previously denied to me, had at last made contact all these years later. I give thanks to God for that! It was strange that after all those years since the break-up with Shirley that I was able to spend time with my daughter who, up to then, I had only been able to picture vaguely, and that was when I chose to recant that part of my life that I had found very upsetting.

Oh, why do we go down roads that apparently come to a dead end? Then another door opens and we find we are looking at the past in a very different light! Life can be strange - but also rather nice sometimes!

About this time I started receiving phone calls which when I answered no one replied. I wondered if it was any of my disgruntled ex-girlfriends, or even husbands of the ladies maybe. I did not have a clue. One day however, I just had this strange feeling and when no one answered, just asked if it was my mother. The phone went down and I had no more calls of that nature again. I knew that maybe I should go and see her but I did not want to be faced with any more rows or even bump into my brother, so I decided against it. Again it was my way of ducking the problem such was my self-esteem at that time.

I'm Satisfied With You…

Hank Williams
You don't dress up in satin
And you don't wear diamond rings
But I'm satisfied with you.

THE FUEKER 51 AIRCRAFT FLIGHT 234 was one of the three times a day flights from Bristol to Schipol Airport, the main airport in Holland. Arriving after the two-hour flight, I looked around for my Dutch contact, Edo, and was a little concerned when no one was there holding up my name as you would expect. Great start!

I walked round to the reception area and still there was no sign of my new colleague. I was just about to contact my UK office when the smiling face of Edo, with his Omar Sharif moustache, walked up to me and explained that they had put the incorrect arrival gate number on the board. 'No problem,' I replied with some relief, as I certainly did not relish the thought of spending my first day in Holland in a busy airport and me not speaking a world of Dutch. Although that would not have been too much of a problem with the majority of Dutch people speaking excellent English. Within ten minutes of spending time in Edo's company I knew I was going to like this handsome individual. He had a charming manner which I took to immediately. He explained that we would be checking into a local hotel in Amsterdam and from then on we would be travelling around Holland visiting the waste paper companies who had the company's baling equipment in situ. Being driven around and being fed and watered with a few beers, that's got to be a hard thing to do in my first week of employment of Bollegraaf Machinery. I guess I could just put up with that!

After a light lunch we left Amsterdam to go to the first site; we saw machinery that was working away, baling paper into large one-ton blocks. Edo was an excellent guide and his instructions on the basic fundamentals of the machinery were excellent but, my goodness, there was certainly a lot to learn. At the end of the day my head was swimming with facts and figures about the new machinery that I was expected to sell. I had a few doubts that I would be able to accomplish this with such a short appraisal time. Arriving back in Amsterdam was a relief, we had dinner at the hotel and then Edo said he would show me the sights of Amsterdam. I took in the sights of Amsterdam and when Edo took me into the red-light district, we saw the girls with their 'big boobies' in their little booths. I thought this cannot be bad!

The week included a visit to the Dutch company's Head Office and an in-depth look at the extremely modern manufacturing facility, which I viewed with awe. The huge computer-controlled robots cutting out the enormous footprints of the baling machines – six at a time. An incredible sight! The company had a superb drawing office and the staff were very friendly and soon made me very welcome. Returning to Amsterdam at the end of the week, we met up with Kim-Ann in the American Hotel in the centre of Amsterdam and soon we were cracking jokes and having a really nice time. Going back to Bristol, even to see my new partner Lisa, was going to be just a little tame after such an exciting and interesting week. Yes, Holland, you certainly get my vote!

Catching the plane back to Bristol I found I was rather tired and realised that the one thing I had not bargained for was that I would not be restricted to just one building as with the entertainment centres but I would be on the move all the time. My target area was the whole of the United Kingdom and I realised that I would now be motoring many miles every week in an attempt to achieve my targets. Returning home to Lisa it was nice to relax and I now found my time split between working from home and travelling to the UK Head Office in Corby. My UK boss, David, was a great character and, when we went out visiting sites, normally I would have to drive. I soon found out that he liked to do one thing when out: he loved to have his chicken and chips. Travelling back one day after already stopping for lunch, he wanted to stop yet again for some food. I really could not face another lunch so, when he was on the mobile telephone, I sped by the last motorway services thinking I could get away with it. He said, 'That's a funny way of handing in your notice.' Oops! I thought he was joking – well I hoped he was!

I found I had to visit Holland approximately once a month, and for a week at a time. It was no hardship and I soon got used to the routine of getting to the airport, waiting, and getting on and off the plane. It was really strange to leave at three o'clock UK time and being sitting in the bar in Amsterdam with Kim-Ann at six thirty the same evening having a drink. I soon found out that, while it was fascinating to visit the red-light district, which we used to call the 'Cook's Tour' because nearly every one of our 'clients' loved to visit the district after they had been around our sites, it became just another drudge as far as I was concerned. Many times it would be raining and it does lose its appeal somewhat when you are getting wet, trudging around the same places. I got used to seeing all types of people going into the 'booths' to visit the girls and I can honestly say I never had the urge to take advantage of the services available.

I was content with my love life; Lisa and I got on well with the exception of her attitude to Kim-Ann, but now with Kim-Ann living in Holland it gave Lisa the 'comfort' that my daughter would not monopolise me - quite silly really.

I was in Amsterdam doing the 'Cook's Tour' and was utterly bored with the evening out. It had been raining; I had two clients with me and I had shown them into a peep show, which consisted of a pretty girl cavorting on a revolving stage showing off her wares, which after a while is really not that exciting. You had to put coins into the machines to ensure that the little sliding door stayed up in place. For one guilder you got about one minute. I waited outside, just looking aimlessly at the milling crowds that were frequenting the area. I was wishing I could just finish the day off and get to my bed but 'work' comes first and, if my customers cared to party until dawn, then so be it.

They finally came out and I asked, 'Did you enjoy the show?'

'Darn right,' they replied. 'We would never see two people 'at it' in England.'

I looked at them and asked, 'What do you mean?'

'Well, they were at it. Bonking,' came the reply. Heck, they had changed the floor show! Trust me to miss out!

When I was back in Corby office, I used to stay at a nice pub, bed and breakfast in a village close by. I used to enjoy the food and the company of the licensee, a Scottish chap called Archie, a good old Scottish name. He had an apartment in Portugal and, when he offered to rent it to Lisa and me, we jumped at it. It was one of the first holidays we had together and we certainly enjoyed the sunshine and bars of Vilamora, where the apartment was situated.

I found that eating good food and drink at Archie's soon increased the waistline and I had to look to my diet as I had put too much weight on. It does show nothing nice comes without its problems.

I managed to entice one of the buyers, a chap called Robbie, to come to Holland to view some of our machines that would eventually, we hoped, be used in his company's distribution centres. He set out some strict conditions: he could only travel on a Sunday afternoon, and he had to be back in England at the latest on the Wednesday following. OK, the problem was we had to travel from Luton Airport which meant me leaving early Sunday morning to meet him at the airport, even though he also lived near Bristol. I met him and straightaway it was talk, talk all the way over on the plane. I moaned silently to myself; normally most of my clients would be in a more congenial mood going to Holland of all places. No, he would only do this and not that so it was with some trepidation that I booked him into the hotel. We then met Edo for the evening meal. Rising early next day found us motoring north.

Robbie appeared to start thawing out just a little bit. Edo was not the type of guy who stayed quiet and he was a good host. Our presentation went well and returning to Amsterdam, after a quick wash-up, we embarked on the, by now, customary 'Cook's Tour'. Edo had to return to his home, so I was left to act as tour guide. I enlisted Kim-Ann's help and, while she was much nearer Robbie's age, I knew that she in no way fancied him. I did, however, leave them talking and went back to the hotel on my own…I must be getting old. Next day Kim-Ann remarked that Robbie maybe had the idea that she may have been the dessert, but that was soon squashed without any upset.

One of the great places to eat in Amsterdam is the Sea Palace, a floating Chinese restaurant that seats seven hundred people. Situated on the docks, it has a great appeal to the tourist and fortunately to our clients. We found that after an excellent meal at the Sea Palace we invariably managed to sign up a deal. Edo had rejoined us the last evening of Robbie's visit and we visited the Sea Palace and pulled out all the stops to try to get the deal which was to be for three baling machines, with more to follow. After a meal we did the tour again of the red-light district. Knowing we had to get up early the next day at five o'clock to take Robbie to the airport I suggested we called it a day and got an early night. I left the two of them talking and went back to my room at the hotel. Nice and easy!

I awoke with the alarm clock ringing in my ears and managed to get a shower and shave before going to make sure Edo was up. Then we would see how our guest was doing. Edo was dressed and made a strange comment: 'Is Robbie back?'

I could not understand this and remarked, 'Back from where?'

Edo then asked me to check his room, which was quite close to mine. I went to Robbie's room, and pushing the already open door even further, I entered the room. It was an eerie sight that confronted me: the shower was dripping as if half on and off. I went further into the room and, in the half-light, I was amazed to find our guest, sprawled out on his bed. He was face down and completely naked. It crossed my mind you could park one of Holland's many cycles in his butt.

I was taken aback and, after trying unsuccessfully to rouse him, I scurried back to Edo to report my findings. Edo was concerned and upon our return to Robbie's room he set about trying to wake him. He only managed to do this by placing a loud smack onto our guest's posterior! I was not very comfortable with that; after all he was our client, and one does not normally smack their arses to wake them up!

Robbie fortunately responded to this apparently effective treatment and sat up. We hurriedly handed him his underclothes and he proceeded with some difficulty to get dressed. He started singing a gibberish song. I guess it made sense to him as he proudly announced that he was 'singing Dutch'. Oh my God, Edo was now finding things quite funny after being a little concerned when he first entered the room. As we packed Robbie's overnight bag, Edo informed me that he and Robbie (at his request) had gone to a local whorehouse where Robbie had taken up with some of the girls. Three ladies, in fact. Edo had tried hard to get him to come back to the hotel but, with Robbie insisting he wanted to stay longer, Edo had returned alone to the hotel. How, and what time, Robbie had returned to the hotel was a mystery, but I did remember hearing some disturbance around four o'clock which meant if that was true, he certainly would have not had much sleep. The half-hour drive to the airport found Robbie slightly more with it but still very much a mixture of being rather drunk and most likely very tired.

We got out of the car and, after Robbie hugged Edo, I managed to steer him to the check-in desk.

'Where's your passport?' I asked Robbie.

There was considerable fumbling in his pockets to no avail, out then came everything onto the check-in counter. Still no sign of his passport and by now the number of people in line behind us had started to increase, with the waiting passengers rather bemused, but now intently watching the unfolding floor show. With what can only be described as a triumphant gesture Robbie announced that someone (looking around) had stolen it, as it was only a little book! He indicated the size with his hands as if to prove what he was saying was a fact.

More embarrassed looks from the check-in staff and not to mention my own as I watched the increasing number of customers waiting to be checked in for their flight back to Bristol.

Robbie then gave another resounding bellow! 'I know where it is,' he exclaimed. 'It's in the safe!'

I looked at him in disbelief. 'Not the one in the hotel?' I asked almost dreading the answer which surely must come.

'Yes,' replied my now sobering up hero.

I then remembered that he had insisted in his usual exacting manner, that everything of value should be put in the hotel safe in his room, with him taking care of the combination as you would expect him to. I started to retrieve my bag and reservation but Robbie cut me short. 'No, Ken, you catch the flight, I'll go back to the hotel. I fancy another day in Amsterdam!'

This was the man who had insisted he had to be back in the UK on that particular day and could not possibly miss it. I started checking in and my last view of my errant customer was him trudging off to get a taxi all the way back to Amsterdam to retrieve his passport. I was about to call Robbie the next day to enquire how he had managed, when I received a phone call from him saying he had received a call from his credit card agency querying a large amount of three and half thousand guilders that he had apparently signed for, a few days before. I called Edo who said he would go by the 'house' and find out what had happened and make sure he got the money back if this was in any way out of order. I phoned Robbie and he thanked me for the promised assistance and said, 'Don't worry, getting into Amsterdam was no problem, but getting out – now that was a problem, ha!' He evidently had gone back to the hotel, gone back to bed and then returned on a much later flight. We did get the order and Robbie had at least some of his money returned.

We breathed a sigh of relief and when we were congratulated by the boss for a job well done, we both kept quiet about the strange if not hilarious time we spent with the man who had found Amsterdam just that little too much to handle!

One day Lisa and I found out from a friend that a nationwide builder was offering a renovated house at a discounted price due to earlier building faults. We had already decided to sell our house at Frenchay and knew that the house on offer would be much more larger and modern than the one we were in.

We called up Jim, the man in charge of the renovations, and arranged to meet him at the site office. We met and I asked what the final price of the renovated houses would be. He replied, seventy-five thousand pounds, which was extremely reasonable considering the original properties had originally sold for around one hundred and thirty thousand pounds! This was before certain faults had been found which were mainly due to a poor concrete mix, nothing that could not be easily remedied. Trying not to show my obvious pleasure, I remarked that maybe a more attractive price would be nearly fifty thousand pounds as I knew there had been a lot of bad publicity about the houses when they were first sold.

Jim said that he was not too keen on my appraisal of the houses. I replied that maybe if future clients saw that we had purchased the house (which just happened to be the first) then maybe they would have the confidence to buy one of the other fifteen houses. At least he would have monies available to repair the others. I knew from my experiences in Wales that, even all these years later, the cost of building a completely new house would not cost that much. The company had to re-point most of them and would also give a new ten-year building warranty. He looked at me and said, 'Fifty-five thousand and we have a deal.'

We shook hands and for once the cards in my hands had paid off. Just like that!

As we were sitting in the soon to be newly renovated show house, I said, 'Great, we would like this one. When can we move in?'

Jim replied, 'Just as soon as we complete the building work, clean the carpets and curtains and replace all the white goods.'

It got better and better. We arranged the cash and the deal was done. Within three months Lisa and I had moved into the detached three-bedroom house, newly decorated, with new carpets, curtains and new fridge etc. I sent a message to him: 'Can you landscape the rear garden?' but he sent back another: 'Don't push your luck!' which I thought was fair enough!

We found that, as the site filled up with eager buyers, we had a few people who liked to rent for a short time which of course suited the company doing the repairs as it gave them an income while they completed the renovation of the other houses. We had quite a few good parties in the close where we lived but fortunately not the ones that entailed throwing the keys on the table. I used to joke that the last time I did that they left the wife and took the car! An old joke from the club days.

Lisa had been working as a silver service waitress on a part-time basis, but now she wanted a more demanding job, so I suggested she tried getting a position as a sales representative. She said she did not think she could handle such a position, going in and meeting new people all the time. I said, 'Rubbish' as she had no problems dealing with clients when we worked together.

In due course she attended an interview and got a job (with a car) visiting clients to sell oil. As this turned out to be for only two days per week, she also obtained a further position selling tools to stores which supplied electricians and builders. At first she worried about the travelling but fortunately I was able to combine some of my calls in the area she was due to work and I took her round so that she got used to the location of the stores.

Like many ladies, her sense of direction was not the best. However, within a short time, I could sense that she was getting very confident in her skills of selling and locating the whereabouts of the stores that she was supplying. Her companies were very pleased with her and she was always being awarded prizes for her efforts.

One of her awards was a great success and it entailed flying to Paris for a weekend in Disneyland! I agreed to go as long as she did not tell anyone. Ken West at Disneyland?

I would never live it down! We caught the flight from Heathrow and soon caught the train which would take us to the nearest exit for Disneyland.

Finally, we arrived at the New York Hotel on site and spent three days enjoying the delights only Disneyland can aspire to typical good old American showbiz. I had managed to acquire some reward points on my Amex so we went into the 'Wild West Show' which was simply amazing. We gasped when the riders drove out about twenty buffalo which took off at high speed towards the end of the rather short arena. The riders easily turned them and all was well but I would not have liked to be the people at the end of the arena the beasts were heading for. Talk about wet knickers! And – pants!

We were fed chicken, chilli con carne and crackers which brought back many memories of my chow days in the American Air Force. It was my favourite snack late evenings at the Commissary after a good night's drinking at the airman's club.

We both enjoyed the fantastic parades that occurred daily and the many adventure lands which littered the show park. I know that years ago when I first ventured into the new world of the United States one thing the Americans always shone at was their staging of events. I learnt a lot about the presentation of everything and it must be said the Americans are masters at doing such things. The Disneyland in Paris was a copy of the one in the United States but it must have given a nice feeling for all the European youngsters (and adults) who eagerly visited the magical land of Walt Disney. Not all exports from the United States involved the use of a tommy gun. Mind you, the Elliott Ness of Untouchables fame certainly had been good viewing when it was first shown and Al Capone added his own type of magic to the cinema screen, but did we really appreciate just how bad a person he was?

It was a nice interlude which came about solely due to the success of Lisa's efforts with her new job. That was from a lady who said she could not handle meeting the buyers of many companies.

The Blues Come Around...

*Hank Williams
Once I was happy as I could be
But I let a girl make a fool of me.*

Some of the most pleasant times that Lisa and I had were going to the dinner dances that came with the involvement of selling machinery to the paper trade. We always stayed at the best hotels whether it was in London or even Dublin. There were several dances each year and even one at the Belfry Golf Course which was nice for the golfers in the trade. We, however, were more interested in the social side of things and we spent many evenings enjoying the good companionship with my fellow English and Dutch associates. Problem was, of course, a new dress every time we went to one of these events. I guess now and again we did buy one for Lisa as well!

In addition to the social events we managed to get away on holidays, going twice to Portugal at Archie's place, and one Christmas to Germany. I had been on holiday to Germany before but this was the first time at Christmas. Arriving there we eagerly awaited our opportunity to witness just how the Germans celebrated Christmas. We were a little disappointed when we found that, basically, they shut up shop and retreat with their families to celebrate privately at home. We had to make do with a band and disco put on by the tour operators – where had all the locals gone? Oh well, the local brandy was very acceptable.

With my own family growing up and courting, it was not long before my daughters, Tanya and Natalie, both got married but, with Claire's feeling still not healed completely, I found that it was not possible for me to attend either of the weddings, which was of great disappointment to me. I guess there are many types of payment and atonement that go with the territory of deceit and divorce. As for my now immediate family, Rosa, Lisa's daughter, was growing up fast and while I clearly supported her financially, her father had no such trouble keeping in touch with her and managed to see her whenever he wanted. No such luck with mine however. I know time heals most ills but it was only many years later that I managed to attend my son's wedding. I had to attend alone as I knew that it might be unwise for the two ladies to meet – even after all this time!

Claire had married her boyfriend and seemed content which I was pleased to hear. She did do a strange thing – on the day she actually got married she sent Lisa a lovely bouquet of flowers. I was just about to say that they were nice and we should put them in water, when Lisa screwed them all up. I was amazed at this and could not quite figure out exactly how these two ladies' minds were working that day. That is, if you could figure them out anyway!

One year Lisa and I got to have a nice holiday together. It was the year that Rosa's father offered to take her to Disneyland so, with her shooting off to the United States, Lisa and I booked a holiday by air and coach to Italy. It was great to relax and just have the two of us with no one else to worry about. Travelling around Italy by coach brought back memories of my trip down from New York to the Blue Ridge Mountains of Virginia, which was the start of my adventures in the USA. Now, years later and with yet another lady on my arm, I was seeking out new adventures but this time in a more sociable and relaxed manner which was very nice. That's amore!

We enjoyed our trip around Italy, visiting the sights of Rome and, of course, throwing coins into the Trevi Fountain, which must be a good income for someone. The surrounding sights of Tuscany must surely be amongst the best in the world with its sweeping hills, many mixtures of colours and fantastic old vineyards and grand old houses. It seemed a fitting end to our nice romantic holiday when, over the coach PA system, we heard the music of the Italian tenor Andrea Bocelli. He was singing 'Con Te Partiro' (Time to say goodbye!). As we sat in the coach holding hands, we both felt very close that beautiful sunny day as we sped back to our waiting plane.

Working for Bollegraaf was proving very satisfying; we had a good product and, with several sales in the UK, mainly thanks to Edo and my own efforts, we were soon branching out in the wider market of MRFs, (Material Recycling Facilities). Waste recyclables, sent to the plant, would be resorted and passed on to be made into something else. After lengthy negotiations I managed to get together a deal that really made the boss happy. Over two million pounds! - a nice order. It was the largest MRF at that time in the UK and, for my part, I would get around twenty thousand pounds in commission. As you can imagine, Lisa and I were quite chuffed about it. Having obtained the order, we waited for the commission. However, we found some hesitancy from the Dutch boss in the payment of these monies. We knew he had received over ninety-five per cent of the money, but he said he was waiting to receive the other five per cent which could take months due to final clearances in getting the plant passed as fit for purpose. We replied, 'Don't worry, we'll have just ninety-five per cent of the money and wait for the rest.'

Weeks passed and then months and still no payment of the cash from our parent company. Many discussions followed, but still the boss insisted he wanted to have the 'final' payment before parting with the commission. I guess when you are due amounts of money like this you tend to lapse into a false sense of security; you perhaps spend more than you would normally. Lisa and I, after assurances that we would eventually get the money, spent money on this and that and soon we found that we had spent too much and needed to put our finances in order. We again asked the boss for the commission money. The UK boss David was also getting extremely concerned at the delaying tactics of his partner. How would this end?

It ended with me being approached by Bollegraaf's biggest competitor, Boa, and I was asked to join them. The deal offered was excellent and I accepted the offer. Now, as they say in the trade, I was 'changing hats'. This was not something I was happy with but I knew I could not change the hold up because it was up to David to get the money first. I would then get paid by him. I knew of course, he was reluctant to do this just yet as the partnership was an ongoing one and suing the Dutch boss would cause a problem and would be bad PR in the trade.

Moving hats was not too difficult. My new Head Office was still in Holland and my potential customers were still in the UK. I did, however, find it hard to end my association with Edo. By now we had become really good friends and of course it meant that he was my business competitor now! I liked my new colleagues in Boa, Martin and Paul, and it was a start of a friendship that would last even to this day. I also remained friends with Edo, which did not please the 'old boss'! It made us all feel better though. David also kept in touch and we always shared a beer at the trade shows that we both attended. Good friends are hard to find and I made some good friends in the waste paper trade.

Boa used to sponsor the Military Horse Show in Holland similar to the Badminton Horse Show in the UK, and the boss of Boa was Mrs Dennibone who loved being involved with such events. She even had the pleasure of meeting Princess Anne at the Dutch event. This was an international event and Lisa and I went over several times as it was held every year. We marvelled at the organization. I guess there were at least thirty thousand people each day of the three-day event. While a lot of people drove there, it was amazing to see how the walking visitors were able to get on the free buses laid on by Mrs D, and spirited away to their destinations. Within an hour and a half they were gone, except of course for a few stragglers. The food and drink laid on was fantastic and no one went away hungry. There would have been no need for young Oliver Twist to ask for more!

I found that the working part of my life had not really changed at all: my trips to Holland and the red-light district were still, apparently, an essential part of the 'business trip' for my clients, although no one ever sampled the desserts on offer. I liked the days off when Paul, Martin and I would often go to different restaurants which were bountiful in Amsterdam. Of course the Banana Bar was not really one of the normal visits but I understood that Paul had a life membership there, the dirty dog!

I had an amusing episode with three Irish guys who wanted to see the Boa equipment and we finished looking around the red-light district as usual. After a tiring evening the guys just wanted to have one last drink and I found a late night watering hole which, as it happened, sold 'Happy Cake'. I had some small knowledge of this cake that to the normal eye looked just like Madeira cake. It was of course laced with small amounts of cannabis. The guys purchased the remaining seven slices of the cake and I ate one of these. The three guys were already in high spirits and the apparent effect of this cake was to increase their jovial manner. I waited for some effect to take hold. I sat in the bar sipping my beer and looked around. It was late but the most I could show for this feast was for me just to yawn longer and more often. I guess I needed that extra slice. Either way I had a sneaky suspicion that the café owner had most likely sold just normal cake to the unsuspecting revellers. Talk about the power of suggestion.

The trips to the red-light district, while completely innocent and part of the extremely successful sales pitch we had adopted both with Bollegraaf and now Boa, were a good talking point for them when back in the UK. It was after one such trip that Lisa remarked that perhaps I was enjoying the trip around the red-light area just a little too much. I, of course, denied any such intimate pleasure had ever taken place and, when she persisted that it could not be a nice place, I challenged her to come with me and see for herself.

We could not go on a company visit so we paid for the trip ourselves, but after we had made the arrangements we found that we had to take Rosa with us. Not to worry, as there were lots of parts of Amsterdam which were ideal and we could have a nice three days there walking around the canals and perhaps visiting the Anne Franks museum. We arrived in Amsterdam and booked into one of the best hotels, close to the Leidseplein which was one of the busiest tourist areas, where we could see the performing artists and students who all helped to make up the magical atmosphere of Amsterdam.

We had lunch and I pushed the boat out and purchased gifts for both Lisa and Rosa, which were well received. In fact we were having a great time until I mentioned that one of the reasons for coming to Amsterdam was that Lisa could see where I was visiting on my 'business' trips with my clients. We arranged for Rosa to stay in the hotel room for an hour or so and we would walk around the district and then return, collect her and go out for some dinner. No problem until, as we were walking out of the door, Rosa pleaded to come as well. Now, she was fourteen years of age, so she was not too young for such a visit as I knew even 'Cook's Travel Agency' arranged family tours of the red-light district.

We caught a tram to the red-light area and I followed the normal route I often followed when leading my eager customers into the 'dreaded den of iniquity'. We had not even ventured twenty feet into this 'wicked' place when Rosa pleaded with her mother that 'the one and only girl' we had seen at that point, had 'looked' at her! I am not sure where else the girl should look. It was early, not even six thirty in the evening and was very sunny, and not at all scary to say the least. I must admit to being extremely annoyed with her antics and told her so but what followed did catch me by surprise, when Lisa agreed it was not a good place to go. 'Don't be daft,' I said, 'it's not even dark and we haven't even entered the red-light district properly.'

We still were on the outside. We sat down on the edge of the 'terrible place' and I purchased a drink for everyone. I was perplexed and extremely annoyed Lisa had nagged me on several occasions to show her what the red-light district was like. One of the main reasons for this trip to Holland was to show her that although it was a very intriguing place to visit, there had always been the tourist side of this area which was often visited by organised groups arranged by travel agencies. In fact, I had visited years previously with my family on a 'Thomas Cook Tour'. Now this had happened and we were all in a deep sulk, especially me! We caught the tram back to the hotel, and as we approached I said to Lisa, 'I'm going to have a drink at the bar. If you want to, join me later and we'll have dinner.' I left the tram without receiving any answer.

I waited for two hours. Then, realising I was going to eat alone, I went to a nearby restaurant and had several drinks and a steak. Arriving back at the hotel and entering the room I was met by a deadly silence. There seemed nothing I could do and, getting into bed, I was amazed to receive the two presents I had purchased for them earlier thrown in my direction, just missing my ear. I picked them up and put them under the pillow. That turned out well, didn't it?

Going on our previously booked canal boat tour did not improve things and it was spent not romantically as previously imagined, but in total silence with the two girls in my life apparently sending me to Coventry. Checking out of the hotel I found that the two girls had not gone without: they had cleared out the mini-bar for good measure. The trip had turned out to be a disaster and worse to come was the bill which of course was my own responsibility. It would have been better to say yes, I had visited the girls. At least it would have been some value for money, but of course for once, I had not been guilty of any wrongdoings. This time!

I found that there are many spin-offs with getting involved with the recycling machinery, such as the sorting of plastics by infra-red. I had been trying to sell such a system to a large company in Milton Keynes and we had to take the representatives of the client company to Norway. We flew to Oslo and met with the parent company representative, Tom, who straightaway took us around the factory which manufactured the product. It was extremely interesting and our clients were very impressed.

Returning to the hotel, Tom took us to one of the many attractive restaurants which lined the shore. Oslo has a great atmosphere all of its own and, while I was used to Amsterdam, I soon found that as long as you liked prawns, the best place in the world to eat prawns was certainly Norway. We found that the starter Tom ordered for us had around sixty prawns – on each plate. I just hoped that prawns did not have the same effect as oysters are supposed to have!

Leaving Oslo, we flew to Germany for several on-site visits so we could observe the equipment in situ which again was most impressive as we saw waste plastics being identified and processed at a rate of five tons per hour. Upon returning to the UK, we finally were able to secure an order for seven of the machines in the new recycling set-up built by our new clients which was the first in the UK. Sometimes we did get it right.

Every year in the UK there were two recycling events, one of which was always held in Paignton in Devon. For many years the company used to display our machinery in one of the many stands which were for hire. We used to stay at a small bed and breakfast hotel in Paignton called the Bella Vista which was owned by Rod and Jackie. They became firm friends of ours and that friendship, I am pleased to say, still continues until this day. Of course every year, when the event was held, was a delight for the owners of the hotels in the area as thousands of waste sales personnel came to the event.

This was the time for the bosses to come to the UK and attend the show. It was quite funny to see my old boss trying to keep out of the way from my new bosses. It was as if he could not face me in case I asked him for the money he still owed me. One year found our stand actually positioned directly opposite theirs and the old boss went to complain. He actually said he thought that I had stage-managed the placing of our stands which of course I had not. My fellow Dutch colleagues certainly had fun when they heard what he was complaining about. Where was his Dutch courage?

While the horrendous Dutch visit faded and peace returned to the West family household, Lisa and I could not reconcile her attitude to Kim-Ann. I found it more and more depressing that she just would not go out of her way to make friends with Kim-Ann or even be civil. It became a subject I could not bring up without it ending with an intense argument. Kim-Ann offered to call her and speak with her and try to be friends but Lisa would not have it. I remember being in bar having a Sunday drink and the subject was brought up and Lisa reacted in her usual volatile manner and I got up and left. She caught up with me in her car but I waved her away. I felt so evil towards her. The problem was that neither Kim-Ann nor I could ever figure out just how this problem occurred in the first place. They had always talked before the split with Claire.

It was a sore in our relationship and, when I was due to go to a social meeting with Debbie who wanted to meet the rest of the family, I found I could not attend and had to leave Kim-Ann to explain to Debbie that we had some family problems.

How embarrassing was that! I felt sad because this would have been a great moment for me but I could not face another row, not in front of Debbie. As usual by now, I was just going through the routine of ducking any confrontation that might face me. The Top Gun had had his wind severely taken out of his sails and his face was often grim. When he walked, he had the walk of a very dispirited man.

The good years were being replaced by uncertain years again and I was starting to feel that perhaps my present world was breaking up. This feeling continued for some time and started to feel that perhaps changes were about to occur which might cause me some considerable heartache – again.

Why Don't You Love Me Like You Used To Do...

Hank Williams
How come you treat me like a worn out shoe
My hair's still curly and my eyes are still blue
Why don't you love me like you used to do?

The days began to drift by and soon I found that, while my work was very rewarding, at home, bringing up a young teenager, could have problems, especially not one your own. I had kept mainly in the background when any correction of the young Rosa was needed. Several things occurred which caused us concern and I know if I had been more assertive at the time perhaps things might have been different but, as nothing stays the same, Lisa and I found ourselves arguing more and more over the antics of the now very grown-up Rosa.

It came to a head when the company found that my home phone bill was in excess of six hundred pounds (over the budget). I could not believe it, but as the phone bills never actually came to me; they were just sent by British Telecom directly to the company's UK office, so I had no way of monitoring them. However, on looking at the actual invoices, I soon realised the problem was caused by excessive use of mobile phones, Rosa's in fact. It was not actually her phone that caused the problem, it was when her friends called her and she would call them back straightaway on our phone. This of course resulted in the high phone bills. I moaned at Rosa but when I found her still doing it I hit the roof and shouted at her, and then, of course, Lisa took her daughter's side. After all Boa paid for the phones, didn't they?

Lisa suggested we go to Relate, an organisation that specialises in mediation which is supposed to assist in mending stressed marriages. I immediately brought up the problems of Lisa and Kim-Ann but this was vetoed by the mediator as not really relevant to the problems and it seemed to become 'them' against me so I refrained from any more visits. Ladies v Man sticking together? By now I guess the stage was set for events to run their course.

From then on it seemed war was breaking out nearly every day and when Lisa suggested we split for a while to have a chance to sort things out I, in my usual bullish manner, said, 'No, enough is enough, we should get divorced!'

I was a little surprised at my own behaviour. While I had been married to Claire for twenty-five years; I had now been with Lisa for over fifteen years.

The next few months were difficult with no side apparently trying to make amends and of course Ken West suddenly found his old 'sod it' self. He would not give in; if Lisa wanted to admit she was in the wrong, then so be it! It was the Pauline scenario all over again! I was not in the wrong and what followed just underlined that perhaps I had not really learnt much about how adult people should behave. I just looked around for a way out and, well, why not another lady to fill my life!

Perhaps I could have acted better in the breakdown, but then I have never been blessed with sensible responses when faced with matters of the heart. Pauline, Shirley and Claire could vouch for that!

After a difficult Christmas we knew that the uneasy peace that prevailed could not go on forever. I was now sleeping on my own. After vacating the bedroom I used as an office, Lisa had moved into it. We purchased a new bed for her and actually tried to act as if nothing was going on. However, without the normal activities that go with married life, we found that we were drifting further apart as the days passed. In the end Lisa said she would see a solicitor and I agreed. Go to it!

The coming of the new millennium was not a happy occasion in the West house; we had all been walking on eggshells just to keep the peace

I knew from past experiences that the only one definite thing which would emerge from the divorce was that it would cost money and, also from past experience, I knew it was normally me that was the worst off financially. The new year was viewed with great expectancy by millions all over the world, but I suddenly realised that the dawning of the New Year meant that I had been slowly but surely getting older! Oh, how time flies when you are enjoying yourself! I had now been married three times and was approaching my third divorce. I must be doing something wrong.

Three months later found us exchanging solicitors' letters even though Lisa and I lived under the same roof, and it was a situation that could not continue. I went to a couple of company exhibitions and social evenings and in the end I had to admit that Lisa and I would most likely be separating, which was of course the truth.

It was amazing that, after all those years of bringing up her daughter, I found that I had no tolerance level when it came to coping with Rosa's antics. I guess also in Lisa's eyes I was now the enemy who was unfeeling to her daughter's wants but I just could not condone such ridiculous expenditure and I am sure no other father would have put up with it either! Perhaps Lisa was now looking for a way out as well?

I had a call from my friend Paul from Holland who informed me that he was also going through a divorce, so we found we had some common ground for commiseration with each other.

For my part, I put up the usual defences and let things take their course. We got the house valued for the forthcoming split. I knew that with Rosa now over eighteen and working there would be no child support payment from me to Lisa. We divided up the furniture, Lisa having the dining set, TV and other selected items. We agreed a one-off payment to her and on one occasion I even went with her to select a house. She later informed me she had chosen one actually situated in the next road. All nice and civil, but a bit close!

One good thing happened: with the assistance of my old friend Edo I managed to get hold of the commission money that was owed me. I offered to make immediate payment of the settlement money and also pay for the divorce. Lisa was then able to make a down payment on the house she wanted. The divorce duly came through and I resigned myself to another period of being on my own. Lisa's daughters were by then living with her. The problem was they also took the dog. I loved that dog. I still miss it!

While I had been getting in and out of my relationships my daughters and son had been increasing their own families and now my daughter

Tanya had produced a daughter, Laura and a son, Liam. Curtis and his wife Dee were not far behind with two sons, Mitch and Terry. I learnt also that my other daughter Natalie had a son so the family were increasing their families which was nice. I had lost touch with Debbie for a while so I did not know how she was doing. Kim-Ann, of course, loved all their offspring but was content to give them back to their parents as she was more interested in a professional career and enjoying herself in Amsterdam.

I, in the meantime, contacted some dating agencies and in due course signed up with one which seemed to have some nice ladies on their books. Talk about great expectations!

The Dutch company informed me that they were holding a high tech meeting at the company offices and that I should attend. I caught the plane to Schipol Airport and then caught the train to Enschede, the town in which the company was based. It was a three-hour journey and, being alone, it seemed to drag on forever. The Netherlands has numerous pretty towns full of lovely houses and when passing in the train you certainly know you are in a different country. I daydreamed as the towns passed by with all their inhabitants living in an apparently different world and that it could be quite possible that someone even there could be experiencing events similar to what I was going through at that time. But they surely could not all be as hurtful as mine; I sincerely hoped not. I arrived at the hotel that the company had booked for all the attending managers and agents.

We had several meetings to go to and I marvelled at the ease with which the senior managers of the company communicated with all their different race associates. They instructed in German, English, and even French. Gosh, how my earlier schooling at Newtown in Reading had missed out on this important part of life - foreign languages! I knew the Dutch people had to learn the different skills of talking with their neighbours; otherwise they would not have been able to trade so easily. In the United Kingdom it was different; we were an island and was it not true that the world revolved around our Sceptred Isle.

We had one more day with even more technical subjects and I was, I admit, more than distracted from what was going on and would often just recant in my mind what had happened. Finishing up, we returned to the hotel and this is where you certainly miss your wife or partner. I was accustomed to having Lisa with me and I found myself missing her – just a little.

When Alex, one of my colleagues, suggested we do the sights and bars of Enschede, I readily agreed. I felt like a drink to blot out the silly thoughts that I had of missing Lisa over the last twenty-four hours. Silly billy!

With a couple of other guys we set out and started hitting the town's numerous bars and my thoughts drifted back to one of my earlier bar crawls in Columbus, Ohio and my blurry vision that had occurred on that occasion. I suddenly realised that the years had drifted by and, while I had been used to taking clients around the red-light district in Amsterdam, I felt out of place with my much younger colleagues. They went out of their way to make me feel welcome and we certainly had more than a few beers. I was just about to call time on our tour of Enschede. I knew I had a long train journey back to Amsterdam unless I could catch a lift.

'No, let's have one last drink at the Latin Club,' remarked Alex.

'Fine, but I guess for me this had better be the last,' I replied.

We entered the club and found the usual half-dressed ladies cavorting around. I soon realised that Alex had brought us into a rather high-class brothel! We sat at one of the round tables which were stationed around the dance floor. We were soon surrounded by some extremely attractive ladies, and for a while I managed to excuse myself from getting involved with any of them. But I guess the manager would not be beaten and he brought in the crème de la crème. What a despicable thing to do! How could he do this to an ageing rejected male who was swiftly losing the will to think straight!

Carla was around twenty-six; she was gorgeous, long black hair all down her back, 'none on her head'. I do jest of course, and being very petite she managed to snare herself somewhere between the table and my right leg. Carla was there if I wanted her to be there or not. I found myself looking into the deep dark wells of the sexiest eyes you could imagine! I found myself agreeing to the new round of drinks that suddenly appeared. Twenty-five guilders that was not too bad, but could I claim it back on the expenses? I must admit at that time I was really not bothered, and I continued gazing into the eyes of this lovely creature that had invaded my space.

I was fast losing the plot - again. I was quite enthralled with the proceedings, having long ago lost the will to give up the night's drinking and return to the safety of the hotel. I looked up and suddenly found my drinking mates had vanished and I asked Carla, 'Where did they go?' I think she managed to translate the slurring words and simply replied, 'Upstairs.'

I looked around as if I expected to see the 'upstairs'. Carla knew that if ever the time was right she had to move now. I apparently did not wish to be left out of the proceedings and I knew that my next move would most likely entail following this delightful young lady upstairs! All good sense had simply vanished with the increased volume of drink, and guess what the drink was now?

The dreaded Canadian Club, my favourite 'drug', which had now become my Achilles' heel, yet again! I found myself asking the question, how much for this lady's pleasure? I was doing what I had previously denied. I was just complying with what I had been accused by Lisa of doing — paying for some sordid pleasure! This was something that happened every day all over the world. The only difference is that instead of paying via your marriage vows you are doing a one-off payment! Easy, when you know how! I tried desperately to barter for one hour for one hundred and fifty guilders instead of the half an hour permitted. Even in his befuddled state Ken West was trying to get a better deal. Talk about lost causes, because as it was pointed out Carla was a special lady and I should remember that! Oh great, now I was apparently expected to believe the sales blurb that went with the deal. I paid the money and ascended the stairs to lose any of my dignity that I might have left!

On awaking the next morning I was not at all happy with my previous night's actions. I left the hotel and returned to Amsterdam by train which meant I had plenty of time to think. It was not long before I came to the conclusion that, as usual, I had taken the easy option and, by not resisting the temptations I had been faced with, I was just reacting in my own self-interested way. I remember years ago reading an old school report of my father's which recorded the words that he was 'manly and trustworthy' and he would grow up to be of good bearing! Like father, like son! Hardly! Where had I gone wrong and why was I incapable of following in my father's footsteps? My old school report had not been that bad!

Returning to the UK I now knew that if I was to turn my life around I guessed my time with Lisa had just about run its course and her volatile manner had not helped, but then I had not even tried to make things better.

I had to stop my selfish ways and try to find someone who might just trust me again and give me another chance, a chance which I must not to mess up again! I guess the bookies would not give me too good odds that I would be able to succeed; they would know a leopard rarely changes his spots!

Honkin Tonkin'...

Hank Williams
When you are sad and lonely and have no place to go
Come and see me, baby, and bring along some dough
And we'll go Honkin Tonkin, Honkin Tonkin
Honkin Tonkin, honey baby, we'll go Honkin Tonkin around this town.

I STARTED HAVING A FEW dates with young ladies who answered my brief which was put in a dating magazine. You know the type: young man barely fifty years of age; wishes to meet a nymphomaniac; has her own house; has a father who owns a brewery. Nice one if you can get it, but unfortunately I never received any replies of that nature. I did, however, meet several ladies who, like me, had been through a divorce which had left them in total disarray. It is like a death because you find that, in addition to losing your immediate family, you can also lose some of your friends.

I was still working many hours travelling around the United Kingdom and also travelling to Holland for meetings. I found that sometimes I became so tired that upon going on a date I was almost dropping off to sleep. This of course was not at all the gentlemanly thing to do, and it was not surprising that I never got past the first date. I did meet one nice young lady, who really took my fancy, I was sitting with her in a hotel bar, and we were laughing and joking. I really thought I was in. I had bought her several drinks and was about to suggest that we should do it again sometime (as you do) when she suddenly announced that she did not think we were really suited.

I was flabbergasted; had I not given her at least three hours of my best wit and had used most of the old chat-up lines that had proved so successful in the past. I was not amused as she had just ordered a large whisky and coke! Why hadn't she made her mind up five minutes before? I wondered if she knew Lisa or Claire. Bloomin' cheek!

I also met one lady who, after having a nice goodnight kiss, informed me that I should go careful with her as she had not done it for sixteen years! I am not sure what she meant by that! Either way, she telephoned and cancelled the date so I was never going to find out. Smart girl!

I did meet a nice girl over a pizza one afternoon and was invited back to her house. We had a cup of tea and arranged to meet at the weekend. I took her for a nice meal and we got on fine. We called a taxi to go back to her place; it was a little embarrassing that when the taxi driver asked me for the address, I had to ask her. He gave us a very strange look.

We got on well and I stayed over for a few nights of mad passionate love, but I think she got a bit tired as she gave me the elbow after one particular night of unbridled passion. Didn't she know I making up for lost time?!

I went on various dates and just as I was feeling I was never going to meet my new 'Miss Right' I received a mailing list which had on it half of what I wanted: a lady who was an ex-landlady. Well, not directly connected with a brewery but one who at last knew how to handle her drink. Or so I thought! I called her up and found an answerphone. She sounded nice on the phone so I persevered, called again, still only to hear the answerphone! Doesn't this girl ever come home? I decided to phone just once more.

I didn't know why, as I would normally give up the ghost and try other numbers; it was not as if there were not any others. I just felt that we were meant to meet. Strange that. I finally got through to her, and found that she sounded nice. She had a nice sounding voice; you know the type of person who would get out of the bath to go for a pee! Yes perfect; she informed me she liked football, and loved music. That was two ticks straightaway! Did she like to drink? 'Occasionally.' Darn, that can't be good; I do like a girl who likes a drink, a laugh and perhaps, eh well, you know what! A pizza!

We arranged to meet at the Gloucester docks and she informed me her name was Christine, nice name, I did have one of those before. Problem was, I could not remember much about the other one! I arrived on time; no sign of any girl that would appear to be looking for a handsome man who was obviously the best catch of the day. Yes, there was a likely one, nice and tall, nice hair, nice figure, nice legs, and looks like she had a bob or two. Now was the time for the nonchalant approach! I moved in for the kill…

'Are you Christine?' I asked eagerly. I looked at her expectantly. After all she was the only one around at that time who fitted my mental image of my new date.

'No, I am not,' the lady remarked indignantly.

'Oh sorry,' I replied. 'You looked like you where waiting for me.'

'That would not be possible,' she replied looking down her long nose. I say that because I was not too happy about her response at all.

'Anyway that would be her loss,' I told myself, and she did have skinny legs!

I was upset I had come all this way for a 'no-show'. Where had the silly girl got to? I walked into one of the cafés which littered the Gloucester Docks and suddenly I felt a tap on my shoulder. Looking around I was quite pleased to see an attractive lady who introduced herself as Christine. I realised straight away of course that she had been hiding around the corner, and most likely she had decided that perhaps I did not look too bad and looked harmless.

'Fine,' I replied and straightaway decided to put her to the ultimate test! 'Come on, let's go and have a drink.'

I should not have worried; off she sped with me trying to keep up with her.

She shouted back to me, 'I know a nice place. It's called the New Inn in the centre of Gloucester.'

When I finally arrived there, I found her sitting at a table, drink in her hand, with a contented smile on her face. I was impressed and when she ordered me a drink I was really pleased. I was not too happy when she then asked me for the money! I decided to persevere, as there was something about this lady I liked. She was slim, really attractive, and she liked football. Can't be bad! I did try to keep up with her, but I had to give up in the end and suggested we eat something. We had a nice meal and I could tell that she was trying to make an effort. She stopped drinking and just kept the money instead. No, I do jest. I had already run out of cash.

I invited her for a drive to a local tourist spot called Ross on Wye and after spending a nice time looking at the town and the lovely views of the river, I asked her if she would like a cream tea. Now, this is how you find out if the person you are with has any breeding or not. If they hold the cup with the little finger slightly lifted and cocked they are of good stock. She crooked her finger as she drank the tea. I was well pleased, until she poured the rest into the saucer and drank it. Ugh!

Christine then suggested that we get a doggie bag so we could take the rest of the scones home. I thought this was an excellent idea because at those prices who could blame anyone for asking for a doggie bag. No, she did have nice eyes and I knew I wanted to see this lady again. I then asked her would she like to come to the next dinner dance that the company was holding in two weeks' time. We would have separate rooms of course, and everything would be all above board.

I was heartened when I thought I saw a glint of disappointment in her eyes when I mentioned the separate rooms, but it disappeared almost as quickly as I noticed it. Maybe I had misread this for tiredness, as it was getting late by now. I took Christine home, and we agreed to meet in two weeks as she had a business meeting the following weekend. Funny time to hold a meeting, but who am I to judge?

I was cleaning my car and my mobile phone rang. It was Christine. Her 'business meeting' had been postponed and we could meet if I wanted to. I readily agreed. It was Easter weekend, I had made no plans with anyone, and it would be nice to have company. I had a good idea: would she like to go south and spend time at the seaside. We could go to Torbay where I had been many times when I attended the annual Waste Management Exhibitions.

I collected her from her home and we headed south on the M5. It was a nice day and I suggested we could stay overnight if she liked. She looked at me and smiled and surprisingly agreed. I said that was good as it would have been a long walk home for her! I guess Christine must have already got used to my silly sense of humour because we did have a very pleasant weekend and started dating seriously from then on. We went to the dinner dance and I introduced Christine to my fellow English and Dutch colleagues and we all had a great time.

It was a busy time after that with me travelling all over the country in an effort to sell companies the machinery.

I wanted to introduce Christine to my daughter Kim-Ann, so we flew to Amsterdam and had a very pleasant weekend staying with Kim-Ann and her boyfriend. It was nice to relax again in the fun city without all the visits to the red-light area, not that it bothered either of us. I suggested to Christine that we should go on holiday together so we booked to go to Italy. It was an all-inclusive coach holiday similar to the one I had been on with Lisa but this time it involved visiting more of the Lakes in the northern area. We visited some lovely places which were quite breathtaking: Florence and Pisa with its leaning tower which at that time was being propped up with steel ropes. Arriving at San Marino, we found a lovely crystal shop and purchased some lovely clocks and other gifts for our families. It was the first time that we had purchased gifts as a couple. Looks like we were getting serious; I mean, gifts with both our names on. We met some nice people on the coach and we had many an evening drink with them. To finish off the tour we travelled to Lake Garda, a beautiful area of Italy and with such spectacular views.

We finally returned to the airport but this time without the strains of Con Te Partiro, which previously may have been a glimpse into the future. As we drew into the airport, I was certainly pleased I did not hear that tune again.

With Christine living in Gloucester and with me in Bristol, I found it tiring travelling back and forth as she did not have a car. She was thinking of selling her house and buying an apartment in the Gloucester centre. I suggested that she might like to consider taking a share in the house I was living. She, of course, was a little bit concerned about living in a house that had a history of another woman and was not far from the previous Mrs West.

We decided to go ahead and, within a surprisingly short time, she had sold her house. It was then that she had to make her mind up because this was a definite commitment. Buying a house with someone was more than dating now and then. By doing this she was agreeing to enter into a permanent relationship and now she was putting her money where her heart appeared to be! Was this a wise thing to do?

Christine had already stayed several weekends so she knew how the house felt for her. In fact she was due to stay for a couple of weeks and was already now in her fourth week! We were getting on extremely well and she turned a blind eye to my reactions when I was faced with bumping into Lisa. Christine was not in any way the cause of the marriage break-up and certainly no one else had been involved. We did have a taste of Lisa's reactions not to Christine living in the house, but when we were out one evening with Terry and Sandra (who had been joint friends of Lisa and me).

Terry and Sandra had been our friends since their work at Snuffy's and of course Sandra had also known Lisa for many years previously.

We were in the local public house, had just obtained our drinks and sat down by the fire. Sandra had gone to the ladies room but she came back flustered; Lisa was in the next section of the bar with a girlfriend.

'So what?' Terry and I asked.

'Well, you know what Lisa is like when something upsets her,' remarked Sandra.

We did not have long to wait because Lisa came into the section of the bar we were in, and just looked at us with what can only be described as a contempt. It lasted a good three minutes, which unfortunately made Terry and me start laughing, which seemed to make her even more upset! She returned to her girlfriend and we put her actions down to the fact that Terry and Sandra still spoke to me. The fact that we were out as a foursome must have annoyed her even more. I guess it was just another casualty of divorce.

With my work carrying on as usual, Christine decided to look for a job in Bristol that was closer than Gloucester. Within a short period of time she obtained a good position with a health insurance company in Bristol and settled in extremely well. We were able to have several trips to Holland as a couple now, and we joined the town twinning group which was connected to France and went on several trips to France.

It was nice when my son Curtis and his wife, my daughter Tanya and her husband all came back into my life. They were not at all enamoured with Lisa and so when we split up they started visiting me on a regular basis, which really made my day. When Kim-Ann came over with her boyfriend, we had a family get-together which was fantastic. Everyone seemed relieved to be back together if, of course, you discount the fact that the last two Mrs Wests were absent. I guess that would have been rather difficult to arrange, not that anyone in that particular gathering wanted to in any way.

My son and daughters had remained in contact with their mother so it was nice that at least the children were at last in contact with both their parents.

It had been a long time and much water had passed under the bridge since the heady days of nightclubs and the upsets which I now had to acknowledge were strictly down to me in many ways. I was introduced to Christine's family: daughter Jackie, her husband Pete, and their young son Ben. They lived in Gloucester it was simple to drive up and meet them. Meeting her son Martin and his partner Vera was a special trip up to London where they lived. I liked them both straightaway. When I said I would not introduce myself too much as his mother would most likely have 'another' man to introduce next week, he laughed and agreed. I hoped he was joking! While in London we took the opportunity to visit her brother Mike and his wife Linda.

I wondered what it was like to have a brother as, of course, my own brother and I had long ago gone our separate ways.

When Christine's family and my family all came to the house at Christmas it was almost as if they had known each other for years. Within minutes Pete and Curtis were joking about football and the girls exchanging tales about their children. Christine and I sat out in the conservatory and watched as this bonding took place. It was great, and no fear of any of our offspring taking offence at the enforced meeting by our association. I was informed by Pete that he would be bringing the many items which he had been storing for Christine down to the house. I asked him to hold off doing this as it was a bit final and I would 'pay' him not to do this. He thought for a minute then said no way, it was too good an opportunity to miss, getting rid of his mother-in-law. He laughed as he said this, but I did wonder!

I did however, come to a conclusion over what may have contributed to some of my past actions, although it was in no way an excuse. Living with Christine, I found that we were both tactile people, and I do not mean this in a sexual manner. We liked to sit and hold hands, almost like we were going back to our teenage years, which of course would have been an extremely hard thing to do.

I was not used to holding hands; mostly my hands were only held when I tried to put them in places which were not allowed and I normally received a slap if I tried!

I realised that perhaps something had been missing during my time with Claire. While it had been a large part of my life (which had produced four children), perhaps my working life had concealed the fact that I did need someone who was more of a tactile person and who would, when possible, touch and hold hands and be that little bit extra close.

I remember that my father used to tickle all of us kids on our backs and that was something which I in turn did to my children. Is this something which might affect the correct choice of partner? No professional bodies ever seem to mention this, yet there are many people who marry and divorce after only a short time. It may be nothing, but I would recommend that everyone planning a relationship of a permanent nature should just take the time to take stock of, maybe once the first passions of the relationship recedes, what is left. You really do need to become soul mates. Anyone can have a sexual relationship which appears to be perfect and perhaps it is - for a while.

I realise now that neither Claire nor Lisa were tactile people. I can never remember seeing either of them cuddling or kissing their children; perhaps they did when I was not present! I remember Claire's mother who, while a likeable person, did not seem to take kindly to any sign of affection that was shown to her when we stayed at her house; it was almost like an embarrassment to her.

Perhaps there is a gene that's passed on to the offspring. It is possibly something to take into consideration, but only if you can see past the sexual part of the relationship. If you are not a tactile person it might never dawn on either party what is missing, until it is too late.

Christine and I spent a lot of money changing things around in the house: new heating system, new kitchen, and a garage conversion, which made a lot of difference to the house. It was nice for Christine to have some input into the changes, particularly in the new kitchen. The changed appearance of the house was immense. We made new friends and even some of the 'old' ones welcomed her; even Lisa's own brother, Steve and his wife Jean. I wondered what Lisa would make of that.

Together with Sandra and Terry, we used to go out for meals and took it in turns to hold dinner parties which always went down well. Steve was an excellent cook and with Sandra and Terry having a catering background, Christine and I always looked forward to such occasions. Christine was no amateur in the kitchen either and, with my assistance, we laid on some nice social evenings. We had the Twinning Association Christmas social night at our house; we had about thirty people in our lounge. We were building up a good social group of friends and we felt quite settled, but would it stay that way?

The Twinning Association consisted of around thirty members and we used to meet once a month to discuss any proposals of visits to and from the French members. We had several friends there which included Helen and James whom we used to go out with for meals and arrange visits to each other's house. One of our members was quite a celebrity. She had a large write-up in a national newspaper, followed by the local paper when she advertised that she was an ex-lady of the night and now was a qualified sex therapist. She had set up an extremely popular business from home. She was a very outgoing character and even wrote a book on the extensive programme that she offered her clients which as usual included a wide spectrum of clients: doctors, lawyers and God knows who else. I guess her database would have made very interesting reading! Either way, she was an extraordinary lady and as she spoke French fluently she was a very welcome addition to our growing numbers of the twinning membership.

When we made our visit to France we stayed with a French airline pilot, Daniel, and his wife Michelle. Michelle was a typical French lady who dressed in skintight leather. You could not ask for anything more. Vive la France!

They made us very welcome and Daniel, our host, brought out a giant bottle of homemade pear brandy, poured us extremely large measure and then told us we could take the bottle to bed with us. We declined as I for one did not want to have a headache the very first morning of our visit. We found their townhouse extraordinary; not one corner or part of the house was wasted. It seemed they had utilized every space for a reason and they had finished it off in natural wood which added to the spectacular effect when you first entered the building.

We were shown many local places of interest and when Daniel asked if we would like to visit the Eiffel Tower in Paris, we eagerly accepted his invitation. He then did an amazing thing: he parked his car on the main boulevard to the tower and just read his newspaper while we visited the Tower. Only an airline pilot could do that; he certainly must have known someone! Lining up after the visit to kiss all the French ladies goodbye was a pleasure; well, kissing the young ones was - including Michelle! Ooh la la!

Then Sandra and Terry dropped a bombshell; they suddenly mentioned they were thinking of moving to Spain. I had been to most places but never to Spain, wasn't that the place for the 18-30 crowd? We agreed to go with them to spy out the land and see what the houses were like. Nice excuse for a holiday and some sun!

With Claire now married it seemed that everyone was now going their separate ways, and the past was, at last, the past, and life goes on. At this time we heard that possibly there would be some changes in the head office staff of our Dutch office and although it would not affect me over in the UK, some of my colleagues, mainly Paul and Martin, had decided to leave the company and look for alternative employment. Clash of personalities, I think it is called. Myself, I was quite happy with the company but I was sad to see Rod, the chief executive, leave as I used to get on well with him.

It is said the time flies when you are enjoying yourself and I can only relate that it certainly seemed to fly by with Christine and me.

As time passed by, having Christine with me on a constant basis was becoming much more beneficial than I had ever imagined. She had a most relaxing way and instinctively realised that the person she had casually met had many more hidden problems that he chose to admit. On the surface I was my usual bullish self, always with a smart reply to any given subject. It was some years since she had had to face the numerous problems connected with divorce. At least she had not been denied access to her children and she patiently gave her advice when asked or when she thought it was needed.

Fortunately for me, Christine's presence and responses quietly put into effect a healing process which would greatly assist me in the months to come. A process that I would be greatly thankful for.

We had enjoyed holidays in France, Portugal and Italy, but I guess the time we went with Sandra and Terry to Spain would prove to be the most significant. We arrived a week earlier than Sandra and Terry and had booked into a hotel at La Zenia, on the Mar Menor with my daughter Kim-Ann who had flown in for a few days. We enjoyed the sun and good wine which were plentiful in such a lovely country. We met a couple of gay characters who ran a beach bar near the hotel and had a nice time sampling the vino and food. The evening ended up with the two girls playing 'Sand Angels' at one thirty in the morning. I had to almost carry them both back to the hotel; talk about the blind leading the blind. Blind drunk maybe! It was nice to get up in the morning and find you have sunshine almost every day. I could only imagine that King Carlos must have made a decree that Spain should have sunshine all the year! I thought Camelot was in England!

Sandra and Terry arrived a week later and Kim-Ann returned home to Holland. We spent the week with our friends looking around the area and we all felt we wanted to look at Spain again but further up the coast. We had heard that the area around Denia was very pretty so we all decided to book for another holiday later that year and check out the delights of that area.

Returning back to the UK I heard some good news which cheered Christine and me up. Paul, our old friend in Holland, had met a new lady and they were engaged to be married. Her name was Mariska and within a short time we would be hopefully be meeting her. Mariska was a sister of one of his new work colleagues and they had met on a blind date. It does happen to other people too! We were pleased when they later tied 'the knot'. They are extremely happy together and I was pleased that Paul who is still one of Christine and my closest friends had at last found a good soul mate, of that there is certainly no doubt. To add to their happiness within a year of getting married they produced a lovely little girl, Eva Sophia, to make their happiness complete.

I have made many references to the music of Hank Williams who made a big impression on me from the early part of my life. This has continued throughout the good and not so good parts of it. It seems Hank had many bad times in his life and most of that involved ladies, mainly his wife. I am pleased that my life was not as sorrowful as apparently his short life was. His unfortunate mishaps in love were maybe self-inflicted through his attraction to drink, but what comes first, the chicken or the egg? I certainly had extremely bad experiences with drink but mine started with the Utopia of my apparent success in the club business, not because I was so unhappy with certain ladies in my life. I would never blame any of them for that. Well, maybe Pauline on one occasion, but that only lasted fortunately one evening. I certainly did not relish the situation I found myself in when I took a certain young lady for a midnight ride. That was obviously drink-fuelled, plus being stupid!

While it does sometimes blunt your senses, your good sense should always prevail. Sounds good on paper, but in reality? Like most people, I do like to celebrate the good times but the worst you get after doing that is a fat head and you deserve that!

My trips to Holland on business continued and one evening I found myself in Amsterdam again with a couple of clients and showing them the delights of the red-light district, including the now compulsory peep show. This had the usual cavorting naked lady on a revolving podium, showing her wares to anyone who wished to put their guilder in the slot thus enabling the small sliding door to remain in the 'open' position. It was raining outside and I was joining in the fun; if you can't beat them, join them. I hasten to add however that I had never repeated my previous disastrous sexual encounter with the ladies of the night.

All the viewing windows were tinted in order that the viewer had some anonymity; however, you could still make out faces and forms, if you looked carefully. I was attracted by some movement from one of the booths nearby and I looked at the booth to see what had attracted my attention. It was a Roy Orbinson lookalike, minus a guitar, but a good likeness nevertheless. I placed more guilders in the slot as my own morbid curiosity took over. It looked like it could better be than the actual floor show! He also had a fawn-coloured raincoat on which was buttoned down from the top. You could only see his face and of course the top part of his body.

I was transfixed by this strange-looking individual; he was himself in turn mesmerized by the female on the revolving podium.

He certainly did not have any problem with guilders. I concluded that he had put quite a bit of money into the cash slot in order that his little door would remain constantly open. As he enjoyed the view, he was enjoying himself! I could not of course see the lower part of his form but it was clearly obvious that he was doing what came naturally to young boys in their early years. Years ago my friend Blackie had informed us boys all about the birds and the bees. The only difference of course was that he was clearly in his late twenties. I suddenly felt very sorry for this person who had to live out his sexual fantasies at the cost of a few guilders, but then perhaps this is what the red-light district was all about.

It had an extra meaning to some people who obviously had other needs; other than to show a few inebriated businessmen a few laughs in order to obtain an order!

It is also possible to find out to one's detriment that sometimes your earlier actions do come back to haunt you at a later date. My absence from my family either by working away or being driven away due to my questionable behaviour may cause the children of the family to react to you in later life. Perhaps they just do not pick up the phone as often as they might have done. You are no longer the centre of their universe and this is why it is important to try to keep that special closeness as much and for as long as possible. I remember my parents asking quite often when they were going to see me when they came to live in Weston. I guess I was just too busy to hear what they really meant: spend more quality time with them. I know that now as many parents have found out to their sorrow. After all we are all only passing through!

I Saw The Light...

*Hank Williams
I wandered so aimless,
Life filled with sin.*

As I grew up I was taught to believe in Christian values, and I am happy to relate that maybe, just maybe, I have now 'seen the light'. My mother and father would most likely say, 'Ken, it's about time too!'

If you reflect at certain times and if you take time to link up the events, you soon realise that you are just part of a large world with everyone apparently going in different directions. Sometimes, when you touch someone, you can have an effect on part of that person's life, good and bad. We are all just passing through and we all have a destiny to achieve. If you try to do your best then maybe, just maybe, you bring joy to yourself and the ones you touch. It seems to me that certain parts of your life are laid out for you. You would not normally change these parts because at the time they feel right. It only changes when you start to feel they are not right for you. It is our choice and we tend to act when faced with these choices. We all have to face up to these times when they arrive.

I cannot understand though, when you see people like my own mother and father, the original Darby and Joan, that they appeared to live solely for us children and each other. I remember the day my father passed away after having a second stroke. He had been in a coma for twelve hours, and the doctor had informed us that he would not recover. Just before my father passed away, he appeared to wake and he asked me to 'look after your mother'.

No words came from his lips and yet I knew exactly what he was saying and replied, 'Yes, Dad.' He was even thinking of her as he passed away. That was true love, so why were all four of his children seemingly incapable of doing the same?

I can only imagine that when I started my first romance with Pauline I expected to experience the same long-term love which would result in marriage. How cruel can this be when you are twice faced with the 'bite of the cherry' relationship with someone which in real terms is a relatively short time and yet it has a drastic effect on your life. I am convinced that my meeting with Pauline was, in my own mind, the real thing, but perhaps our destinies were not meant to be so.

They say the 'first love' of your life is the most intense and perhaps it is, but at what cost to your future relationships when you possibly keep this love in the back of your mind. Does this mean we settle for second best when entering further relationships?

I can only draw the conclusion that perhaps you might subconsciously blame any future new partner for what has happened in the past.

This does seem quite drastic but then love is a drastic thing, nice when it is going well but not so nice when it is not. I guess an extreme example of this is when someone decides that they cannot live without their partner and then takes action to ensure that no one else will have them either. That conclusion does not even bear thinking about, but it does happen. It takes a brave person to admit to themselves that all the relationships in their lives have been blighted by an earlier one. I hope this was not the case but it cannot be ruled out!

The songs that Hank Williams used to sing and the words seemed to indicate an apparent true life experience: 'Why don't you love me like you used to do, my hair's still curly and my eyes are still blue'. Why don't you love me like you used to do? So what has changed? Perhaps in most cases, it was the straw that broke the camel's back!

Christine and I had booked another holiday in Spain. Sandra and Terry, at the last minute, were unable to join us so we went without them this time. After a good flight we collected the hire car and found our way to the apartment that we had rented for the two weeks. The company that had rented the apartment to us also sold houses, so when they asked us if we wanted to look around some properties we agreed. We informed them, however, that we were not really in the market just yet and that we were looking around mainly for our friends. It would be nice to have a look around the area without me having to drive.

Looking at properties can be quite exhausting and after a while we were glad to have the weekend off and relax in the numerous bars and restaurants which line the main beaches which, at the resort we were staying, were at least ten miles in length. We happily resisted all properties on offer, until we looked at an older property with a lovely garden with nine palm trees in it, swimming pool, four bedrooms, three bathrooms, garage and two car ports. Not bad for a holiday home and maybe a good investment?

We looked at each other and bearing in mind that we were shortly to become senior citizens, we paid the deposit and set the wheels in motions to purchase the house we had both fallen in love with. We called our family and friends in the UK, including of course Terry and Sandra, to tell them that we had made a commitment in sunny Spain.

I guess that the unexpected commitment we both made to purchase the villa made me think that perhaps we should at least think about tying the knot and I asked Christine if she would be interested in marrying me. I knew I had not been viewed by many of our relatives as a particularly good risk as, having been married and divorced three times, it was a little weak to respond to questions of how you managed that was that you liked wedding cake! Either way Christine surprisingly agreed that she would like to!

I was a bit surprised because up to that time I had considered her to be a lady of sound common sense! When ringing Sandra and Terry we told them that in addition to our surprised purchase that we had got engaged as well. Unknown to us, this caused our friends some concern and they actually spent some eighteen hours worrying that perhaps we had been kidnapped and the sudden news of the engagement was my way of asking them to get help! Terry reasoned that no way would I ever get engaged again and so soon, due to the many conversations he had had with me on the subject when breaking up with Lisa!

Either way, the next day, when they called early we had to convince them that no we had not been kidnapped and we actually meant both pieces of news. Oh well, nothing stays the same! Returning to the UK we started advertising our newly acquired property, letting out our downstairs apartment which was self-contained with its own BBQ and of course access to the pool.

We did very well and were happy to continue with this new business. Of course we had several visitors including Terry and Sandra and Helen and James. I guess the attraction of Spain proved overwhelming as they all decided they would like to eventually purchase homes in Spain for themselves. Will there be anyone left in the UK?

It came to the time however when Christine and I started to feel that perhaps we were maybe in the wrong place. We had a nice house in the UK, but an even nicer one in sunny Spain.

So we sold our house in the UK and, after a short time renting, packed up all our worldly goods, resigned our employments and moved south and I mean south literally.

We had a Mercedes motor car already in Spain which I had purchased from the owners of the villa, but we had bought another car from our hairdresser David, due to the fact that when I left my position with my company I of course lost the use of my company car. We decided to drive over from Portsmouth, via Madrid for an overnight stay, and then onto our final destination.

We were one hundred and thirty-seven kilometres from Madrid when the car we were driving, an old Vauxhall, decided that perhaps the heat was a little too much and it gave up, with steam arising everywhere. As if to remind us that we were still not going to have it too much our way, it started raining, and I mean raining.

It was fortunate that we had taken out road coverage with Green Flag because, after we managed to canter into a small off-road motorway services, Christine was able to ascertain exactly where we were and we called the number for the breakdown service.

It was her first introduction to communicating with the Spanish people and she handled it very well. Me, I guess I would let her handle the communication from now on. What happened next was simply amazing. We were collected by a Spanish mechanic who spoke no English. It was good that we knew how to communicate with our hands which was quite amusing. He took us to his garage where he passed us the phone and we spoke to an English-speaking Green Flag receptionist who not only arranged a taxi to Madrid but one which was also very willing to take the numerous boxes which we had in the back of our car.

We thanked him but we just could not see the smart hotel in Madrid being too happy with us setting down around twenty boxes in their hotel entrance. Next day the breakdown service arranged a hire car and we drove back to the service area to collect the majority of our belongings.

The mechanic told us he would let us know when the car would be fixed and we drove the long distance to our villa in a new car, but in the safe knowledge that we would most likely make it this time. Sandra and Terry had come over for a final look round. We had given them a separate set of keys to the downstairs apartment and they were there waiting, rather worried due to our late arrival but pleased to have been able to relax in the lovely surroundings.

We had the hire car for twenty-one days and were able to drive our guests back to the airport before I finally, with the assistance of Len a relative of Christine's who already lived in Spain, undertook the long trip back to the service station to retrieve our car. The 'B' roads we travelled on were first-class and we made excellent time and eventually arrived at our destination and collected the car. We asked the mechanic if the car would last and he proudly pumped on his chest and said in his pidgin English that he guaranteed it. We were still a little bit sceptical but can only admit that he had done a fantastic job with the repair, and the car lasted in perfect order until I sold it on two years later. Well done, El Mecanico! The amazing thing about this adventure, admittedly inconvenient to say the least, was that the whole cost to us both was the grand sum of thirty-two pounds. Nice one, Green Flag!

We have settled extremely well into the villa and now accept the sunshine as a normal occurrence even though we do sometimes wonder if it is for real. It does rain in Spain but when they say mainly on the plain that it is not really true as it does for several days everywhere. However, as if to honour King Carlos's decree, it soon stops and out comes the sun. Just like magic!

We have found that the Spanish people love to celebrate. Fiestas are bountiful and seem to occur almost every week – somewhere! They take their religion very seriously and, more importantly, their love of their children. They have their children's first communion and also one for their coming of age. In the villages it seems that absolutely everyone turns out to see even the most distant relative get married, engaged, and, in some cases, buried. Yes, people pass on over here in spite of the sunshine. If they wish to put up lights for these occasions they just ask their councils to do it and it is done almost free of charge, such is their desire to create and maintain the community spirit which is in abundance. It reminds me of my younger years at Albany Road, but where are the close-knit communities now that we see in the weekly episodes of the soap opera, Coronation Street?

Close by we have Terry and Sandra who also made the move to the sunshine and Helen and James who sold up and moved just up the coast. We are not all in the same town but near enough to visit and spend time together. England is just two hours away by air and we can visit the children and of course the grandchildren. We spend most of our days driving around the numerous resorts that are within a short distance of our home.

Christine and I have settled down together quite easily and I reckon the good work she evoked all those years ago has paid off quite well because I am happy to do everything she allows me to. I think! I am in the process of trying to lose some of the pounds that I have put on due to the rather excessive amount of vino that I have consumed since our arrival. Food and wine are considerably cheaper than in the UK and of course I can even purchase my favourite drink Canadian Club, which I do now drink on exceptional occasions, but not on every occasion as I used to.

I have Hank Williams music on my car CD player, which makes it just 'purfeck' as Pa Larkin would say. Christine has managed to survive the revelations which have emerged from the record of my time in Uncle Sam's Air Force, and since.

I guess someday she should receive a medal for doing this and perhaps also my daughter Kim-Ann who, as much as she thought she knew everything about me, must have still shook her head in wonderment when reading parts of this account.

I think she is also pleased secretly that at least it appears she has been spared parts of the insanity that have gripped her wayward father, or has she? Time will tell!

It is nice to walk on the soft sandy beaches with the water lapping over your feet, or even go swimming on Christmas Day in the lovely clear water, something that we had not experienced before. We often sit around the pool, sampling the various wines and eating the fresh fruit which is in abundance all year round. Life is just perfect with the exception of the occasional mosquito that joins us on our late night safaris by the pool.

We also know that when we plan a BBQ for the next day it is odds on that the sun will not let us down at the last minute! Nice to have the odds on your side for once!

Watching from our veranda we can see our grandchildren when they visit, jumping in and out of the pool and getting nice and brown in the process.

And we often say to each other, 'Well it's been a tough fight but we've made it!'

Pauline, eat your heart out!

About the Author

Ken Wise has led the kind of life that usually only appears in Soap Operas. Now he has settled down to a more sedate lifestyle in the sunshine of Spain he is putting his story telling talents to good use by pen to paper in his first novel. Based on the surprising and sometime humorous events of an Englishman in the American Air Force and the experiences that shaped the adventure that was to become his life.